SECRETS

GRAND STREET
66

SECRETS

This issue of ***GRAND STREET*** *is dedicated to the memory of* ***DOMINIQUE DE MENIL***, 1908–1997 & ***ZBIGNIEW HERBERT***, 1924–1998.

FRONT COVER
Arturo Herrera, Untitled, 1997–98 (detail). Mixed-media collage on paper, 12 x 9 in.

BACK COVER Bruce Nauman, video still from *Green Horses*, 1988. Two color video monitors, two videotape players, one video projector, two videotapes (color, sound), one chair. Dimensions variable.

TITLE PAGE Marcel Duchamp, *With Hidden Noise (Ball of Twine)*, 1916. Assisted Readymade: ball of twine between two brass plates, joined by four long screws, containing a small unknown object added by Walter Arensberg, 5 x 5 x 5 1/8 in.

TABLE OF CONTENTS Packing lettuce near Bakersfield, California, 1996. Photograph by Daniel Rothenberg.

Grand Street (ISSN 0734-5496; ISBN 1-885490-17-8) is published quarterly by Grand Street Press (a project of the New York Foundation for the Arts, Inc., a not-for-profit corporation), 131 Varick Street, Room 906, New York, NY 10013. Tel: (212) 807-6548, Fax: (212) 807-6544. Contributions and gifts to Grand Street Press are tax-deductible to the extent allowed by law. This publication is made possible, in part, by a grant from the New York State Council on the Arts.

Volume Seventeen, Number Two (*Grand Street* 66—Fall 1998). Second-class postage paid at New York, NY, and additional mailing offices. Postmaster: Please send address changes to Grand Street Subscription Service, Dept. GRS, P.O. Box 3000, Denville, NJ 07834. Subscriptions are $40 a year (four issues). Foreign subscriptions (including Canada) are $55 a year, payable in U.S. funds. Single-copy price is $12.95 ($18 in Canada). For subscription inquiries, please call (800) 807-6548.

Grand Street is printed by Hull Printing in Meriden, CT. It is distributed to the trade by D.A.P./Distributed Art Publishers, 155 Avenue of the Americas, New York, NY 10013, Tel: (212) 627-1999, Fax: (212) 627-9484, and to newsstands only by Bernhard DeBoer, Inc., 113 E. Centre Street, Nutley, NJ 07110, Total Circulation, 80 Frederick Street, Hackensack, NJ 07601, Ingram Periodicals, 1226 Heil Quaker Blvd., La Vergne, TN 37086, and Ubiquity Distributors, 607 Degraw Street, Brooklyn, NY 11217. *Grand Street* is distributed in Australia and New Zealand by Peribo Pty, Ltd., 58 Beaumont Road, Mount Kuring-Gai, NSW 2080, Australia, Tel: (2) 457-0011, and in the United Kingdom by Central Books, 99 Wallis Road, London E9 5LN, Tel: (181) 986-4854.

GRAND STREET

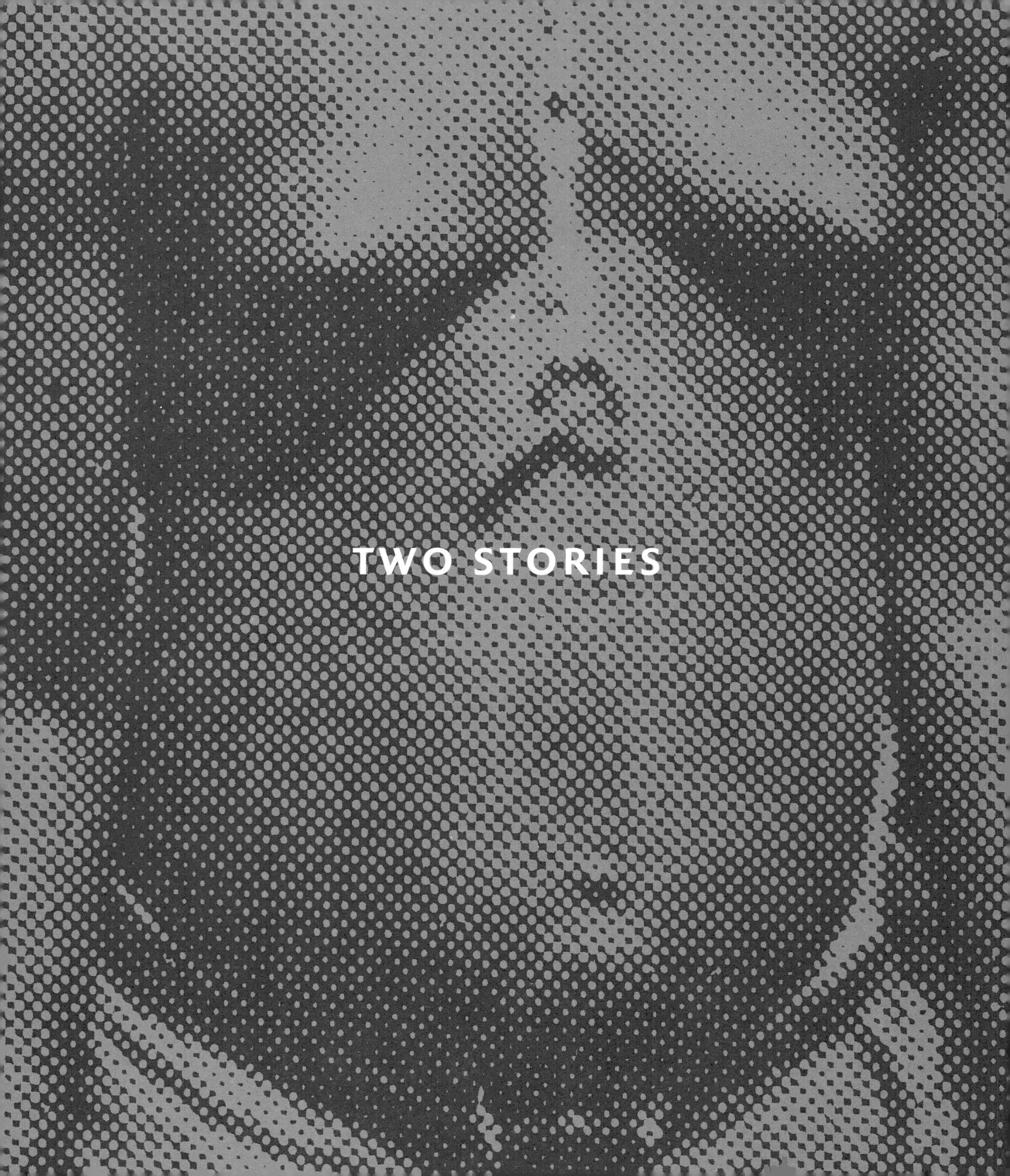
TWO STORIES

RIANNA SCHEEPERS

Barter

The store owner hears the dusty shuffling of feet outside the open door of his store. He puts down the bookkeeping he's working on and comes out of the small office in the back. He goes and stands behind the bar and leans with his elbows on the eroded wooden counter that runs the whole length of the store.

Two women come in out of the sharp sunlight. Each has an *ukhamba* on her head. They duck down, their hips and knees straight, their spines and necks stiff, so that the earthen pots on their heads don't knock against the iron pails and the bicycle wheels hanging from the ceiling. They stop and lean against the wall to accustom themselves to the dimness inside the store.

The store owner waits.

The women stand there like dark statues sculpted of wood. They do not speak. They stand still and sniff the smells of the store: bales of hay stacked all the way to the ceiling, rolls of cloth, fried fat, and the sweat of Africa baked in the dim heat of the store's corrugated iron roof. They see the store owner behind the counter. They lift their dark arms to feel if the earthen pots are still standing straight, but they don't put them down.

The store owner watches them.

Both women are wearing wide, colorful skirts, their torsos bare in the tradition and the heat of this land. Like all the women, their heads are draped with cloth. The bracelets around their upper arms and necks are woven of grass, with bright beads and red seeds woven in.

The store owner is no longer leaning on the counter. He is standing by the cash register, his thumbs hooked into his belt. The heat makes the odor of his body steam. His shirt is half unbuttoned, and his big stomach pushes out his hanging shirt flaps. His blond chest hair is sweaty, his skin glistens.

The store owner looks at the two women.

He is a Scottish immigrant who came seeking the dark mystery of Africa after his thin, sickly wife died in England. In his rattling pickup truck he drove over and across the country's dirt tracks, but when he saw how openly the black women walked with exposed undulating breasts, he decided to set up shop in the oppressive heat of the Zululand hills. He makes his living selling tea and sugar, which he measures out into little 10- and 20-cent paper bags. He weighs his coffee beans on a scale with iron weights. There is a pyramid of weights, piled up smaller and smaller to the top, on the counter next to the scale. If the scale beam doesn't even out, he bites a coffee bean in half.

The store owner also barters his wares for the yield of the land that the black people bring him: lard, and green ears of corn, and eggs, in exchange for sugar, and cloth, and pieces of mottled soap.

"*Ufunani?*" the store owner asks. He talks to them in Fanagalo Zulu, the pidgin of the mines, with a heavy, wild accent, but his clients know the rituals of barter.

"*Sizothenga.*" They want to buy.

The store owner beckons them over to the counter. The women bend their knees lightly, and carefully take down the pots from their heads without inclining their necks. With the lifting of their hands and the lowering of their pots their round breasts sway. The store owner watches. With his dim eyes he grabs at the heavy mass of the brown breasts with the large nipples. He looks at their arms with the woven bracelets of grass and bright beads. He caresses the mud texture of the skin where their stomachs make ripples on their flanks. He tastes the sweat of their armpits. His mouth hangs slightly open.

The women put the earthen pots down on the counter in front of him. He leans forward, his eyes still on the swaying breasts and the arms close to him. He looks down. The dark interior of the cool earthen pots is buffered with dry grass. In the shelter of the grass lies a batch of oval, brown-speckled eggs, like in a nest. The store owner picks up an egg and weighs it in his hand. The egg lies cool against his warm skin. He closes his hand completely over it.

He carefully takes the eggs out of their nest and puts them in a basket. There are eighteen eggs altogether. The women want sugar in exchange for the eggs. And tea. And soap if there is still any bartering left for the eggs. The store owner puts the preweighed bags on the counter in front of the women. And a small bit of mottled soap. The women don't haggle. They carefully pack the goods into the earthen pots and push the soap between the bags and the soft grass.

The store owner knows that all the women's men are away. He knows that the men are working in the coal mines, the gold mines, the uranium mines, and that the money they send every month cannot cover a whole month's necessities. When the women come bartering, the store owner knows that the men's wages have already been spent. He wonders why the women always come to barter with eggs, why they don't eat them themselves. The store owner doesn't know that the women are not allowed to eat them. As long as a woman sleeps without her husband, lying alone on the *icansi* in the hut, she may not use the power of the eggs for her own body. She will eat them again when he returns. With his dark glasses, and his shoes with the white tips, and much money. Easter week. And Christmas.

The women have what they need, but they still stand there. The store owner sees how their black eyes touch the goods on the shelves. They look past him at the rolls of cloth and the jars and the exotic merchandise that they can never see close up. They don't have enough money. He knows that; they do too. He watches their raised eyes search the shelves. He caresses the women's necks, their shoulders, down to their breasts. He takes their breasts in his hands. He rolls their nipples between his fingertips. His hands sweep over the curve of their stomachs, disappear under the heavy cloth of their skirts. He feels their thick thighs; the moist creases of their groins. He turns around.

The store owner takes a glass jar from the shelf and puts it down on the counter between him and the two women. Vaseline.

The women giggle and speak faster in their clicking language. When they speak so fast he cannot catch what they are saying between the many clicks. Their hands reach for the jar, they want to look, they want to smell, they want to dab it on their skin, but he picks it up and holds it in his hand. He looks them in the eye.

The women look at each other and speak furtively in a dialect he cannot make out. One of the women lifts her *ukhamba* from the counter and positions it on her head. She turns around and walks out of the store into the sun. The store owner watches her swaying walk as she leaves. Holding the jar of Vaseline in his hand, he walks to the end of the counter. He claps up the hinged countertop. The woman who stayed follows him silently, her *ukhamba* in her hands, past the counter gate, which he holds open for her and then carefully pushes shut behind her. The store owner makes sure his clattering cash register is locked and goes into his office. He leaves his store with the door wide open without even looking back. He knows every sound of his store; he won't miss any shuffling footsteps.

The store owner's office is a jumble of old tattered books, unpacked produce, and dust covering everything like flour. The sunlight shines through the grimy panes and falls like a pool of water on the chaotic desk. There are no curtains at the window, but a stack of old order books lies on the window ledge. Bits of ill-fitting linoleum of different shapes and colors cover the floor. The store owner grabs an old overall hanging on the back of the chair and hangs it on a nail above the window. The grimy light darkens. He turns around. The woman is behind him. He takes the earthen pot out of her hands and puts it on the desk among the merchandise. The woman is standing still, her eyes lowered.

The store owner opens the jar. With his two forefingers he scoops out a gob of the thick greasy ointment. He comes closer to the woman, starts slowly rubbing the ointment over her breast. The breast, like amber, like polished wood, starts glowing. The woman still does not move. With one hand the store owner keeps stroking and clutching the thick folds of skin beneath the woman's breast, his other hand unzips his bulging fly. His organ, large and freckled, thrusts its way up from between his legs. The store owner grabs at her with both hands.

He pushes her down onto the floor.

With his knees he pushes her skirt out of the way.

The store owner pulls back.

He watches the woman on the floor as she first gets up on her knees, and then, steadying herself with one hand on the floor, stands up. Her wide skirt falls back over her hips and legs, and down into its swinging pleats. He watches her take the round grass-woven *inkatha*, on which she balances her earthen pot, out from between the packets in the pot, and firmly press it down on her head. She lifts the *ukhamba* from the desk but puts it down again. She bends over and picks up the jar of Vaseline. The store owner hears the lid scrape over the glass jar's grooves as she twists it tight. Then she presses the jar firmly between the packet of tea and the bag of sugar in the *ukhamba*. She picks up the earthen pot again and slowly puts it, as she has done so many times before, onto her head. Her neck and her shoulders rock the pot into balance.

She turns around and walks out without looking back at the man behind her. In the store she reaches with lightning speed over to a glass jar on the counter and grabs a bright orange apricot sweet. She stuffs it into her mouth.

The store owner hears her footsteps over the dusty floor. He hears her earthen pot bump lightly against the iron tubs that are hanging on a roof beam by the door. He follows her and stands by the door, his arms akimbo. The woman walks along the twisting path up toward her town, which lies at the foot of the hills. Her neck and shoulders have the airiness and pride of a woman who knows that she has struck a good bargain.

Second Child

Lord God, the missionary's wife shouted.

The missionary's wife gave birth to a son in the warm hospital building of the Nongoma mission. *Umngoma*. Witch doctor. Ancient dwelling place of the *Umngoma* and *Isangoma*.

This is her second child born in the mission hospital. She had given birth three hours after her husband brought her here in the jolting Ford over the two-lane track, leaving her in the hands of the black nurse and the Lord.

She had already washed herself carefully at home, shaved herself, and, stopping every so often, her cramps getting stronger, tied back her hair in braids. Her husband helped her. She wondered whether she would have more milk this time than with her first child.

The nurse had helped her onto the bed and waited by her side. The Dutch mission doctor came back in time from the eNdunu hills where he was treating festering eyes. The missionary had a horse sent out to him.

The birth of the missionary wife's son is without complications and easier than the one before—the big first baby had been dragged and pulled out of her.

The breasts of the underfed girl were barely formed.

They were like unripe medlars, hard little buds that had not grown bigger, but had swollen crookedly from the child within her. Her body was thin, her pointed shoulders sharp and bony like the mongrels in the village. Her hipbones under her tanned-hide skirt were still too stiff, too narrow, too thirteen-year-old to force out a child.

The missionary's wife heard the girl being brought to the hospital. The terrible screeching. And the flurried voices. The doctor had sent the nurse out to see what was going on. The screeching was like a child's shrieks of fear. The hospital building is small, she could hear it clearly. She wondered what kind of brawl had started up again. What kind of slash in the head or stab in the body could it be that made this creature shriek like this? But she herself was giving birth, and later the screeching had stopped.

You're going to owe me for this one, Lord, says the missionary's wife.

The black nurse and two hospital workers had to hold the shrieking girl down on the high hospital bed, her eyes rolling wildly up into her head. When the doctor came in and saw her emaciated body with the knife slashes on her pregnant belly, he knew that there would be trouble. He gave her an injection and went to prepare the operating room.

The village in which the girl grew up lies high in the hills, jammed against the slope on the sun side. Early morning and late afternoon the women walk down the winding path to the river to get water for their huts, their hips swaying, their breasts like armfuls of ripe papayas. The village is small, just a few huts.

The field of corn behind the huts is already harvested. The plants stand bent in the sun. Two goats wander about among the rocks and aloe plants, and a group of tattered chickens are in the yard. And the thin mongrels that must find their own fare on the veld. The mottled cow with twisted horns that they used to have had fallen down the precipice one day because the little *umfana* who was supposed to watch her got lost in the thick fog that had suddenly risen. The *Isangoma* had come and marked the place where the cow had smashed against the rocks. He had also marked the *umfana*.

On a clear day from the top of the hills the people of the village can see the cross of the church. But they never go to the church.

They just go to the store, where the white man comes from out of the darkness behind his counter to look at the eggs in their grass baskets, which they barter for sugar and tea and cloth. They also know about the doctor who lives by the church. But they will not go to him.

Even the first time he arrived at the village on his horse and with his black bag, they wouldn't have anything to do with him. They saw him coming from a distance along the footpath, and they had gone into their dark huts in dead silence and waited with drawn breath. Even the mongrels on the veld had been silent. The women waited till he stopped calling to them and was far away before they peeked out through a slit in the door. They will not come near him. Not look at him even once. Never.

Nor at the *umfundisi* from the church with the cross, even though they can hear the sweet-sounding songs that rise from the church building in the valley.

The huts and the hills around them see and hear and know the breath of the *Isangoma*. The *Isangoma* sees and hears and knows every breath the village takes. Also the wild games of the children between the rocks.

The messenger sent by the missionary to fetch the doctor had found the girl in the veld on his way back through the foothills. He had heard the moans and, curious, had gone to look behind the aloe plants.

She was alone, squatting on her haunches, clutching her belly in her hands. Her eyes were large and wild, and her mouth open and dry. He had seen her large belly. He had seen the slash marks of the *Insangoma* on her body, and was horror-struck. For a few moments he had held his hands over his eyes. He didn't want to look at her. He wanted to forget what he had seen. He wanted to climb onto his horse and go away from this place where the *Isangoma* still plied his ghastly trade, but the girl's face and her moaning made him turn back.

He had tried to pull her up from the ground, but she threw herself down screaming, clutching her belly with her thin arms. Her legs and her animal-hide skirt were wet, the tepid smell of birth fluid and urine and excrement sharp in his nose. He wouldn't be able to get her onto the horse, he didn't want to take her, he didn't want to touch her—he feared the *Isangoma*. He couldn't leave her here; he stood helplessly between the girl and the horse. He couldn't go to the hamlet she came from for help. Not that village. He left his horse and hurried toward the path.

The group of women that were heading to the store along the path, their earthen pots on their heads, went with him to see. Clicking and swaying they looked and spoke with fear, but didn't want to touch her. The messenger took his horse and rode off to the mission to get help.

The missionary took the Ford from out of the shadow of the tree and had the messenger drive with him. The Lord God is stronger than the devil's power of the *Umthakathi* and the *Isangoma*, he told his baptized, weeping parishioner on the way.

The Dutch mission doctor cuts a cesarean section wide over the girl's taut stomach skin, right across the slashes of the witch doctor's knife. He can see the throbbing life beneath.

The girl dies under anesthesia. The hospital isn't set up for such operations. The worst illnesses here are the black people's eye sickness and TB. The women usually give birth to their children as easily as squatting down in the veld. Even if she had lived, she wouldn't have had milk for the child, the doctor thinks. Either way it is a miracle that the baby is alive.

Later that day the nurse comes to tell the doctor that the orphan can't keep down the watered cow's milk from the bottle.

I care for these creatures here, Lord, says the missionary's wife. I don't chase them away, I give them food, and plant pumpkins, and together with my husband preach the gospel to these pagans. Lord, here stands our church. Lord, here stands Your church on the spot where Zululand's witch doctors used to squat together in their grass huts. Here stands Your church on the battlefield where Dinizulu and Zibephu murdered each other with assagai spears.

I don't mind that my sons swim white-buttock black-buttock with the little *abantwanas* from the village in the muddy river. I don't mind that my sons and the *abafana* pee together against the wall of the cow pen. I don't mind when they play in the straw huts and come home smelling of straw huts. That together they scoop with their fingers from the black pot pasty clumps of meal and eat them. Lord, I am a girl from the Huguenot Valley, but I will work here by my husband's side. I love the fog that pours into the creases of the hills, and the smokiness of the fires. But Lord God, must I share these creatures' wretchedness in such a way?

The missionary's wife sees her husband standing next to her narrow bed. he knows of the pretty Dexter cow standing in the pen, with its black hide and its round udder, and the rich milk it gives.

You owe me for this one, Lord, says the missionary's wife.

You must watch over my child. You must make my blond son bigger and stronger with the Dexter cow's milk than he would become with my own.

Now that I'm giving my breasts to the savages.

Translated from the Afrikaans by Peter Constantine

JUAN CAMERON

Imitation of Pavese

Would it be a sin to lie beside Giullia and drowse with her
like a blind man stretched on the grass with his guide?
Would it perhaps be a betrayal of the movement
a transgression   to the cause
to carry her by bicycle to the Café Siesta
or go past the library and from among the columns
gaze at each other like this during mass?
Would it be a sin to embrace her suddenly   greet her
touch her nineteen years on the cheek
say to her this is me   take her by the hand?

Translated from the Spanish by Cola Franzen

GIVE THE GIFT OF IMAGINATION AND {SAVE}

Name

Address

City State Zip

Gift subscriptions to:

Recipient's Name

Address

City State Zip

Recipient's Name

Address

City State Zip

Signature *(a gift card will be sent in your name)*

$40 First Gift or New Subscription

4 issues at $11.80 off the cover price

$34 Additional Gifts

4 issues at $17.80 off the cover price

All foreign (including Canadian) orders $55 per year, payable in U.S. funds. Institutional orders $50 per year.

○ Payment enclosed

○ Bill me

PLEASE CHARGE MY:

○ American Express

○ Mastercard

○ Visa

Account Number

Expiration Date

LAST MINUTE? FOR IMMEDIATE SERVICE CALL

1-800-807-6548

NO POSTAGE
NECESSARY
IF MAILED IN THE
UNITED STATES

BUSINESS REPLY MAIL

First Class Mail Permit No. 301 Denville, NJ

Postage will be paid by Addressee

GRAND STREET
Subscription Services
P.O. Box 3000
Denville, NJ 07834-9878

NO POSTAGE
NECESSARY
IF MAILED IN THE
UNITED STATES

BUSINESS REPLY MAIL

First Class Mail Permit No. 301 Denville, NJ

Postage will be paid by Addressee

GRAND STREET
Subscription Services
P.O. Box 3000
Denville, NJ 07834-9878

A CONVERSATION

PETER BROOK

ON MOZART'S DON GIOVANNI

"Music is a language related to the invisible by which nothingness suddenly is there in a form that cannot be seen but can certainly be perceived." PETER BROOK, *The Empty Space*

PETER BROOK | LAURENT FENEYROU

The following conversation took place on May 7, 1998, at Aix-en-Provence, France.

Laurent Feneyrou: How wide, in your view, is the gap between *Don Giovanni* and *The Marriage of Figaro?*

Peter Brook: *The Marriage of Figaro*, *Don Giovanni*, and even *The Magic Flute* have one thing in common: they defy classification. They cannot be summed up in a word or a definition. Not one of these works is entirely "funny," "serious," "frivolous," or "solemn." At the same time, they do share a common element: each one of them is Mozartian. Mozart was the very essence of vitality and this vital exuberance was evident in his everyday life, in his letters and in the little that we know of his conversation. It was the one factor that unified his entire musical output.

From the outset, Mozart accumulated a vast range of impressions to do with human life, not only those gathered from the outside, from the observation of other people, but also from the inside scrutiny of his own being. Each and every person is constantly in a state of flux; feelings, images, colors, sensory impressions, theories, thoughts, ideas, all these are constantly present. They remain in a form that is hardly accessible to the individual in question. The composer, however, is able to capture these impressions and express them in the shape of vibrations of the utmost delicacy.

Mozart's personality displayed in succession despair, the awareness of death, humor, joy, derision, speed of thought, and the ability to see life at one and the same time on the social level and on the cosmic level. Death is a presence. In the face of death, our feeling for life is for a moment unbelievably reinforced. Throughout his music, Mozart constantly comes back to a contemplation of this presence. His compositions in their entirety lie between two poles: the joy of living and awe in the face of death.

> *... I have received a piece of news which greatly distresses me, the more so as I gathered from your last letter that, thank God, you were very well indeed. But now I hear that you are really ill. I need hardly tell you how greatly I am longing to receive some reassuring news from yourself. And I still expect it; although I have now made a habit of being prepared in all affairs of life for the worst. As death, when we come to consider it closely, is the true goal of our existence, I have formed during the last few years such close relations with this best and truest friend of mankind, that his image is no longer terrifying to me, but it is indeed very soothing and consoling! And I thank God*

PAGE 17: Peter Brook in a rehearsal of *Don Giovanni*, Aix-en-Provence, 1998.

> *for graciously granting me the opportunity (you know what I mean) of learning that death is the key which unlocks the door to our true happiness. I never lie down at night without reflecting that—young as I am—I may not live to see another day. Yet no one of all my acquaintances in my company could say that I am morose or disgruntled. For this blessing I daily thank my Creator and wish with all my heart that each one of my fellow creatures could enjoy it.*
>
> WOLFGANG AMADEUS MOZART
> letter to his father, 1787

Mozart was free, entirely free when it was a matter of writing or imagining music. In the space of three bars, he could introduce speed, light, derision, tenderness, and a deep sense of tragedy.

Let us examine what happens with any good pianist. When any note is played, the musician must relax his body and free himself so that he can attack the following note in an entirely different fashion. A bad actor, under the sway of emotion, launches forth and throughout ten sentences goes on saying the words with exactly the same feeling. What is marvelous in the case of Shakespeare or of Racine is that the subtlety of their writing is such that from one moment to another, feelings change color, sometimes only slightly, at others drastically. The performer has to do the same thing, going immediately from a tragic word to an almost insignificant word, to a word without any importance.

To use another analogy, in *Don Giovanni*, Mozart is somewhat like Chekhov. Chekhov loathed the falsity of overcharged sentiment—he himself was a man of deep feeling. Whenever a character becomes overemotional, he immediately introduces a comic effect in order to break up this emotion. This device is to be found in most all of his plays. But when it seems that the comical atmosphere is about to become permanent, Chekhov introduces a moment of truth, an emotional truth that takes your breath away. In *The Cherry Orchard*, for example, Varya comes onstage *through tears*. During the initial rehearsals, the actress began to cry. Chekhov stopped her immediately: "Although I wrote *through tears*, this wasn't to be taken literally; all it means is that there is a degree of sadness. But if you really cry, you can't simply come out of that a moment later."

With Mozart, if you talk about *opera buffa* or *dramma giocoso*, you are introducing distinctions and categories. Such and such a moment is *buffo*, another is drama. This is not at all the case. Within a phrase, or from one phrase to another, there is freedom of movement. If you do not know the content, you might gain the impression that the music is incredibly gay. But a light and rapid tempo sometimes accompanies a very sad moment, and vice versa. So I believe that you have to approach Mozart in a state of awareness that makes it possible to perceive these transitions, which are inseparable from intimacy.

This is what links *The Marriage of Figaro* to *Don Giovanni* and even to *The Magic Flute*.

> *There are two extremes to be avoided, and once you have escaped from the dangers of these reefs, you are well on the way to mastering the art of Mozartian navigation. The first consists in not seeing the depths that lie beneath apparent lightheartedness; the second one is much more difficult to avoid and it consists in ignoring this lightheartedness once you have understood the poignancy that can lie within its magic aspects.*
>
> JEAN-VICTOR HOCQUAID
> *La Pensée de Mozart*, 1958

Laurent Feneyrou: Beneath the mere entertainment, does Da Ponte reinforce the drama, does he underline the cruelty of the relationships and the bitterness of the situations? And does Mozart distance himself from his librettist? Is his Don Giovanni aware of depravity and the cruel games of desire?

Peter Brook: That is a very interesting question, because I think that the answer to it is both yes and no. Da Ponte does not give us the same Don Juan as Molière. Don Giovanni is not the great sinner. He is a man who plays the moment and who, as we see him before us, lives each moment with incredible verve. He doesn't give a damn about the consequences, rather like the great gangsters you see at the cinema. They are often heroes. They kill right and left, before dying themselves at the end of the film. But they are not presented as examples of men who are evil incarnate. Da Ponte writes his comic scenes with extraordinary cruelty. Behind the laughter, the winks exchanged between men, the way he treats the women is very cruel. When Leporello in disguise seduces Donna Elvira once again, the fact that she falls so easily into his arms is a hard and nasty idea. To a certain extent,it is macho and today it would be looked upon as unforgivable.

This is not denied in the opera. Mozart recognizes and identifies the situations in his music. But he transforms Da Ponte and goes well beyond him. If the libretto were to be performed simply as a play, it could be made into something very lively and very funny, but it would be nothing more than a sardonic, cynical, and rather nasty little comedy. We wouldn't come away from it with the strange joy we feel after looking through the window onto life that Mozart gives us. In rehearsal there is everything to be gained from coming back to the words in detail, for very often they are very precise. Mozart is faithful to Da Ponte in the recitatives both as to meaning and to the intimate relationship between the content of a word and the tiny twist of the musical phrase. But within, there are a thousand shades of meaning available to the singer who looks for them. These shades of meaning are musical but they are inspired by those contained in the words.

This marriage in the recitatives is very intimate. But just as soon as the recitative moves into an aria, a transformation takes place and another quality becomes evident.

Laurent Feneyrou: "Ah! Already the villain is fallen . . . " sings Don Giovanni on the death of the Commendatore, underlining the gentle weight of the body in the face of the grave. What is the meaning for you of the trio with which the first scene of the opera comes to an end?

Peter Brook: I am sure that Da Ponte was incapable of foreseeing this moment. *Don Giovanni* begins rather frivolously. Leporello is grumbling. He's having a real moan. You can easily imagine him in a film by Marcel Pagnol sitting at table with a few friends, pastis in hand and complaining: "This won't do!" His anger at the beginning of the second act is entirely different. The recitative here is a sung recitative. Leporello's violent outburst against his master and the argument they have come over very strongly. There is nothing to indicate, however, that Leporello is a Figaro in revolt. There is a social relationship between Don Giovanni and his servant and there is a hierarchy, although it is a highly unusual one. It is different from the situation of Figaro who appears at the historic moment when servants are beginning to assert their rights and he therefore stands up against the laws of the Count. But the Count remains the master and Figaro remains a servant. Many commentators have underlined the quasi-twinship between Leporello and Don Giovanni. Peter Sellars even went so far as to have the two roles sung by twin brothers. Although there is a real social difference between the two, one of the pair having been brought up in a peasant and laborer's background and the other as an aristocrat, they are nevertheless very close to each other in the way they interact.

> *Throughout the action Leporello appears as an irresponsible, innocent, gross, and excrementitious element in the personality of Don Juan while Don Juan appears as a fragment of the rascally Leporello become brilliant and aggressive but with a conscience convicted of sin. Leporello soothes Don Juan, who in turn animates Leporello. It is not enough to emphasize the state of interdependence which constitutes the Don Juan-Leporello character: we must pursue our investigation a little further with the assertion that within that character there is love—love for oneself, who is at the same time oneself and one's alter ego.*
>
> PIERRE JEAN-JOUVE
> *Le Don Juan de Mozart*, 1942

In the second act, when Don Giovanni gives money to Leporello and the latter accepts it, the difference between the two is restated in a most contemporary manner. He can be bought. But the reason why he can be bought is once again the form of identification that constantly appears. He has the same sexuality. He plays the game. He goes along with it. But the first scene is not a scene of revolt. The music is light.

The next scene, with the entrance of Donna Anna, a woman who is like a tigress, provides a dramatic impression musically, not in the manner of Verdi but as the expression of an immense vitality and energy. A man who we don't yet know is running away from a splendid woman in an extraordinary state of rage. Don Giovanni's instincts then lead him in two directions. Firstly, we feel that his carnal desires turn him toward Donna Anna, but at the same time he wants—at any price— to be rid of a woman who is stronger than he is.

To some extent, all this is funny. You can see this scene like one in a film by Quentin Tarantino in which a woman is chasing a man in a New York bar. She is furious, she screams, smashes a bottle, and threatens him. The man asks his friends to protect him at any price from this woman. The situation is a genuine one; it is dramatic but it is not tragic. There again, we are taken from comedy toward melodrama in the noblest meaning of the word. And then the Commendatore appears. Don Giovanni teases him. You can't help but find something funny in Don Giovanni's complete lack of concern. He is very *cool*. He provokes him. And then he kills him. The situation has been neither heavy nor oppressive, but suddenly death, the black thread that runs throughout the opera, appears in all its mystery. What inspired Mozart was Da Ponte's line when Don Giovanni says: "Already I see his soul departing from his heaving breast, I see his soul parting." He does not say: "The poor old man is dead, I have killed him." At this precise moment, Don Giovanni and the Commendatore are confronted by the reality of death as a transfiguration, like a mystical event. And Leporello is face-to-face with his own terror. The beauty of this seriousness is it comes as a complete break with the preceding situations. As with Chekhov, the intensity of this feeling is subsequently broken by the insolence of the recitative, which once again leads to another change, to another rupture.

Peter Brook's production of *Don Giovanni*, Festival international d'art lyrique, Aix-en-Provence, 1998.

Laurent Feneyrou: During the recitative of the second scene of the first act, Leporello exclaims: "Hurray, two charming undertakings! Forcing the daughter and murdering the father." He then asks himself, "But Donna Anna, what did she ask for?" The only reply to this question is Don Giovanni's annoyance. Is Da Ponte conveying here the impossibility of uniting desire with liberty?

Peter Brook: Maybe. But what desire, what liberty? These questions go way beyond the scope of our conversation.

Laurent Feneyrou: Is *Don Giovanni* the opera of the loss of all compassion? Is the hero simply a man of laughter, a man who can mock at suffering, a *dissoluto punito* who is nevertheless attractive and not in the least ridiculous or humiliated?

Peter Brook: Music is an absolutely indispensable language for human beings, from Gregorian chant to the most popular music, that of Piaf and rock and roll. In popular music, the words always convey feelings that everybody understands and shares and that can be summed up in just a few words. Take, for example, "Je ne regrette rien." It's an absolutely precise observation. But the meaning is vastly enhanced by Piaf's singing. The words are not enough in themselves. I cannot express myself fully if I say: "I have no regrets." That could very well give the impression of total indifference, or amorality and pretentiousness. When Piaf sings "Je ne regrette rien," there is no question at all of pretentiousness. You really understand something. You could approach the same idea from every possible angle and even write a whole book about regret, but this would be far less direct than listening to her singing.

It's along these lines that it seems to me that there is something in Don Giovanni's character that arouses a feeling of sympathy. Mozart would never have accepted the commission to write an opera that would involve portraying a character that he detested. There are composers today who could do such a thing without the slightest difficulty. It's perfectly possible to imagine an opera being written on Hitler or Stalin, rather like the case of Brecht and *Arturo Ui*. Mozart accepted the commission because he felt compassion for Don Giovanni and had an intuitive understanding of him. This does not mean that he did not have any compassion for the other characters. As with "Je ne regrette rien," he follows the action, he lends expression to everybody and he puts Don Giovanni into situations that from our point of view are shocking and even sickening. And he expresses something else. I believe that it is Mozart's compassion that removes any idea of a mean and indifferent character, or that of an out-and-out frivolous creature.

> *When he welcomes his three masked guests, Don Giovanni says to them with the utmost banality:* "E aperto a tutti quanti, viva la libertá!"*—and the conceptual meaning of his words is aimed at the sole liberty of not revealing one's identity in order to take part in the festivities where everybody can behave as they please. Da Ponte's libretto says nothing more, but Mozart's music draws in all the voices to join that of Don Giovanni in a triumphant and brilliant apotheosis; it bestows upon this declaration of liberty a new density and in consequence a more intimate meaning. It would of course be absurd to see in this an affirmation of the political liberty of the French Revolution; all the same, it is well and truly the liberty to live as a man according to his natural being that is being demanded here.*
>
> BRIGITTE MARACK
> *Mozart*, 1970

There are two keys to this libretto. One is "Viva la libertá!" If you listen to this statement in its context, it has nothing to do with the French Revolution. If Mozart had put it into the mouth of Leporello, if Leporello had had an aria entitled "Viva la libertá!," the link with Figaro and Beaumarchais would have become patent. But it is Don Giovanni who is speaking during an evening's entertainment put on in his own dwelling with the one and only aim of seducing Zerlina and possibly a number of other young girls. In other words, it's the *dolce vita*. And this *dolce vita* is provided for this very reason among peasants, for there is nobody as puritan in a society of this nature as a peasant. Masetto is a firmly upright being. "Ho capito." Then there arrive three members of the aristocracy who also have their own morality. It is Don Giovanni's wish that during this night of debauchery, the key of the door he is opening should be that of liberty. Mozart lived at a time when society was in the process of opening up. To this extent, a direct link can be found between the customs of the end of the eighteenth century and May 1968, without Mozart having been influenced either by Sade or the French Revolution. May 1968 was not so much a political movement as an authentic affirmation of "Viva la libertá!" Why do we accept what is imposed upon us by a society that provides us with no reason to believe in its values? In the end, Don Giovanni arrives at real purity in his need of liberty. Without forcing the comparison too far, he incarnates the reason for which Sartre called Genet a saint. He goes right to the end with such insistence that he becomes a curious sort of saint. This rebel has his own purity.

> *The great ball scene in the first act is not mere musical virtuosity with all its three separate orchestras on the stage, and the complicated cross-rhythms of the dances. Each of the social classes—peasantry, bourgeoisie, and aristocracy—has its own dance, and the total independence of every rhythm is a reflection of the social hierarchy; it is this order and harmony that is destroyed by the attempted rape of Zerlina offstage.*
>
> CHARLES ROSEN
> *The Classical Style*, 1978

The other key for a satisfactory performance is the word *moment*. The *momento*. Life in the moment. It is for that reason that Don Giovanni must be performed by a singer who is also a good actor. To sing Don Giovanni, it isn't enough to be handsome with a fine voice. The acting demands are just as important as the vocal and musical demands. What is needed is an actor with the ability to change, one who can live the character of Don Giovanni moment by moment. Don Giovanni's error, his Achilles' heel, lies perhaps in his living to such an extent the wealth and joy of the moment. He is endowed with nearly every quality: charm, energy, and the attractive nature of the free man. Yet he cannot see that the present moment is inseparable from its influence over the following moment. In the immense kaleidoscope of his qualities, there is one essential thing lacking, the understanding that every act has consequences. This is precisely where the freedom of each one of us is inevitably hedged in. In *Crime and Punishment*, Raskolnikov naively believes that everything is allowed to the man who is free. We come across the same problem, alas, in the case of twelve-year-old children who commit appalling crimes. There is the child who kills a classmate and who six months later remains cold and indifferent before the judge. This is a pathological case. And the other case is that of a child who is absolutely heedless.

You cannot say that Don Giovanni is an exemplary being, that you can seduce and kill because it is funny.

That is not liberty at all.

But when Don Giovanni talks about women, he talks not merely about desire and the joy of voluptuousness but truly about love. When he gives himself body and soul, at that moment he is talking about love. This desire makes him irresistible. In "Là ci darem la mano!" he is a professional seducer with immense charm. But when Zerlina falls into his arms, the duet they sing together is a little love duet of great purity. And it is precisely here that you find all the dialectic and fascinating sides to the character. From a certain point of view, it represents a joyful expression of liberty. But there is a flaw in Don Giovanni's personality: he never foresees the terrifying consequences of his acts. He refuses even to recognize them.

> *But what is the force, then, by which Don Juan seduces? It is desire, the energy of sensuous desire. He desires in every woman the whole of womanhood, and therein lies the sensuously idealizing power with which he at once embellishes and overcomes his prey. The reaction to this gigantic passion beautifies and develops the one desired, who flushes in enhanced beauty by its reflection, the object of his desire, who blushes in response to it.*
>
> SØREN KIERKEGAARD
> *Either/Or*, 1846

At the end of the opera, if one listens to the music, it is clear that once again the presence of the mystery of death is infinitely more important than the idea of punishment, even though Da Ponte wrote *punito*. At that time, when devils came on stage, the audience used to laugh. They were not in the least terrorized by their appearance. Here, the music does not play along with the church by invoking Hell. It goes much further than that, for the feeling is deeper and more serious, as in a requiem.

Laurent Feneyrou: So Don Giovanni is apparently uncalculating; but in addition, he has no memory, plan, or method. He seems to be absolutely spontaneous. Unaware of the future, he seems forgetful of his certain fate, thus freeing himself from such a vision. In your view, are his moments hermetically sealed?

Peter Brook: I believe that this is absolutely so. His moments are inseparable from the flaw, from the one thing that this man lacks, the capacity at any precise moment to remember what has gone just before and to understand what is to come. If his memory had been totally developed, he might have found within himself the moral consciousness that even without external moral pressures, would have changed his behavior toward others.

Laurent Feneyrou: Does this mean that his forgetfulness lends legitimacy to the incessant renewal of his desire?

Peter Brook: Yes, I believe that to a certain extent, women for him are like a meal. Even though we may not have the experience of *mille e tre* women, everyone of us has enjoyed the experience of *mille e tre*, if not more, dinners or glasses of wine in our lives. The memory of a glass of wine does not help us to refuse another glass the following day. The glass of wine is an experience that passes. And somewhere in his digestive system, Don Giovanni behaves in this fashion with women. Each experience passes.

ABOVE:
Claudio Abbado (right) and Daniel Harding, conductors of Peter Brook's production of *Don Giovanni*, in rehearsal, Aix-en-Provence, 1998.

BELOW:
Peter Brook's production of *Don Giovanni*, Festival international d'art lyrique, Aix-en-Provence, 1998.

Don Juan is a man who represents what is possible. His desire is power and all his relationships are relationships of power and possession. That is why he is a myth of modern times. But this is only the outside appearance. Because he is a man of desire, Don Juan is a being who lives in the sphere of the fascination that he exercises and exploits and in which he delights; at the same time he maintains, by means of his mastery and constant betrayal, the desire-driven liberty that he does not wish to relinquish. Don Juan knows very well that he is welcoming impossibility with desire, but he asserts that impossibility is none other than the sum of what is possible and that it can therefore be mastered in the same way as a number and it matters not at all that this number should be one thousand and three, or even a few more or a few less. Don Juan could very well commit himself to one woman only, whom he would possess but a single time, always provided that he could desire her, not as the one and only woman but as the single entity summoning the infinity of repetition.

MAURICE BLANCHOT
The Infinite Interview, 1969

Laurent Feneyrou: In the last scene of the first act, Donna Anna, Donna Elvira, and Don Ottavio come on stage masked. Did Mozart find the essence of the theater in these characters without a face, in the hidden and concealed being of the characters? Is not Don Giovanni also the "fertile satiety of the carnival"?

Peter Brook: What fascinates me in nearly all works of art is that they go a great deal further than the most gifted of their authors could possibly explain. A number of contemporary authors such as Pinter and Beckett have always refused to provide the least explanation. They claim that they don't know, that they haven't the least idea about their characters. "What happens after the play?" "But there isn't an end." "What happened before?" "But there wasn't a before. The character said only what I wrote."

Generation after generation, century upon century, layer upon layer get added, which have nothing to do with the author's intentions. A great many works can be interpreted in countless ways. When the interpretation hits the right note, the overall impression that emerges is that of an absolute truth, one which was always there. It may well be that this interpretation escapes people from another epoch or culture. At the same time, another aspect can appear as something self-evident. All great works are things in movement. Some of their constituent parts are hidden in the subconscious of the works. As a result of the fluctuating conditions of our lives, new readings come to the surface, other readings disappear. I believe that today, we are much less in sympathy than we were fifty years ago with the commedia dell'arte and the pantomime humor.

It is for this reason that we are wrong to attribute to any given author philosophical or analytical intentions that we might well discover later. Even though Mozart had penetrating and highly intelligent ideas on the theater, I cannot for a moment think that when he was writing a scene with masked characters he was giving much thought to masks. He wrote in the intuitive movement of an act of creation. The case of Pirandello on the other hand is quite different. He had thought a great deal about illusion on the stage and he tried to express in his plays a number of ideas about the theater and about life.

There are masks simply because there are characters who do not want to be recognized. Although we may respect those people who write about a particular work, it has to be said that literary analysis is somewhat dangerous for a director and for an actor in so much as it introduces didactic or theoretical concepts. And a singer, just like an actor, can think of nothing else save the ideas that he is expressing. They have to find life, moment by moment.

> *In Don Giovanni, taking off one's mask is no longer a matter of acknowledging a concealed identity, since in any case, the other being is no longer identical with the original self. It is a matter of casting aside a dramatic convention and revealing a face which is no longer that of an identity, outside all other possible faces. At the end of the first act, Don Giovanni is preparing to give a reception in his mansion in order to seduce Zerlina. Laughter is wafted through the dense air of the night, occasional fragments of dance music and snatches of conversation can be heard. The lighted windows are like cutouts against the darkness and they attract passersby like moths to the trap set by Don Giovanni. We know that the three dominoes who come onstage are Anna, Ottavio, and Elvira, all of them intent on ruining Don Giovanni's erotic schemes. When they remove their masks simultaneously and sing aside an appeal to divine justice, they are not revealing their stage identities but removing themselves from their dramatic condition. What they are showing is their inner face, that of a reality which reveals them and which is no longer their vengeance. The settings of the masquerade, the festivities, and the theater are superimposed and the revealed identity is transformed into a person that the being disintegrates. Through the intervention of the mask and behind the hollow shape of the face, Mozart lends substance to the invisible, bereft of its nonface, its double identity.*
>
> MICHEL TAMISIER
> *Don Juan et le Mythe du théâtre*, 1975

Laurent Feneyrou: In your view, why are all Don Giovanni's promising plans frustrated as soon as the Commendatore has met his death?

Peter Brook: Da Ponte opted for the best dramatic sequence. Given the speed of events—everything takes place within the space of twenty-four hours, with a statue that the funeral undertakers of the time miraculously managed to produce within the same twenty-four hours—the theatrical tempo is never allowed to falter, never allowed to let up. It is wonderful. And within the setting of the plot, the comic situations depend entirely on this permanent frustration. It would have been far more ponderous to display a series of seductions. The dominant idea here in the plot is that nothing can go right. The devil is at hand and it's the moment of truth. Don Giovanni's time is up. That very day he began to career wildly to his death.

Just as he is about to catch Zerlina a second time, Masetto appears. This scene can be played either as a moment of frustration, or as a slight frustration, dispelled by the considerable delights of danger. Masetto has appeared. Don Giovanni is well aware just how much Masetto wants to get him. And there you have Don Giovanni in his entirety, in his absolutely primitive, intuitive, animal, and ferocious joy over finding himself, like Zorro, in great danger. It's like what happens in kung fu films. It's the same situation as Bruce Lee meeting a pretty girl. He's attracted. Then suddenly five thugs turn up. Of course, he's disappointed about not getting the girl, but he is overjoyed at finding himself confronted by five nasty and dangerous individuals. This is at work in the scene with Masetto in the second act. If the scene is played too lightly, it turns into operetta, "Offenbach," or a farce with a deceived husband and armed idiots. But if it is thought that Masetto and the villagers are powerful thugs who have every reason to kill Don

Giovanni, then Don Giovanni, even in disguise, is in a dangerous situation. He provokes them. Who goes there? He could escape, say something else, but he pronounces his name: "I am Don Giovanni's servant." Masetto replies: "Leporello." That does nothing to avert the danger. Don Giovanni stokes up the situation to such an extent that to extricate himself, his only possibility is to add: "That scoundrel." He says it with such vehemence that Masetto is convinced that he is on their side.

That is what leads into the rest of the story. And it is a pretty dreadful story. Don Giovanni, disguised as Leporello, asks Masetto and the villagers to find Leporello, disguised as Don Giovanni, to give him a good beating and then kill him. He provokes an extremely dangerous situation for his servant. This is ferocity à la Bruce Lee.

Laurent Feneyrou: Is there a place for God in *Don Giovanni* and in the death of its hero?

Peter Brook: There are two completely different gods. There is the god of religions. That particular god is always a god to whom the different religions, churches, and sects have given a face and attributes. And there is the mystical god, a god who has no form and who is not the Catholic, personal god to whom one speaks literally as to a father. And if Mozart's god, after having been the god of Freemasonry, becomes the god who has no name, no form, no face, who cannot be named or expressed in words but who can be evoked as a reality by means of music, then I would say that that is the god of Mozart in all his religious music. But I would make a complete and absolute separation from the didactic god of religion who is of use to the church by stressing good, evil, punishment, paradise, hell, and all the rest. Mozart's music is neither doctrinaire nor didactic. A profound spirituality is common to both *The Magic Flute* and *Don Giovanni*. In a way, there is as much spirituality in *Don Giovanni* as there is in *The Magic Flute*. The two operas are complementary. At first sight, *The Magic Flute* is more mystical than *Don Giovanni*. The religion in it is shown in its finest colors, the colors of an illuminated paradise, in spite of the darkness and obscurity embodied in Monostatos. *Don Giovanni* has the same spiritual depth, but it does not shine. The two works span the whole range of the private and intimate feelings of Mozart's spirituality. It is the same composer who is making his way along the same path.

Laurent Feneyrou: Does the experience of the void run through the whole of *Don Giovanni*?

Peter Brook: The mysterious scene in the second act, set in a dark courtyard, is one which seems to take place nowhere. There is no realism to justify Leporello taking Donna Elvira to the very place to which Donna Anna, Don Ottavio, Zerlina, and Masetto will make their way a few seconds later. It is a scene that takes place in a mysterious spot, in a situation of dramatic farce where the music is very intense and of great beauty. Leporello in disguise is revealed for who he is. The characters wander around in this no-man's-land. What a powerful impression of sadness emanates here from an opera that is otherwise positive, affirmative, and strong!

You cannot imagine how long the time seemed to me, away from you! I cannot express my feelings, but it's like a void—which hurts me—a sort of languor which is never satisfied and which later is never appeased—which lasts forever and even grows day by day.

WOLFGANG AMADEUS MOZART
letter to his wife, 1737

Laurent Feneyrou: In the last scene, vengeance, rage, and spite have lost all their point or impact. The punishment is aimless. Although Donna Elvira, Donna Anna, Don Ottavio, Zerlina, and Masetto had hitherto existed only through their fascinated attachment to their master, they are all now afraid of the desire-filled liberty that Don Giovanni has revealed to them. Is Don Giovanni a sort of vanishing point, a horizon whose loss leaves man on his own, wandering and abandoned?

Peter Brook: That is absolutely so! All the characters are splendid, touching, profoundly touching because in their own ways, they are all lost. Don Giovanni himself is a lost soul without realizing it. Every individual who lives the feverish sort of life he did is bound to come to a sudden stop. There is perhaps an absolute void. For Leporello, there is nothing completely satisfying. It is perhaps for that reason that he is very human, because, like everybody, he leads a life of compromise, with his blend of dreadful cowardice and eminently likable qualities.

Laurent Feneyrou: Exhausting desire, desiring in a vacuum, desiring nothing save music, the source of life and energy, is that how Mozart composed?

Peter Brook: If we come back to the fact that music is the one language of humanity that touches the most fundamental truths, all musicians are extraordinarily lucky. After the saints and the great mystics, the people who are the luckiest in the world, even though they may endure appalling trials, are those who enjoy the genius of music. The musician hears what is inaccessible to others. When he enters into this inaccessible sphere, his joy is extraordinary.

The composer has access to a world to which most of us have no access. But almost anybody can feel a taste for music. It is for that reason that music does not exist only in the head of the composer. It is bound up with the generous need to share. We cannot enter the mind of Mozart but we can go fairly deeply into his experience. Before the act of composition, there is no shape or form. Then music adopts a certain shape, one which has yet to become a vehicle. Mozart writes his score. And we approach him, we climb a mountain with him. Our own vision is no longer the one we are accustomed to experience every day. But he himself had no choice. He was born like that, even if his genius endowed him neither with the rights nor the powers of great adventurers and great financiers. It was beyond his control to create the material conditions of his life. Quite the opposite was true, and the art of Bach and of Mozart could not spare them day-to-day troubles, creditors, and the inevitable difficulties with wives and children. On the other hand, what the composer bears within himself provides him with permanent access to another level of human existence. And in the end, this is far more important than anything else.

Or else, taking away and giving back, privation and restoration, these also represent the division between the two states of the code: language and music are both symbols but opposed as to the economy of the body. In both instances, you have retrenchment, creation of absence, and theft. But where language restores only an almost abstract vibration to which there still adheres, together with the intelligible, the whole misfortune of articulated mourning, music restores to this stolen body a system of vibrations which bathe and envelop, provoke resonance, touch at every fiber, remaking for you by means of caresses a body without fortuity or weight, a transfigured body. Singing which soars above the historic misfortune of speaking, and music which resolves the farewell that lingers in the singing, that is what opera is. Mozart knew with the absolute certainty of his bodily being what music had to say about itself through him. Further back: abducted by music and trained to say farewell through it; further on: leaning toward music to derive consolation. What had the law on its side had to have love on its side, too. Don Giovanni *is no less of a miracle for having this as its justification.*

LUDOVIC JANVIER

"L'Impatience et le Deuil," in *L'Avant-Scène*, 1979

Laurent Feneyrou: You wrote in *The Shifting Point*: "Opera was born fifty-thousand years ago when people came out of their caves uttering sounds. From these sounds there came Verdi, Puccini, and Wagner. There was a noise for fear, for love, for happiness, and for anger. It was opera on one note and atonal to boot. At that precise moment, it was a natural human expression which turned into singing. A long time later, this process was codified, given structure and turned into art." Is it the desire for sound between "the plumbing and the water which flows through it" that animates *Don Giovanni*?

Peter Brook: Man has developed an extraordinary instrument, that of conceptual language, which to a great extent is an expression of the functioning of the brain, of mental processes. But before that, there was a first language that came from the language of animals, the language of feeling. The cries of animals express in a very primitive manner feelings to which they give outward expression by a sound. Before expression, ideas, and concepts, early man expressed his state of being and the state of his emotions by sounds and cries. These were cries of pain, of distress, of warning, and of joy. Later, the first word for *happy* did not suffice to express a feeling of unlimited joy. A sound was added to it, coming before, with, and after the word.

In the work I have carried out with actors, we have been able to see how a need for expression can spring from a single note, an absolutely necessary note. Then, as with the most primitive melodies, there comes a phrase with two notes, then three. A form is in the making. There is nothing artificial about the evolution of this form into what we call opera. Quite the contrary, for it is the most natural way in the world to enhance a mere word, which in itself is incapable of expressing the whole range of feelings that it suggests. The statement "Je ne regrette rien" is a generalization. But Piaf—just as Mozart in *Don Giovanni*, each in their own way—expresses word by word the inner and hidden shades of meaning.

Translated from the French by John Sidgwick

JOSEPH CORNELL : *L'agriculture pratique*

LA SEMAINE MÉTÉOROLOGIQUE

Du 23 au 29 janvier 1911 (OBSERVATOIRE DU PARC SAINT-MAUR.)

JOURS ET DATES	PRESSION à midi.	TEMPÉRATURE Minima.	Maxima.	Moyenne	Ecart sur la normale.	Vent.	Durée de l'insolation.	Hauteur de pluie.	REMARQUES DIVERSES
	millim.						heures	millim.	
Lundi... 23 janv.	775.2	—1°.9	0°.0	—1°.0	— 3°.2	S	0.0	0.2	Temps couvert, neige fine après-midi.
Mardi.... 24 —	775.2	0.0	2.5	1.0	— 1.2	S	0.0	»	Temps couvert, brouillard le soir.
Mercredi.. 25 —	775.6	—1.1	2.7	1.0	— 1.3	S	0.0	»	Brouillard et gelée bl. le matin, t·mps couvert, bruine le s.
Jeudi..... 26 —	776.5	2.7	6.6	4.3	+ 2.0	S O	0.0	0.1	Bruine le matin, temps couvert.
Vendredi.. 27 —	776.5	4.0	6.4	5.0	+ 2.7	S	0.0	»	Brouillard le matin, temps couvert
Samedi .. 28 —	776.1	—1.0	6 3	3.3	+ 0.9	S E	0.0		... m., beau et ... soir.
Dimanche. 29 —	772.1	—1.9	7.9	1.8	— 0.6	N E	7.8		...ouill. le ...rnée,
Moyennes ou totaux......	775.3	0.1	4.6	2.2	»	S			
Ecarts sur la normale.....	+11.6	0.0	—1.3	—0.1	»	»			

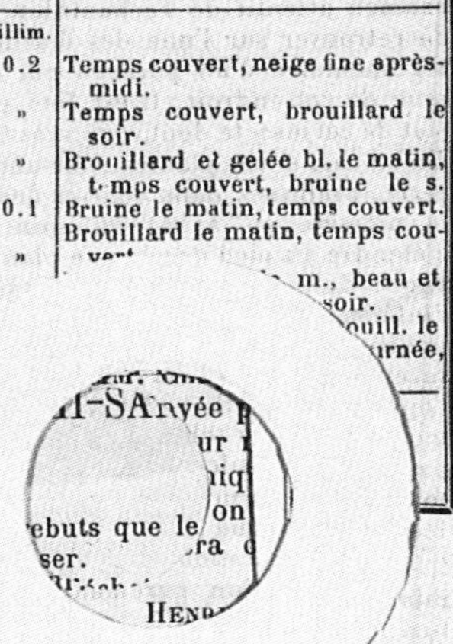

REVUE COMMERC

COURS DES DENRÉES A

Situation agricole. — Depuis quelques jours, le baromètre marque des pressions élevées, le temps est clair et le froid très vif. Aux environs de Paris, la température est de 3 à 4 degrés au-dessous de zéro. Le mois de janvier a été assez favorable aux travaux des champs; dans plusieurs régions, on a poursuivi l'exécution des emblavures de froment et l'étendue à cultiver en blé de printemps sera peut-être moins importante qu'on ne le pensait.

Toutefois, on ne sera fixé à cet égard que dans un mois, car certains blés, attaqués par les limaces et les rongeurs, devront être refaits; d'autres, semés tardivement dans un sol saturé d'eau, n'ont pas levé, la semence ayant pourri en terre. Les premiers blés semés sont, en général, assez beaux; en quelques endroits, ils sont un peu étiolés, mais l'application en mars d'une petite quantité de nitrate de soude leur rendra leur aspect normal.

On continue à préparer les terres à ensemencer en blés de printemps; souhaitons que le beau temps permette de mener à bonne fin la tâche du cultivateur, car c'est de la réussite des blés de printemps que dépend l'avenir de la prochaine récolte.

A l'étranger, en Russie, des neiges abondantes sont tombées dans le sud; les perspectives des récoltes sont excellentes. En Angleterre, les travaux des champs se poursuivent par un temps sec et froid. Dans l'Inde, les nouvelles des récoltes sont satisfaisantes et l'on prévoit pour les mois d'avril et de mai, de fortes expéditions de blé.

Blés et autres céréales. — Les exportations de blés de la République-Argentine, d'Australie et de l'Inde sont très actives. En Amérique, aux Etats-Unis, les cours des blés ont fléchi de 30 centimes par quintal; sur les marchés européens, la faiblesse des prix du blé est g... ...0 kilogr. les blés sur les marches ...23 à New-York, 18.36 à Chicago, 19.72 à 20.87 à Londres, 25.56 à Berlin.

En France, les offres sont peu nombreuses sur les marchés, les beaux blés sont rares et ceux de qualité moyenne se vendent à des prix faiblement tenus.

On paie aux 100 kilogr. sur les marchés du Nord : à Angers, le blé 27.75 à 28 fr., l'avoine 20.75 à 21 fr.; à Angoulême, le blé 28.75 à 29 fr., l'avoine 20 fr.; à Beauvais, le blé 26.50 à 27 fr., l'avoine 17 à 20 fr.; à Besançon, le blé 24 à 25.50, l'avoine 16 à 18.50; à Blois, le blé 27.50 à 28.25, l'avoine 19.50 à 20 fr.; à Bourg, le blé 28 fr., l'avoine 19.50 à 22 fr.; à Bourges, le blé 26.50 à 27 fr., l'avoine 18.50 à 19.50; à Chartres, le blé 27.50 à 28.25, l'avoine 20 fr.; à Châteauroux, le blé 27.50 à 28.25, l'avoine 19.25 à 20.50; à Chaumont, le blé 25.50 à 26 fr., l'avoine 15.50 à 16 fr.; à Clermont-Ferrand, le blé 27 à 28 fr., l'avoine 20 à 20.50; à Evreux, le blé 27 à 27.50, l'avoine 18.25 à 19.50; à Laon, le blé 26 à 26.25, l'avoine 18 à 19.25; à Limoges, le blé 27.50 à 28 fr., l'avoine 20 à 20.50; à Moulins, le blé 27 à 27.25, l'avoine 18.50 à 18 75; à Nancy, le blé 24 fr., l'avoine 17.50 à 19 fr.; à Nantes, le blé 28 à 28.25, l'avoine 19.75 à 20 fr.; à Nevers, le blé 26 à 27.50, l'avoine 19.50 à 20 fr.; à Orléans, le blé 28 à 28.25, l'avoine 20 fr.; à Rennes, le blé 28 à 28.50, l'avoine 20.50; à Rouen, le blé 26 à 26.75, l'avoine 18.25 à 21.50; à Saint-Brieuc, le blé 27 fr., l'avoine 20 fr.; à Troyes, le blé 25.50 à 26 fr.; l'avoine 19 à 20 fr.

Sur les marchés du Midi, on cote aux 100 kilogr. : à Nîmes, le blé 26 à 28 fr., l'avoine 20 fr.; à Tarbes, le blé 28.75 à 29.25, l'avoine 22 à 23 fr.; à Toulouse, le blé 25.75 à 29.25, l'avoine grise 21 à 21.50.

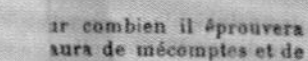

POMPE DE JARDIN A COMMANDE ÉLECTRIQUE
151
A une distance de 30 mètres du puits on a
s parallèles, de 6 mètres de
pportent un réservoir prisma-
e 3 mètres de hauteur, con-
s cubes d'eau.
pe employée est montée sur
A
B
C
r
n
a
E
Mariée
Fig. 27. — Pompe à commande électrique, employée au jardin potager de la Norville.
en appuyant le galet B sur la jante de la roue A.
On voit dans la figure 27 le gros câble souple E qui renferme les deux conducteurs électriques soigneusement isolés; le courant passe au rhéostat de démarrage r avant de se rendre au moteur C. La pompe ne présente
153
Alfred Gallier.
EURS

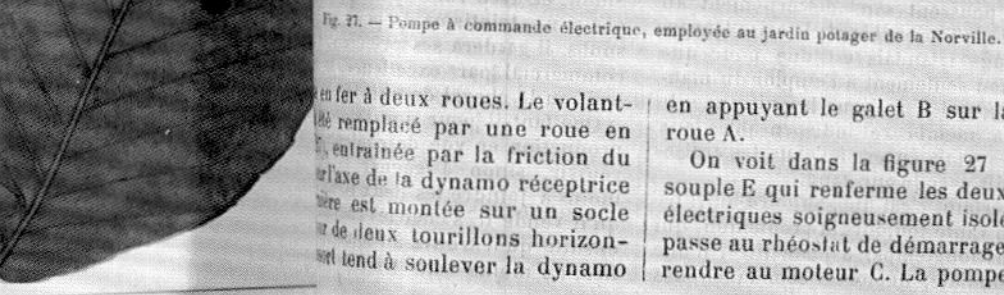

des principales étapes de l'activité du Service que dirige M. Chapelle. Mais ces associations ne peuvent rendre les services qu'on en attend qu'à la condition de travailler dans les [illegible]ditions les plus parfaites.

C'est po[illegible]quoi MM. Chapelle et Ruby ont eu l'excellente [illegible]nsée de rédiger un guide complet sur l'art d[illegible] faire de la bonne huile d'olive. Tel est l'obje[illegible] de l'ouvrage qu'ils viennent de publier sous [illegible] titre *L'Huilerie moderne, extraction de l'hu[illegible]olive* (1). Ecrit par des spécialistes [illegible] ce livre sera précieux non s[illegible] qui possèdent des mou[illegible] sont appelés à en diri[illegible] tous ceux qui s'intéress[illegible] rapide analyse suffira po[illegible]

Il ne suffit pas, pour [illegible]e huile, de travailler rationnelle[illegible]ves: la première condition à remplir est que les fruits soient de bonne qualité et qu'ils aient été conservés dans les meilleures conditions. C'est pourquoi MM. Chapelle et Ruby commencent par fournir des notions précises sur la constitution même des olives, ainsi que sur les règles à observer dans leur récolte et dans leur conservation jusqu'au moment o[illegible] elles sont triturées. Ce sont des indications qui sont en quelque sorte préliminaires, mais qui sont essentielles.

Le bon aménagement du moulin et l'emploi d'un matériel bien choisi sont les conditions d'un travail régulier. A cet égard, les auteurs décrivent avec un soin rigoureux les appareils les plus perfectionnés, et ils donnent des détails précis sur les progrès méthodiques qui ont été réalisés tant en France que dans les autres pays, notamment en Italie où l'oléiculture occupe une grande place.

Les mêmes descriptions des innovations les plus récentes se retrouvent à l'occasion des méthodes de fabrication des huiles d'olive, de conservation et de filtration, comme d'utilisation des sous-produits.

Appuyée sur des plans et des devis d'huileries modèles, cette documentation copieuse fait de l'ouvrage de MM. Chapelle et Ruby, suivant l'expressi[illegible]yée plus haut, un véritable guide [illegible]r moderne, qui [illegible]oit s'appuyer [illegible]nique rigoureu-se[illegible]ment ordonn[illegible] que le co[illegible]ont rendu ainsi un [illegible]ouveau se[illegible]ra certainement appré[illegible]ié à sa valeu[illegible]

HENRY SAGNIER.

LA SITUATION A[illegible]E DANS [illegible]'AVEYRON

LA [illegible]UE[illegible]

25 [illegible]

Nous avons eu une assez abondante [illegible] neige, le 2 janvier. Sur une notable partie[illegible] département, cette neige est restée jusqu'à [illegible] jour, parce qu'il n'a pas cessé de geler. Parfo[illegible] se montre un beau soleil, qui réchauffe la tem[illegible]pérature aux bonnes expositions; mais, à l'ombr[illegible] le thermomètre se maintient toujours au-dessous de zéro. Impossible d'ouvrir le moindre sillon.

C'est grand dommage; car les semailles d'automne n'ont pas pu se faire à moitié; et celles qui furent faites ne promettent rien de bon. Il serait donc très à souhaiter qu'on pût dès maintenant s'occuper des céréales de printemps.

Chez nous, comme dans maintes parties de la France, la cachexie fait de grands ravages parmi les troupeaux de bêtes à laine.

On en cite qui auraient déjà perdu plus de la moitié de leur effectif.

Les propriétaires et fermiers qui savent leurs brebis atteintes se hâtent de les vendre pour la boucherie, à n'importe quelles conditions.

Mais souvent les brebis meurent, sans que rien ait révélé d'avance leur état de maladie. Et puis, [illegible]s cadavres, on trou[illegible] dans le foie [illegible] douves. Les pluies et les [illegible]nda[illegible]ntes de l'été et de l'automne furent cause de tout ce mal. Il apparaîtra bien plus encore en février et mars, aux premières herbes, et au fur et à mesure que se continuera l'agnelage.

En ce moment, les agneaux de lait se paient en moyenne 95 fr. les 100 kilogr. de poids vif. Les années précédentes, à pareille date, ils étaient un peu plus chers. Cette différence vient, dit-on, du prix des peaux d'agneaux qui, de 28 fr. la douzaine en 1910, sont tombées actuellement à 18 fr. chez les gantiers de Millau. Pour la viande d'agneau elle est aussi chere que l'an passé.

Quant à la campagne laitière de Roquefort, elle débute mal. En outre du mauvais état de santé de beaucoup de troupeaux, et de la qualité généralement défectueuse des fourrages, il y a des faits d'un autre ordre qui exercent une action défavorable aux producteurs de lait.

La concurrence active que se faisaient, ces dernières années, les industriels de Roquefort sur le marché du lait de brebis avait fait beaucoup augmenter le prix de cette denrée, passée par étapes successives, en un quart de siècle, de 22 fr. à 25 fr., à 28 fr., à 30 fr... et finalement à 35, 36 et même 37 fr. l'hectolitre.

(1) Un volume in-8° de 208 pages avec 83 figures et 5 plans d'huileries. — Librairie Béranger, 15, rue des Saints-Pères, à Paris. Prix : 4 fr.; franco-poste, 4 fr. 50.

Les principales maisons de Roquefort ont voulu mettre un terme à cette concurrence, qui avait pour résultat de surélever dans de pareilles proportions la matière première de leur industrie. Elles ont engagé des pourparlers en vue d'une entente.

Et un beau jour (c'était dans le courant du mois de décembre dernier), propriétaires et fermiers producteurs de lait de brebis apprenaient avec effroi, et avec indignation ... tente était conclue ... les trois ... la So...

où le prix de 35 fr. est encore pratiqué à l'heure actuelle, soit parce que le lait, dans ces parages, est plus riche en caséine, soit aussi parce qu'il s'y trouve des fromageries appartenant aux Sociétés non fusionnées, pour maintenir un peu de concurrence.

Au lieu de se répandre en récriminations aussi stériles que violentes contre les gros industriels de Roquefort, contre leurs accaparements, contre leurs *trusts*, les producteurs de lait de brebis ... leur exemple, s'entendre comme ... communaux ou pa... et reunir en... fédérations ... par arron...

— N° 7483 (*Seine-et-Marne*). — Vous voulez installer un petit **atelier de menuiserie** comprenant : *a*, une scie à ruban à chantourner avec poulies de 0m.60 de diamètre ; *b*, une mortaiseuse; *c*, une raboteuse de 0m.40 de large, pouvant faire dégauchisseuse sur 0m.25 de largeur ; *d*, une toupie à moulures.

Les machines devant travailler simultanément sont *a* et *b*, puis *c* et *d*.

Un **moteur** de 5 chevaux-vapeur peut évidemment convenir, car tout dépend de l'avancement qu'on donnera aux pièces de bois à travailler ; c'est cet avancement, constituant un frein, qui détermine surtout le travail mécanique néces-

saire par seconde pour enle... de bois dans le même temps.

Il ne faut pas songer au m... ir ... de 5 chevaux ou plus; vous ... verez de fabrication courante. Il e... même le moteur à gaz pauvre, qu... avantag... qu'à partir d'une dizaine de ... et pour travail continu, toute la jou... omme c... d'une usine ou d'un atelier. ... us cons... lons l'emploi d'un moteur à pé... mpant, sera plus économique qu'un ... à esse... minérale.

MM. Petit, Collard et Cie, 19, ... aux Fleu...

A signaler encore les plaquettes en argent attribuées à M. Charles Camille, à Sceaux (Seine), pour un lot de pigeons romains chamois, et à M. P. Paquis, à Cliron (Ardennes), pour un lot de lapins béliers d'un développement exceptionnel.

Beurres et fromages. — L'exposition des beurres était fort intéressante. La multiplication des laiteries coopératives dans plusieurs régions est le fait saillant des dernières années ; elle a donné au concours un caractère accentué, à raison du nombre très important de lots exposés par ces associations.

C'est d'abord l'Association des laiteries coopératives des Charentes et du Poitou, dont la haute influence est [illegible]

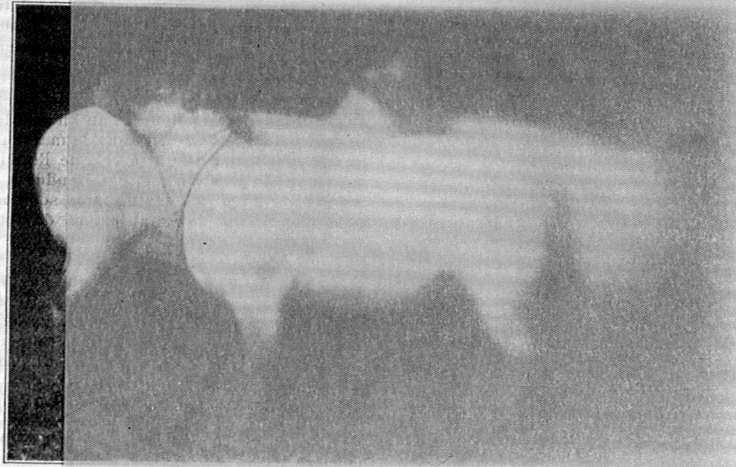

Fig. 49. — Lot d'agneaux [illegible]

jours la plus nombreuse. [illegible] tique nouveau n'est [illegible] neur sont décernés : [illegible] M. Doublet, à Préaux [illegible] fromages de Pont-l'Évêque [illegible] classe, à M. A. [illegible] Dôme), pour un fromage d'Auvergne. [illegible] ler quelques bons lots de fromages des Pyrénées exposés [illegible] et de bons lots [illegible] fromageries coopératives des Vosges.

Produits divers. — [illegible] en ce qui concerne [illegible] prement dits, [illegible] très belles collections [illegible] Andrieux forment [illegible] section. A côté, on remarquait [illegible]

ciétés locales y so… d'une valeur de 1… conclure qu'un tiers… est réassuré, ce qui… Il est permis d'ajou… de réassurance, il e… situation assez préc… variés. Il en est, au c… une grande vitalité, … assurance des arrondi… et de Wassy (Haute-Ma… une fédération de 220 … ital de près de 8… part, l'Union f… son activité, avec … ur plus du tiers du … fait abstraction de … on doit constater q… il est encore trop peu … rop précaire dans nombre de circo… quand elle existe.

…e saurait exprimer la m… opinio… *assurances contre l'incen…* De… s situations sont beaucoup … précises. Les 2 187 so… stant au 30 septembre … dhérents effectifs pour u… le 508 374 563 fr., et 36 845 membres … nts devant assurer un capital de … 190 fr. à l'expiration de leurs polices. On compte encore 23 départements … ossèdent pas d'assurances mutuelles … incendie ; mais, si l'on tient compte … es les sociétés actuelles ont été … ns les dix dernières années, on doit … er une fois de plus, comme nous … ait à maintes reprises, la rapidité … uelle le mouvement s'est accéléré.

…ôté, la réassurance fonctionne beau… s normalement que pour les assu… ntre la mortalité du bétail. En 1910, … ciétés locales étaien… s de réassurance… nales ; pour u… ns. D'autre p… degré fon… ns très imp… e part, par l… l'Union ce… rs de F… oir la… tre … lteurs … Paris, dont …

…la grêle res… tuation que … réparties …

entre 23 départements, assuraient, en 1910, un capital de 28 millions de francs.

Quant aux *assurances mutuelles contre les accidents du travail agricole*, elles sont encore … nombreuses que celles contre la grêle. … rt officiel constate que de petites so… les ne sauraient assurer les res… t les charges imposées par les … il 1898 et 30 juin 1899, et il … alités qui se sont créées … des risques très limités … indemnités peu impor…

… gé… du rapport du mi… gricultu… la suivante :

… ats obten… des plus satisfai… rent que … r les idées de … e solida… t davantage … rofon… mocratie ru… l'e… est consi… re be… p à faire pour … de l'assurance agricole. … s'en … compte par ce fait que les d'assurances contre la mortalité du bé… ont, nous l'avons vu, de beaucoup les … nombreuses, ne représentent à cette heure qu'un capital assuré de 532 millions, soit à peu près le dixième du cheptel de la France ! D'une part, les sociétés locales font encore défaut sur bien des points et, d'autre part, plus de la moitié de celles qui existent ne sont pas fédérées ou réassurées et se trouvent, par suite de leur isolement, exposées à de graves éventualités.

C'est pour remédier à cette situation que le Gouvernement a déposé, avant la fin de la dernière législature, le projet de loi qui tend à l'institution d'une caisse centrale destinée à réassurer les sociétés locales de réassurances mutuelles agricoles.

Cette Caisse qui doit être gérée par la Caisse des dépôts et consignations, et qui sera alimentée annuellement par les cotisations des caisses affiliées et par une subvention de 300 000 fr., prélevée sur le budget du ministère de l'Agriculture, bénéficiera d'un fonds initial de dotation de 1 800 000 fr. constitué par un prélèvement sur le produit des jeux dans les cercles et casinos, en exécution de la loi du 15 juin 1907. … caisse centrale se consacrera tout d'abord à … réassurance du bétail dont l'organisation offre déjà des bases solides puisqu'il existe 58 caisses locales de réassurance. Mais des lois ultérieures pourront l'autoriser à étendre successivement ses opérations aux autres risques agricoles lorsque les ressources disponibles le permettront et au fur et à mesure des besoins qui se manifesteront.

Il n'est pas douteux que cette caisse qui servira de régulateur et de soutien à toutes les caisses affiliées n'exerce une influence considérable sur le développement de ces institutions en stimulant les initiatives et en dissipant les dernières hésitations. Ce sera la consolidation et le couronnement de l'œuvre que le Gouvernement de la République a entreprise lorsqu'il a résolu d'assurer par l'application des principes mutualistes la sécurité et la prospérité de nos agriculteurs.

Le projet de loi que M. Raynaud rappelle a soulevé d'assez vives discussions dont le Congrès de la Mutualité, qui s'est tenu à Rouen au mois de septembre, a recueilli les échos, comme on s'en souvient. Il paraît peu probable que la discussion devant le Parlement en soit prochaine.

Sucres et mélasses pour l'alimentation du bétail.

Des décrets en date du 29 décembre ont fixé de nouveaux modes de dénaturation pour les sucres et les bas produits, en vue de bénéficier des dispositions de la loi du 5 juillet 1904, relative à l'emploi du sucre destiné à l'alimentation du bétail :

A 100 kilogr. de sirops de turbinage, mélanger aussi intimement que possible : 1° 2 kilogr. de sel marin ; 2° 20 kilogr. de cossettes épuisées de sucrerie (pulpes humides).

A 100 kilogr. de sucres cristallisés titrant moins de 95 degrés saccharimétriques, ou de sirops de turbinage, mélanger aussi intimement que possible : 1° 2 kilogr. de sel marin ; 2° 20 kilogr. de farine de maïs ou de fèves ou de riz.

Ces modes de dénaturation s'ajouteront désormais à ceux qui ont été fixés antérieurement.

D'autre part, sur l'avis conforme du Comité consultatif des arts et manufactures, le ministre des Finances a autorisé, à titre d'essai, le nouveau procédé ci-après pour la dénaturation des mélasses destinées à l'alimentation du bétail :

A 80 kilogr. de mélasses épuisées, mélanger aussi intimement que possible 20 kilogr. au moins d'une ou plusieurs des substances ci-après : bas produits de mouture, coques de cacao ou d'arachides en poudre, radicelles de malterie, paillettes de lin, cossettes épuisées de sucrerie (pulpes humides).

L'administration des Contributions indirectes rappelle qu'en raison de l'intérêt que présente pour l'agriculture la diffusion des produits mélassés, elle s'est appliquée à réduire autant que possible les formalités qui incombent aux dépositaires de ces produits. Ceux-ci ont simplement à représenter aux employés les acquits-à-caution ayant légitimé le transport des produits qu'ils reçoivent et à tenir note sur un carnet des livraisons qu'ils effectuent, celles-ci n'impliquant la délivrance d'aucun titre de mouvement. Il est possible de dispenser de la formalité du cautionnement les dépositaires qui présenteraient par eux mêmes une surface suffisante. Enfin, eu égard aux garanties qui résultent de la dénaturation préalable, le contrôle à exercer chez les dépositaires de mélasses dénaturées peut être moins fréquent et moins strict que chez ceux recevant de la mélasse en nature.

Admission temporaire des amandes.

Le *Journal Officiel* du 30 décembre a fixé les règles à suivre pour l'admission temporaire des amandes douces avariées et des amandes amères, en vue de l'extraction de l'huile fixe. Cette mesure avait été autorisée par la loi du 29 mars 1910 sur le régime douanier. Voici ces règles :

Les amandes douces avariées et les amandes amères devront être présentées sans coque.

Sont considérées comme amandes douces avariées celles qui sont impropres à l'alimentation, telles que les amandes moisies, les amandes véreuses ou piquées par des vers, les amandes rancies ou dont le goût a été altéré par des émanations ou par le contact de marchandises à odeur forte.

Le service des laboratoires sera appelé à constater, pour chaque introduction, l'état des amandes douces présentées comme avariées.

Les déclarants s'engageront, par une soumission valablement cautionnée, à réexporter ou à mettre en entrepôt, dans un délai qui ne pourra excéder six mois, les huiles provenant du traitement desdites amandes.

Les quantités d'huile fixe à représenter à la sortie comme compensation sont fixées à 55 kilogr. pour 100 kilogr. d'amandes douces avariées ou d'amandes amères sans coque importées.

L'entrée et la sortie devront s'effectuer par le même bureau de douane. Le bureau de Marseille est le seul ouvert actuellement pour ces opérations.

Nécrologie.

Nous éprouvons le regret d'annoncer la mort de M. François [illegible] ident honoraire du Comice agr[illegible] dissement de Lille (Nord), dé[illegible] à Paillencourt, dans sa soi[illegible] année. Agriculteur très est[illegible] uvre à des études et d[illegible] appréciées.

Not[illegible]
vien[illegible]
Ru[illegible]
m[illegible]
a[illegible]

Joseph Cornell

An avid reader since childhood, Joseph Cornell discovered the joy of browsing in the bookstalls along New York's Fourth Avenue during the 1920s. Characteristically, browsers proceed in a leisurely and exploratory fashion and on a solitary basis, whether in privacy at home or in the public domain of bookstores and libraries. For many, browsing retains its casualness. For others, it inspires bibliomania, the collecting and preserving books as objects in and of themselves.

Cornell identified closely with the concept of bibliomania. At the time of his death in 1972, his personal library included some three thousand vintage and contemporary books and periodicals that attest to his encyclopedic interests in the arts and humanities. Literature and poetry are the subjects of at least a third of these publications, a percentage that is not surprising given the abundant literary allusions in his artworks.

However, unlike a traditional bibliophile, Cornell did not hesitate to alter, sometimes even destroy the books and magazines that he collected. The papered surfaces and poetic imagery of his boxes and collages owe much to the publications from which he tirelessly cut illustrations, reproductions, and printed text. Yet Cornell also transformed books, adapting them as the armatures and containers for a small group of artworks that he called "book objects." Made primarily during the 1930s and 1940s, works such as his Untitled Book Object (*Journal d'agriculture pratique et Journal de l'agriculture*) are studies in surprise.

Between the staid covers of this 1911 volume, we find that at least a quarter of its 844 pages feature Cornell's collage vignettes, inserts, cutouts, and overlays of transparent or opaque paper. Impressions of images—top to bottom, across page spreads, and through apertures, front to back—encourage us to browse long and often. Cornell's typed and handwritten inscriptions, as well as the manner in which he circled or underlined words throughout the text, encourage us to linger even more.

Cornell's modifications in his book objects often have no literal or sequential relationship to the old textbooks that he preferred to use for these projects. In this, his most ambitious book object, however, the cast of artists whom he quotes in word and image—the manuscript illuminator for Le Duc de Berry, Diego Velázquez, Marcel Duchamp, and Salvador Dalí among others—suggests a pantheon of homages registered against the backdrop of an authoritative, encyclopedia-style text. Whether direct or oblique, the multiple references to Duchamp also introduce a tantalizing subtext.

The two men had met at the Brummer Gallery in New York City in late 1933 and they enjoyed a friendship based on mutual respect and affection for the balance of their lives. Here we see one of Cornell's earliest acknowledgments of Duchamp not just as an artist who transformed modern art but also as an artist whom he referred to as a "unique personality," and regarded as a mentor.

Lynda Roscoe Hartigan

YEHUDA AMICHAI

My Son Was Drafted

1

My son was drafted. We brought him
to the station along with the other boys.
Now his face has joined the faces of those who say goodbye to me
from the passing windows of the buses and trains of my life,
faces in the streaming rain, faces
squinting in the sun. And now his face.
In the corner of the window, like a stamp on an envelope.

2

In a piazza in Rome near the Coliseum I wash my hands at a public faucet
and drink from my cupped palm, and meanwhile a red-haired woman
in a white dress who was sitting on a folding chair near a closed gate
is gone. When I lift my wet face
she is no more, flown away like a feather laid down upon the world
to check if the world is still breathing. The world
is still breathing, the world is alive
the woman is still alive. We are alive, my son is still alive
the white feather's still flying and living.
I want my son to be a soldier in the Italian army
with a crest of colorful feathers on his cap,
happily dashing around with no enemies, no camouflage.

Translated from the Hebrew by Chana Bloch and Chana Kronfeld

SLEEP

VICTOR PELEVIN

At the very start of the third semester, in one of the lectures on Marxism-Leninism, Nikita Dozakin made a remarkable discovery. Something strange had been happening to him for quite some time now: as soon as the small senior lecturer with the big ears—the one who looked like a priest assailed by blasphemous thoughts—entered the lecture hall, Nikita was overcome by the urge to sleep, as though he were exhausted. And when the lecturer began speaking and pointing up at the light fixture, Nikita just couldn't resist any more, and fell asleep.

At first it seemed as though the lecturer were not talking about philosophy, but about something from Nikita's childhood—about attics, sandpits, and burning garbage dumps. Then the pen in Nikita's hand would mount diagonally to the very top of his sheet of paper, trailing some illegible phrase in its wake, and finally his head would droop and he would plummet down into darkness—only to emerge from it a second or two later, when the same sequence of events would be repeated.

His notes looked very odd and were totally useless for study: short paragraphs of text were cut through by long diagonal sentences about cosmonauts lost in space or a visit to Moscow by the Mongol Khan, all in small, jerky handwriting. At first Nikita was very upset by his inability to sit through a lecture in the proper fashion, but then he began wondering whether the same happened to the other students—and that was when he made his discovery. It turned out that almost everyone else in the hall was sleeping, but they did it a lot more cleverly than he did—with their foreheads leaning against the open palm of one hand, so that their faces were hidden. At the same time they hid their right hands behind their left elbows, so that it was quite impossible to tell whether or not they were writing as they sat there.

Nikita tried sitting in this position and he found that the quality of his sleep changed immediately. Before he used to switch suddenly back and forth between total oblivion and startled wakefulness, but now the two states were combined—he fell asleep, but not completely, not so deeply that he was totally oblivious. His state of consciousness was like morning drowsiness, when any thought is easily transformed into a moving colored picture you can watch while you wait for the ring of the alarm clock you've set back an hour. He discovered this new state was actually more convenient for making notes on the lectures—all he had to do was to let his hand move on its own, allowing the lecturer's mumbling to skip straight from his ears to his fingers, but on no account allowing it to enter his brain—then Nikita would have woken up, or fallen into a deeper sleep, losing all contact with what was happening.

Gradually, balancing between these two states, he grew so adept at sleeping that he learned how to pay attention to several subjects simultaneously with that tiny part of his consciousness that was responsible for contact with the external world. He might, for instance, have a dream in which the action unfolded in a women's bathhouse (a frequent and rather strange vision, including a number of quite astonishing absurdities: on the log walls there were handwritten posters with versified appeals to people to save bread; and thickset red-haired women holding rusty washbasins, dressed in short ballet dresses made of feathers). At the same time he was able to follow the streak of egg yolk on the lecturer's tie, while listening to the joke about three Georgians in space that the student next to him recited constantly.

For several days, waking up after a philosophy class, Nikita was filled with joy at his new abilities, but the self-satisfaction evaporated when he realized that, as yet, all he could do in his sleep was listen and write, but the other student could tell a joke while he was asleep! It was obvious from that special oily gleam in his eyes, his general pose, and a number of other small but telling details. So one day, when he fell asleep at a lecture, Nikita tried telling a joke of his own in reply. He deliberately chose the shortest and most simple one, about an international violinists' competition in Paris. He almost got through it, but stumbled right at the very end and started talking about Dnepropetrovsk geysers instead of Dzerzhinsky's mauser. His neighbor didn't notice anything, though, and chortled in a deep bass when three seconds had gone by without Nikita saying anything, and it was clear the joke was over. What astonished Nikita most of all was the deep, viscous quality his voice acquired when he was talking in his sleep. But it was dangerous to pay too much attention to this, or he would begin to wake up.

Speaking while he was asleep was hard, but possible, and the lecturer served as an example of the extent to which human mastery of this skill could be taken. Nikita would never have guessed that the lecturer was asleep too, if he hadn't noticed that when the lecturer leaned against the tall lectern in his usual fashion, from time to time he would turn over to his left side and end up with his back to the auditorium and his face to the board (in order to justify his impolite pose he would gesture feebly in the direction of his numbered list of premises). Sometimes when the lecturer turned his back, his speech would slow down and his utterances would become so liberal, they incited a fearful joy—but he gave most of the course propped up on his right side.

Nikita soon realized that sleeping was convenient not only in lectures, but at seminars too, and gradually he was able to manage a few simple movements—he could get to his feet without waking up and greet the lecturer, he could go up to the board and wipe it clean, and even look for chalk in the nearby lecture halls. When he was called on, at first he used to wake up, become alarmed, and start confusing words and concepts, at the same time feeling a profound admiration for the sleeping lecturer's ability to frown, clear his throat, and bang his hand on the table, all while keeping his eyes open and actually maintaining some semblance of expression. The first time Nikita managed to answer a question in his sleep it was unexpected and completely without any preparation—he simply became aware at the boundary of his consciousness that he was reciting some "fundamental premises." At the same time he was on the upper landing of a tall bell tower, where a small wind ensemble was playing, conducted by Love, which proved to be a short, yellow-haired old woman who moved with monkey-like agility.

Nikita was given straight A's, and from then on he even took notes from primary sources while he was still asleep, and only reverted to full wakefulness in order to leave the reading hall. Little by little his mastery increased, and by the end of his second year he was already falling asleep as he entered the subway in the morning, and waking up when he left the same station at night.

But something began to frighten him. He noticed that he had begun to fall asleep unexpectedly, without being aware that he was doing so. It was only when he woke up that he realized, for instance, that Comrade Lunacharksy's visit to their institute on a carriage with three black horses wearing bells was not part of the program of ideological studies devoted to the three-hundredth anniversary of the first Russian balalaika (the entire country was preparing for the big date at the time), but just an ordinary dream.

It was all very confusing, and in order to be able to tell whether he was asleep or not at any particular moment, Nikita began carrying a small pin with a big, round, green head in his pocket, and whenever he was in any doubt, he pricked his thigh, and everything became clear. Then, of course, there was the new fear that he might simply dream that he was pricking himself with the pin, but Nikita drove that thought out of his mind as quite unbearable. His relations with fellow students at the institute improved noticeably—the Communist Youth League organizer, Seryozha Firsov, who could drink eleven glasses of beer in his sleep without stopping, confessed that he always used to think that Nikita was crazy, or at least that there was something strange about him, but now it was clear he was a good guy. Seryozha was about to add something else, but his tongue ran away with him, and he suddenly started talking about Spartak and Salavat Yulaev's chances in soccer this year, from which Nikita, who was dreaming at that moment about the Battle of Kursk, concluded that his friend was having a highly confused Romano-Pugachevian dream of some sort. Nikita gradually stopped being surprised that the sleeping passengers in the subway were able to swear and argue, stand on each other's feet and hold up those heavy bags filled with toilet paper and pickled seaweed—he had learned to do all of that himself. But he was astounded by something else. As soon as they reached an empty seat, many of the passengers in the subway would immediately drop their heads onto their chests and fall asleep—not the way they had been sleeping a minute earlier, but much deeper, completely cutting themselves off from everything around them. And yet, when they heard the name of their station announced through their dreams, they never woke up completely, they slid straight back with astounding precision into the state from which they had previously taken their dive into temporary oblivion.

Nikita noticed this for the first time when a man sitting in front of him wearing a blue overall coat, who was snoring so loudly the sound filled the entire car, suddenly jerked up his head, marked his place in the book lying open on his knees with his travel pass, closed his eyes, and fell into a state of motionless, inorganic torpor; after a while the carriage was shaken violently and the man jerked his head and began snoring again. Nikita guessed the same thing must be happening to the others, even if they weren't snoring.

At home he began observing his parents closely and soon noticed that he could never catch them awake, no matter how hard he tried—they were asleep all of the time. Just once his father, sitting in the armchair, let his head droop and dozed off into a nightmare: he shrieked, waved his arms about, leaped to his feet, and woke up—Nikita could tell that from the expression on his face—but then he swore, fell back asleep, and sat down closer to the television, where the blue flickering screen was purveying some historical epic of communal dozing.

On another occasion his mother dropped the iron onto her foot, giving herself a nasty bruise and burn. Until the paramedics arrived, she sobbed so pitifully in her sleep that Nikita couldn't bear it any longer and fell asleep himself until the evening, when his mother was already dozing peacefully over *One Day in the Life of Ivan Denisovich*. The book had been brought over by a neighbor attracted by the smell of bandages and blood, an old anthroposophist by the name of Maximka, who had reminded Nikita, ever since his childhood, of a decayed biblical patriarch. Maximka was only visited very rarely by any of his numerous criminal grandchildren, and he was quietly sleeping out his life in the company of several intelligent cats and a dark-colored icon with which he argued every morning.

After the incident with the iron, Nikita's relations with his parents moved into a new phase. It turned out to be quite easy to avoid all the scandals and misunderstandings if you simply went to sleep at the beginning of the conversation. One time he and his father discussed the state of the country, and during the discussion Nikita squirmed and shuddered on his seat because Senkievich, the smirking host of "Traveler's Club," had tied him to the mast of his papyrus boat and was whispering something into Thor Heyerdahl's ear. The boat was lost somewhere in the Atlantic, and Heyerdahl and Senkievich were walking around openly in their black Masonic caps.

"You're showing a bit more intelligence," said his father, gazing up with one eye at the ceiling, "only I don't know who can have been feeding you all that rubbish about caps. They have aprons, long ones down to here," his father demonstrated with his hands.

And so it turned out that no matter what form of human activity Nikita tried to adjust to, difficulties only existed until the moment he fell asleep, and after that, without the slightest real involvement on his part, he did everything that was required, and so well that when he woke up he was amazed. This applied both to the institute and to his free time, which used to be something of a torment to him because it just dragged on for so long. In his sleep Nikita devoured many of the books that had previously resisted his attempts to decipher them, and even learned to read newspapers, which finally reassured his parents, who had frequently whispered their bitter disappointment about him to each other.

"It's just like you've been reborn!" said his mother, who loved a pompous turn of phrase. This phrase was usually pronounced in the kitchen, while the borscht was being prepared. As the beets fell into the water, Nikita would begin dreaming of something out of Herman Melville. The smell of fried seaweed would fly out through the window, and mingle with the bovine lowing of a French horn. Then the music would fade away and the radio voice would begin speaking: "Today at seven o'clock we present for your attention a concert by master artists, which sounds, so to speak, the final chord of the symphony of festivities devoted to the three-hundredth anniversary of the Russian balalaika!"

In the evening the family gathered round the blue window into the universe. Nikita's parents had a family favorite: "The World in the Eye of the Camera." His father came out to see it dressed in his gray-striped pajamas and curled up in the armchair. His mother came in from the kitchen with a plate in her hand, and for hours at a time they would sit there enchanted, following the landscapes drifting across the screen through half-closed eyes.

"If you long to try the taste of fresh bananas and wash them down with coconut milk," said the television, "if you long to delight in the roaring of the surf, the golden warmth of the sands, and the gentle sunshine, then . . ."

At this point the television paused intriguingly. ". . . Then that means you long to be among the bananas and lemons of Singapore."

Nikita snored along with his parents. Sometimes the name of the program would reach him, refracted through the prism of his dreams, and the content of his dreams would assume the form of a screen. Several times during the program "Our Garden," Nikita dreamed about the inventor of a popular sexual perversity; the French marquis was dressed in a cranberry-red robe with gold lace trimming, and he was inviting Nikita to go with him to some women's hostel.

Sometimes everything deteriorated into total confusion and the archimandrite Julian, an essential participant for any self-respecting round table, would peer out of his long Zil with the flashing light on the top and say: "Till we meet again on the airwaves."

As he spoke he would jerk his finger upward in a frightened manner toward the empty heavens. One of his parents would change the channel, and when Nikita half-opened his eyes he would see on the screen a major wearing a light-blue beret, standing in a hot mountain ravine.

"Death?" the major would say with a smile. "You're only afraid of that at the beginning, just for the first few days. Serving here has really been an education for us—we've taught the spirits, and the spirits have taught us. . . ."

The off switch would click, and Nikita would go to his own room to sleep under a blanket on the bed. In the morning, when he heard footsteps in the corridor or the alarm clock ringing, he would open his eyes carefully, taking his time to adjust to the daylight, then get up and go to the bathroom, where various thoughts usually came into his head, and his night dreams gave way to the first of his daydreams.

"How very lonely a human being really is," he would think, twisting the toothbrush in his mouth. "I don't even know what my parents are dreaming about, or what the passersby on the street or old Grandpa Maximka are dreaming about. I wish I could at least ask someone why we're all asleep."

Then he would panic at the thought of how impossible it was to discuss the question. Not even the most brazen of the books that Nikita had read had so much as mentioned it, and he had never heard anyone speak about it aloud. Nikita could guess what the problem was. This was not one of the ordinary things that simply go unspoken, it was a kind of universal joint on which people's entire lives turned. Even if someone shouted out that they should tell the whole truth, it wasn't because he really hated things being left unspoken, but because he was forced to by this most important thing in existence being left unspoken.

Once, when he was standing in a slow-moving line for seaweed that filled half the supermarket, Nikita even had a special dream on this subject. He was in a vaulted corridor, where the ceiling was decorated with moldings of vine leaves and snub-nosed female profiles, and the floor was covered with a red runner of carpet. Nikita set off along the corridor, turned several corners, and found himself in a dead end that ended with a painted window. One of the doors in the short cul-de-sac opened and a plump man in a dark suit peered out. His eyes gleamed happily and he waved Nikita in.

Sitting at a round table in the center of the room was a group of about fifteen men, all in suits and ties and all rather similar to each other—balding, aging, with the shadow of the same inexpressible thought on their faces. They paid no attention to Nikita.

"Beyond a shadow of doubt!" said the one who was addressing the others. "We have to tell the whole truth. People are fed up."

"Why not? Of course!" responded several cheerful voices, and everyone began speaking at once; there was nothing but confused hubbub until the one who happened to be speaking smacked the table really hard with a file bearing the inscription Far East Fish—Nikita realized that the words were not on the file at all, but on the tin of seaweed from his other dream. The full surface of the file hit the table, and though the sound was not loud, it was very solid and prolonged, like the sound of a church bell with a muffler. Silence fell.

"Clearly," said the one who had struck the table, "we first have to find out what will come of all this. Let's try setting up a commission, say with three members."

"What for?" asked a girl in a white gown.

Nikita realized she was there because of him, and he held out the money for his five cans of seaweed. The girl's mouth gave out a sound like the rattling and buzzing of a cash register, but she didn't even glance at Nikita.

"In order," the man answered her—even though Nikita had moved on past the cash register, and was already on his way toward the supermarket doors—"in order that the members of the commission can first try telling each other the whole truth."

Agreement was quickly reached on the membership of the committee—it was made up of the speaker himself and two men in light-blue three-piece suits and horn-rimmed glasses, who looked like brothers: both of them even had dandruff on their left shoulders. (Nikita was perfectly well aware, of course, that neither the dandruff on the shoulders nor their simple way of speaking was genuine, but were simply elements of the accepted aesthetics in dreams of this kind.) The others went out into the corridor, where the sun was shining, the wind was blowing, and car motors were roaring, and while Nikita was walking down the steps into the pedestrian passageway, they locked the door of the room, and to make sure nobody could peep in, they filled the keyhole with caviar from a sandwich.

They waited. Nikita walked past the monument to the antitank gun and the tobacco shop, and had reached the huge obscene inscription on the wall of the concrete slab Palace of Weddings—which meant that he had only five more minutes to walk before he was home—when suddenly from inside the room, where so far he had heard only a hubbub of indistinguishable voices, there came a gurgling and crackling, which was followed by total silence. The whole truth had apparently been told. Someone knocked at the door.

"Comrades! How are things going?"

There was no reply. The people in the small crowd at the door began exchanging glances, and a sun-tanned European-looking man exchanged glances with Nikita by mistake, but immediately averted his eyes and muttered something in irritation.

"We'll break in!" they finally agreed in the corridor.

The door gave way at the fifth or sixth blow, just at the moment when Nikita was entering the hallway of his house, and he and the door-breakers found themselves in a completely empty room with a large puddle covering most of the floor. At first Nikita thought it was the puddle he'd seen in the elevator, but when he compared the outlines, he decided it wasn't. Although the long tongues of urine were still creeping toward the walls, there was nobody there, not under the table or behind the curtains, and three empty suits that had been left dangling on the chairs were all hunched over and scorched on the inside. A pair of cracked horn-rimmed glasses gleamed beside the leg of an overturned chair.

"That's the truth for you," someone whispered behind his back. Nikita was already thoroughly fed up with this dream, which showed no sign of coming to an end, and he reached into his pocket for his pin. Trust his bad luck, it wasn't there. He went into the apartment, threw the bag with the cans onto the floor, opened his wardrobe and began going through the pockets of all the trousers hanging there. In the meantime all the others went out into the corridor and started whispering in alarm; the sun-tanned guy almost whispered something to Nikita again, but stopped himself in time. They decided they had to phone somewhere urgently, and the sun-tanned guy, who was given the responsibility of phoning, was already on his way to the telephone, when suddenly all of them began howling triumphantly—the vanished trio had appeared right there in the corridor in front of them. They were wearing light-blue shorts and sneakers and looked ruddy and cheerful, as though they'd just come from the bathhouse.

"There!" shouted the one who had been speaking at the very beginning of the dream, gesturing with his arm. "It's a joke, of course, but we wanted to show certain impatient comrades . . ."

In his fury Nikita jabbed himself several times with the pin, harder than necessary, and he never knew what happened after that. He picked up the bag and carried it into the kitchen, and then went over to the window. Outside there was a summer wind, people were walking along talking happily, and it was just as though each of the passersby really was walking under Nikita's windows, and not actually in some dimension known only to him.

As he gazed at the tiny human figures, Nikita thought gloomily that he still didn't know the content of their dreams, or the relationship between sleeping and waking in their lives. He had nobody to complain to about his recurrent nightmares or to tell about the dreams that pleased him. He suddenly wanted very badly to go out into the street and start talking to someone—it didn't matter in the slightest who it was—about everything that he had come to understand. And no matter how crazy the idea might be, today he was going to do it.

About forty minutes later he was already striding away from one of the outlying subway stations up an empty street that rose toward the horizon. It was like an avenue of lime trees that had been sawed in half—where the second row of trees should have been there was a broad, paved road. He had come out this way because there were quiet places here, places the militia patrols hardly ever visited. That was important—Nikita knew that you could only run away from a sleeping militiaman in a dream, and adrenaline in the blood is a very poor soporific. Nikita walked up the slope, pricking his leg with the pin and admiring the immense lime trees, like frozen fountains of green ink: he was so absorbed in them that he almost missed his first client.

He was an old man with several different colored badges hanging on a decrepit brown jacket, probably out for his usual evening stroll. He darted out of the bushes, squinted at Nikita, and set off up the hill. Nikita caught up with him and started walking beside him. From time to time the old man would raise his hand and move his thumb through the air with a forceful gesture.

"What's that you're doing?" Nikita asked after a while.

"Bedbugs," replied the old man.

"What bedbugs?" Nikita was puzzled.

"Ordinary ones," the old man said, and sighed. "From the apartment above. All the walls here are full of holes."

"You need Desinsectal," said Nikita.

"No need. In one night I'll squash more with my thumb than all your chemicals. You know the way Utyosov sings it: 'Our enemies . . .'"

Then he fell silent, and Nikita never did find out about the bedbugs and Utyosov. They walked on for several yards without speaking.

"Splat," the old man suddenly said, "splat."

"Is that the bedbugs cracking?" Nikita asked, hazarding a guess.

"No," said the old man with a smile, "bedbugs die quietly. That's the caviar."

"What caviar?"

"Well, just think about it," said the old man, livening up, his eyes beginning to gleam with the crazed cunning of a Suvorov. "D'you see that kiosk?"

Standing on the corner there was a newspaper and magazine kiosk.

"Yes," said Nikita.

"Good. Well now, imagine there's a crooked little hut standing right there, and they sell caviar there. You've never seen caviar like it and you never will—every grain the size of a grape, unnerstand? And then the woman serving, that great lazy creature, when she's weighing you out half a kilo she just grabs it out of the barrel with her scoop and slaps it onto the scales. By the time she's ladled out half a kilo for you she's dropped as much on the ground—splat! Unnerstand?"

The old man's eyes stopped gleaming. He looked around, spat, and went across the road, sometimes stepping around something invisible—perhaps the heaps of caviar lying on the asphalt in his dream.

"All right," Nikita decided, "I have to ask directly. Otherwise you can't tell what anybody's talking about. If they call the militia, I'll run for it."

It was already quite dark on the street. The street lamps were on, but only half of them were working, and most of those gave off a weak purple glow that colored the pavement and the trees rather than illuminating them, making the street look like some harsh scene from the afterlife. Nikita sat on a bench under the lime trees and froze into immobility. A few minutes later something that squeaked and squealed and consisted of a dark spot and a light spot appeared on the edge of the hemisphere of visibility that was bounded by twilight. It came closer, its movement interrupted by brief pauses during which it rocked to and fro, giving out an insincerely reassuring whisper.

When he looked more closely, Nikita could make out a woman of about thirty in a dark jacket, pushing a light-colored baby carriage in front of her. It was quite obvious that the woman was asleep: every now and then she adjusted an invisible pillow under her head, pretending through the force of habitual female hypocrisy that she was tidying her piebald hair. Nikita got up off his bench. The woman trembled but didn't wake up.

"Excuse me," Nikita began, angry at his own embarrassment, "may I ask you a personal question?"

The woman drew her plucked eyebrows up onto her forehead and stretched her thick lips from ear to ear, which Nikita took to indicate polite incomprehension.

"A question?" she asked in a low voice. "All right."

"What is it you're dreaming about at the moment?"

Nikita made an idiotic gesture, gesturing at everything around them with his hand, and lapsed into final and utter confusion when he realized that his words had had an entirely inappropriate suggestive note to them. The woman laughed like a pigeon cooing.

"You silly thing," she said tenderly, "I don't like that type."

"What type then?"

"With Alsatians, you silly. With big Alsatians."

She's making fun of me, thought Nikita.

"Please don't misunderstand me," he said. "I realize that I'm stepping out of bounds, so to speak."

The women shrieked quietly, turned her eyes away from him, and began walking quickly.

"You see," Nikita continued, becoming excited, "I know that normal people don't talk about it. Perhaps I'm not normal. But surely you must have wanted to talk about it with someone sometime?"

"Talk about what?" the woman asked, as though she were playing for time in a conversation with a lunatic. She was almost running now, peering intensely ahead into the gloom: the stroller was bouncing over the surface of the asphalt, and something in it was beating against its oilcloth sides.

"I'll tell you what about," Nikita answered, breaking into a trot. "Take today for instance. I switch on the television, and there it is—I don't know which is more frightening, the audience or the presidium. I watched for a whole hour and I didn't see anything new, except perhaps for a couple of unfamiliar poses. One person sleeping in a tractor, another sleeping in an orbital space station, one talking about sports in his sleep, and even the ones jumping from the springboard—they were all asleep. And it turns out I have nobody to talk to."

The woman frantically adjusted her pillow and began running quite openly. Nikita ran alongside her, trying to get his breath back after the effort of speaking, and the green star of a traffic light loomed rapidly toward them.

"For instance, take you and me. I'll tell you what, let me stick a pin in you! Why didn't I think of that before? Shall I?"

The woman flew out into the intersection and then stopped so sharply that something in the stroller shifted bodily and almost broke through the front of it, and before he could stop himself he had flown on several yards beyond her.

"Help!" shouted the woman.

As luck would have it, standing about twenty feet away in an alley there were two men with armbands on their sleeves, both wearing identical white jackets that made them look like angels. Their first response was to back away, but when they saw Nikita standing under the traffic light and not displaying any signs of hostility, they grew bolder and slowly came closer.

One of them started talking to the woman, who was wailing and moaning and waving her arms about and kept repeating the words *pester* and *maniac*, and the second man came over to Nikita.

"Out for a walk?" he asked in a friendly voice.

"Something like that," answered Nikita.

The policeman was a head shorter than Nikita and was wearing dark glasses—Nikita had noticed a long time ago that some people found it hard to sleep in the light with their eyes open. The patrolman turned to his partner, who was nodding sympathetically to the woman and writing something down on a sheet of paper. At last the woman finished what she was saying, glanced triumphantly at Nikita, adjusted her pillow, turned her stroller around, and pushed it off up the street. The other policeman came over. He was a man of about forty with a thick mustache and a cap pulled right down over his ears to prevent his hair from being ruffled during the night, and a bag slung over his shoulder.

"On the money," he said to his partner. "It was her."

"I realized it right away," said the one in glasses, and turning to Nikita, he said, "and what's your name?"

Nikita introduced himself.

"I'm Gavrila," said the one in glasses, "and this is Mikhail. Don't you be alarmed, she's the local idiot. They mention her at all our briefings. When she was little two border guards raped her in the middle of a cinema, during the film *Here, Mukhtar!*, and she's been touched ever since. She's got a bust of Dzerzhinsky wrapped in diapers in the stroller. Every evening she phones the station and complains they're trying to screw her, and she pesters the dog catchers, trying to get them to let an Alsatian loose on her. . . ."

"I did notice," Nikita said, "that she was a bit strange."

"Never mind her. You drinking?"

Nikita thought for a moment.

"Yes," he said.

They sat down on the very same bench where Nikita had been sitting only a few minutes earlier. Mikhail took a bottle of Moscow Special Export Vodka out of his bag, separated the bronzed cap from its fixing ring with a key-ring charm shaped like a small sword, and twisted it off with a single complicated movement of his wrist. He was obviously one of those natural talents you can still meet in Russia who opens bottles of beer on his eye socket and with a single firm slap of the hand can knock the cork halfway out of a bottle of dry Bulgarian wine, so that it can easily be grasped in his firm white teeth.

Perhaps I should ask them? Nikita thought, as he took the heavy paper cup and the seaweed sandwich. *But I'm afraid to. There are two of them, after all, and that Mikhail's a big guy.*

Nikita breathed out heavily and fixed his gaze on the complex interwoven pattern of shadows on the asphalt under his feet. The pattern changed with every gust of the warm evening wind: at first there were clear images of horns and banners, then suddenly there was the outline of South America, or three Adidas stripes from the wires hanging under the tree, or else it all looked like nothing more than the shadows cast by light shining through leaves. Nikita raised his cup to his lips. The liquid that was intended to represent his country in foreign parts slipped down with remarkable gentleness and tact, no doubt in the belief that the action was taking place somewhere in the Western Hemisphere.

"By the way, where are we right now?" Nikita asked.

"Route number three," replied Gavrila in the glasses, downing a cupful.

"You blockhead," laughed Mikhail. "Just because some pig writes something down on the map does that mean it really is route number three? It's Stenka Razin Boulevard."

Gavrila toyed with the empty cup, then for some reason he prodded Nikita with his finger and asked: "Shall we finish it?"

"What do you think?" Mikhail asked Nikita seriously, tossing the cap up and down on his palm.

"All the same to me," said Nikita.

"Well, in that case . . ."

The cup made its second round in silence.

"That's it," Mikhail said thoughtfully. "Nothing else for the workers to look forward to for the time being."

He swung back his arm and was about to toss the bottle into the bushes, but Nikita managed to grab his sleeve.

"Let me have a look," he said.

As Mikhail handed him the bottle Nikita noticed a tattoo on his wrist—

it looked like a man on horseback thrusting his lance into something under the hooves of his horse—but Mikhail immediately hid his hand away in his pocket, and it would have been awkward to ask specially to look at the tattoo. Nikita looked closely at the bottle. The label was exactly the same as on Moscow Special for the domestic market, except that the writing was in Latin characters and the Special Limited Extra Export Product emblem—a stylized globe with SLEEP inscribed on it in big letters—gazed out from the white background like an eye.

"Time to go," Mikhail said suddenly, glancing at his watch.

"Time to go," Gavrila repeated like an echo.

"Time to go," Nikita repeated for some reason.

"Put on your armband," said Mikhail, "or the captain'll raise hell."

Nikita reached down into his pocket, pulled out a crumpled armband and slipped it over his arm; the tapes were already tied. The word *patrolman* was back to front, but Nikita made no effort to fix it. "It won't be for long anyway," he thought to himself.

When he got up off the bench, he felt really unsteady and he was even afraid for a second that he'd be spotted at the militiamen's base, but then he remembered what state the captain himself was in at the end of the last shift, and felt calmer.

The three of them walked in silence as far as the traffic light and turned on to a side street, in the direction of the base, which was ten minutes' walk away. Perhaps it was the vodka, perhaps something else, but it was a long time since Nikita had felt such a lightness in every part of his body—he felt as though he weren't walking but soaring straight up into the sky, borne aloft on currents of air. Mikhail and Gavrila walked on each side of him, surveying the street with drunken severity. Every now and then they encountered groups of people. First there were some empty-headed girls, one of whom winked at Nikita, then a pair of obvious criminals, then some people eating a cake right there on the street, and various other rather dubious individuals.

It's a good thing, Nikita thought, *there's three of us. Or else they'd tear us to pieces —just look at their ugly mugs.*

Thinking was hard. Inside his head the words of a children's song kept flaring up like bright neon lights—with words about how the best thing on earth was to step out side by side across the open country and sing together. Nikita didn't understand the meaning of the words, but that didn't worry him.

Back at the station they found that everyone had already gone home. The duty officer said they could have come in an hour earlier. While Nikita looked for his bag in the dark room where they usually held the briefings and assigned people their routes, Mikhail and Gavrila left—otherwise they would have missed their train. Once he'd handed in his armband, Nikita pretended that he was in a hurry too. The last thing he felt like doing was walking to the subway with the captain and talking about Yeltsin. Once he was out on the street, he felt that his good mood had totally evaporated.

Turning up his collar, he set off toward the subway, thinking about the next day. The grocery order with the two sticks of salami, the phone call to Urengoi, a liter of vodka for the holidays (he should have asked his colleagues where they got the Special, but it was too late now), collect little Anna from the kindergarten, because the wife was going to the gynecologist—the stupid cow, even down there she had something wrong with her—put it all together and he'd have to take a half-day off from German Parmenych for taking today off. He was sitting inside the subway car now, opposite a pregnant woman who was staring hard at him from under her head scarf, drilling holes in his bald patch; he just kept on looking at his newspaper until the bastards tapped him on the shoulder, and then he had to get up and give her his seat, but they were already approaching his station. He went over to the doors and looked at his tired, wrinkled face in the glass with the entwined electrical snakes rushing past outside it. Suddenly his face disappeared and its place was taken by a black void with lights in the distance: the tunnel had come to an end and the train had emerged onto the bridge across the frozen river. He could see a sign, *Glory to Soviet Man*, on the roof of a tall building, lit up by crossed beams of blue light.

A minute later the train dived back into the tunnel and the glass was filled with gesticulating alcoholics, a girl with needles who was finishing knitting something blue under the subway map, a schoolboy with a pale face, daydreaming over the photographs in a history textbook, an army colonel in a tall astrakhan hat, invincibly clutching a briefcase with a combination lock, and there on the other side of the glass somebody had traced out the word YES in block capitals.

Then a long and empty street covered in snow appeared in front of him. There was a sharp pain in his leg. He put his hand in his pocket and took out a pin with a big round green head that had gotten in there somehow. He tossed it into a snowdrift and looked upward. In the gap between the houses the sky was very high and clear, and he was surprised to make out the dipper shape of the Great Bear among the fine sprinkling of stars—for some reason he'd been sure it could only be seen in summer.

Translated from the Russian by Andrew Bromfield

The Widow Dido

Cities burn.
Gangs of the poor, righteous with need, burn.
Inside my little house, inside the air,

I lie awake all day,
surfeited by weather
(as though inside a tiny speckled egg

found floating in the marsh grass.)
I am salt and you are the sea,
I am wine, music, lies

and all this is learning how to die.
The poor? They are my poor.
The rain is my rain, nailed to the wall.

The plum? Mine. The pit inside? Mine.
The rotting is mine;
never rotting is mine.

(Floating in the marsh grass?
Mine.) Cities burn,
there is no need to say so again.

The poor exact their due.
In my tiny house, so small
it shouldn't be, I wear my rage

like an apology. Mine?
Now that you are gone,
all I am is mine.

Susan Hiller

The Secrets of Sunset Beach

Susan Hiller

Susan Hiller, a master of mise-en-scène who presents each new project as a different material, spatial, and often aural experience, chose a modest format for *The Secrets of Sunset Beach* (1987–1988). Originally made at a time when some artists were producing photographs that emulated nineteenth-century salon paintings, Hiller's output seemed, instead, to subtly recall the medium's beginnings, when light first gleamed on photographic paper.

Her method is without a trace of nostalgia. We are fully located in a present time, able to enjoy the renewal of sunlight as it enters a dark room. The allusion to a past moment in visual history probably has more to do with the way Hiller likes to encapsulate fruitful contradictions. Her images allow us to experience the sunlight both as a natural force and as "artifice"—the product of the artificial light, chemical emulsions, and blank paper that make up the photographic process.

The "scene" is a place where a story of human affairs (we cannot tell exactly what) is being acted out. We are half-reminded of the small, light-filled rooms of seventeenth-century Dutch art, where a contemplative quality of pure visual enjoyment is sometimes combined with the unfolding of an intrigue; and half-reminded again of Hollywood film noir, except that the associations of crime and melodrama are returned again to the tranquillity of philosophical reverie.

Hiller has always insisted that she works with cultural artifacts rather than with what are usually called "raw materials." This has been her response to the belief that visual reality is socially constructed. She collects and records things, often deciding only much later how they will be reconfigured. Yet, paradoxically, it is the beauty of the ensemble, conceived as a "painting" or "sculpture" that always stays in mind. There are echoes of anthropology (Hiller worked as an anthropologist before becoming an artist): in other words, the reading of cultures from the study of their artifacts and representations. But anthropology's claim to truth has been richly questioned and enlarged by what might be called an artist's "not knowing," an interest in inconsistencies, marginal insights, the dark side, dreams. I see Hiller as an artist who combines the erudite and the popular in a passionate search for a new kind of collaborative knowledge.

The site for *The Secrets of Sunset Beach* was just such a cultural given, idiosyncratic and charged with meaning. In 1987, while she was on a teaching visit to California State University at Long Beach, Hiller rented a small beach house. The tiny interior turned out to be densely hung with nets, pictures, shells and other mementos of the sea and islands. Hiller projected her own slides into this "private fantasy world of interior design," a kind of abstract script she has often used, the gestures of the writing or drawing hand rendered here as light.

The result is an extraordinary overlay of patterns. The fortuitous projections and reflections of sunlight interface with cultural inscriptions: curtains, wallpaper, blinds, a TV screen, bric-a-brac. Despite their supposedly different values and qualities, the elemental, the sentimental and the artistically expressive mingle, offset and harmonize with one another. At one moment Hiller's script is part of a shimmering impressionism, at another it is darkly reflected in an oval mirror whose presence is intimated only by its luxuriant halo of shells.

Perhaps this little room is a transformation of the camera obscura. The original "dark room" gave a literal transcription of the world by cutting the observer off from it. We cannot "look" and "live" at the same time. In *The Secrets of Sunset Beach* the boundary between inside and outside, in the literal and the metaphorical sense, resonates like a liquid membrane. As Hiller has stated, "everything we perceive is a combination of something externally given and something we bring to it so there is never anything without our subjectivity."

Guy Brett

Somebody Different

I and them. To what extent can they be reached? A poet knows that he is taken by them for somebody different from what he is, and that's how it will be after his death, no sign from the other world arriving to correct the mistake.

Inserting a Meaning

Inserting a meaning occurs constantly, for works of art (of poetry, of painting, of music) enrich the register of existing things, while every existing thing calls for something, and it is not enough to say simply; it *is*. Inserting a meaning into pine or a mountain is very difficult, it is a little easier in the case of the creations of man, that being who incessantly strives, expects, desires. Hence the repeated attempts to name the strivings hidden in an oeuvre.

Yet past events also call for a meaning, as it is difficult to stop at one word, simply saying they were. Was not Marxism just an act of inserting a meaning into the history of the nineteenth century?

And inserting a meaning into one's own life. Something must correspond to something, something must result from something. Perhaps so that things just plain stupid and dishonest find an explanation.

Milder

With age his fierceness abated and there swelled in him, along with tolerance, an all-embracing doubt. He would sit in the dark before the scene of a puppet show and watch their chases, prayers, swaggers, repentances, recognizing in them his own nonsense.

A Desire

A desire to open oneself before people and to tell everything about one's life. Impossible. Unless one writes a psychological novel, which, besides, would be very far from the truth. It would consist in a self-accusing confession, and we know a scrupulous conscience accuses its bearer of smaller transgressions in order to hide bigger ones.

To Wash

At the end of his life, a poet thinks: I have plunged into so many of the obsessions and stupid ideas of my epoch! It would be necessary to put me in a bathtub and scrub me till all that dirt was washed away. And yet only because of that dirt could I be a poet of the twentieth century, and perhaps the Good Lord wanted it, so that I was of use to Him.

I Saw

I was there, and I know, because I have seen. I am surrounded by people who were born later, yet they believe that they must know, at least something, of those things. In fact, they know nothing, one detail or two, at best. It is the same with the particulars of my biography and the books I have written. We imagine we are observed and are of concern to someone. They have heard something, if only vaguely; one of my books fell into their hands and upon it they form a judgment of the others.

A Little Treatise on Colors

The leaves of the oaks are like the leather of bookbinding. How to speak
otherwise of them, when in October they take on a brown hue and are as if
leathery, ready to be set with gold. Why this excessive poverty of language
anytime we deal with colors? What do we have at our disposal when we try
to name the splendor of colors? Some leaves are yellow, some red, and is that
all? But there are also yellow-red, and flame-red, and bull's blood red (why
this recourse to comparisons?). And birches. Their leaves are like small,
pale-yellow coins, sparsely attached to twigs which are of what hue? Lilac,
from the lilacs, and violet, from the violet (again, these unwieldy
comparisons). How does the yellow of birch leaves differ from the yellow of aspens,
underlaid with copper, stronger and stronger, till copper wins. A
copper color? Again a thing, copper. And probably only green and yellow are deeply
in the language, for blue the etymologists associate with *flavus*,
yellow, while red again, in its old Norse forms, goes back to trees, the rowan or
reynir, mountain ash, or perhaps to rust. Is the language so resistant
because our eyes are not very attentive to details of nature unless they serve a
practical purpose? In October, pumpkins ripen in the fields and their color is
orange. Why this recourse to orange, how many eyes saw oranges in a
northern country? I put all this down, for I have encountered difficulty in describing
autumn in the valley of the Connecticut River in a precise and simple manner,
without the props of comparison and metaphor.

Be Like Others

Wherever you lived—in the city of Pergamum at the time of the
Emperor Hadrian, in Marseilles under Louis XV or in the New
Amsterdam of the colonists—be aware that you should consider yourself lucky
if your life followed the pattern of your neighbors. If you moved,
thought, felt, just as they did; and just as they, you did what was prescribed
for a given moment. If, year after year, duties and rituals became part of you, and
you took a wife, brought up children, and could meet peacefully the darkening
days of old age.

Think of those who were refused a blessed resemblance to their
fellow men. Of those who tried hard to act correctly, so that they would be
spoken of no worse than their kin, but who did not succeed in anything, for
whom everything would go wrong because of some invisible flaw. And who
at last for that undeserved affliction would receive the punishment of
loneliness, and who did not even try then to hide their fate.

On a bench in a public park, with a paper bag from which the neck of a
bottle protrudes, under the bridges of the big cities, on sidewalks where the
homeless keep their bundles, in a slum street with neon, waiting in front of a
bar for the hour of opening, they, a nation of the excluded, whose day begins
and ends with the awareness of failure. Think, how great is your luck. You
did not even have to notice such as they, even though there were many
nearby. Praise mediocrity and rejoice that you did not have to associate
yourself with rebels. For, after all, they also were bearers of disagreement
with the laws of life, and exaggerated hope, just like those who were
marked in advance to fail.

Translated from the Polish by the author and Robert Hass

THE INQUISITOR'S MANUAL

If you say it's true then I believe you, Master João, but I don't see why you have to say such terrible things about Senhor Francisco, you know what a mean temper he has, and he's not dead yet, he could still recover from the stroke. Of course it's your business not mine, and you've no doubt talked to the doctors to make sure your father has no chance of getting better and making your life hell, you'd be crazy to risk having the old man back on the loose, threatening everybody under the sun with his shotgun. That's how I see it but what do I know, I was just the steward's daughter, spending my life between the vegetable garden and the stable, milking the cows, cleaning the dovecote, changing the dogs' bowls and tending the hen coop, with no time left over for schools and books. When we arrived from Trás-Os-Montes, Senhor Francisco made a place for us in the barn, with a partition that separated us from the corn, and we made a roof of sorts in order to keep out the swooping bats that talked like people, we put a stove in the corner, we used the sink in the wine cellar for our necessities, and I remember waking up in summer in the dark and hearing the frogs from the swamp, the sleepless dogs, the restless cattle, and my father's snoring, which made the same sound as the windmill. I remember seeing the light still on in Senhor Francisco's office, the oranges that glowed in the August calm, burning slow and steady like the oil lamps of saints, and I felt good, I felt eternal, I felt happy, because it seemed that time had stopped forever and no one would ever die. In the morning the oranges dimmed, the tractor began to drone, and with the return of death

(and, worse than death, time)

they yelled at me to get dressed, and with a milk pail in each hand, skinny as a twig and pushed along by the wind, I walked past the beehives and the pond with geese to the stable, where the animals turned their snouts away from the wall to look at me, and then a sound of boots crossing the wet cement, a cigarillo smell that made me sick, the hand of Senhor Francisco grabbing my neck

"Don't be afraid, little girl"

and I cringing in fear

(he won't get better, will he? swear to me he won't get better, because if he gets better he'll beat my brains out)

Senhor Francisco sprawled out on a sack of seeds, watching me without saying a word, or observing the white foam seething in the buckets, and I without the courage to say

"Let me go"

without daring to say

"Get out of here"

since besides being my father's boss he was some kind of government minister, he was even visited once or twice a year by Professor Salazar

(we knew when Professor Salazar was coming because the farm would fill up the day before with plainclothes policemen who shooed away the workers, snooped everywhere, even under our mattresses, and copied down the data from our ID cards, a National Guard jeep waited at the main entrance, a second jeep by the swamp, and a third one on the other side of the wall, until finally a pair of motorcycles would climb the cypress-covered hill with sirens blaring, followed by an army truck, another pair of motorcycles, and at last the car with curtains of Professor Salazar, dressed in an overcoat, even in summer, the plainclothesmen sprinkled among the rose bushes, a gentleman with glasses would get out of the limousine, open the door for Professor Salazar and lead the way up the steps, prancing all around him as the crows in the distance mockingly cawed, and the next day the police returned to open fire on them)

I without the courage to say

"Get out of here"

cringing in fear because he was the boss, because he was rich, because he was a government minister who had power over a lot of people in Lisbon, and I thought that if I said

"Get out of here, let me go, get out of here"

(swear to me there's no danger or I won't say another word no matter how much you pay, because what good would the money do me?)

he'd order the National Guard to shoot me, just like when he heard about the Revolution on the radio and immediately seized his shotgun to kill us all, pulling back on the breech and aiming straight at us

"Scram, you commies, and I mean now"

as my mother and I scrambled toward the gate with a bundle of clothes and my father held out his pleading arms

"We're not communists, Senhor Francisco, I swear to God we never tried to rob you"

Senhor Francisco all disheveled, his shirttail hanging out of his pants, his hat around his ears, threatening the tractor operator, the chauffeur, the housekeeper, the maids, even the cook who slept with him and hated me, Senhor Francisco hitting us with the barrel of his gun

"Scram"

as we all scrambled down the cypress-covered hillside toward Setúbal, toward Palmela, with the startled magpies flying this way and that, the pigeons frozen with fear, and the German shepherds, let loose from their kennels, biting at our heels, urged on by Senhor Francisco yelling

"Sic 'em"

(before Professor Salazar's last visit a bunch of National Guard jeeps commanded by a corporal spent a week gunning down the crows, leaving dozens of them lying dead in the orchard, and the corporal would kick them over with his boot

"That'll teach you not to make fun of the President")

one of the German shepherds knocked down the housekeeper, who was crying, her suitcase popped open on the gravel, the dogs ran off with her skirts, her sweaters and her shoes, my father wanted to help her but Senhor Francisco wouldn't let him, he pulled back on the breech

"I'll kill you, you swine, I'll kill you"

(when Professor Salazar got out of his car the farm was a cemetery of birds and nobody made fun of him, not even the frogs from the swamp with their seaweed-swollen throats)

the German shepherds growling and snarling at each other as they snapped at the suitcase and Senhor Francisco yelled

"Sic 'em"

my father shielding the housekeeper and vying with the dogs for her sweaters and skirts, and from his face I could tell he was almost weeping

"We're not communists, Senhor Francisco, God strike me down if we're communists, we don't know anything about politics"

the windmill searching for wind and Senhor Francisco waving away my father with the butt of his gun

"Scram"

(Professor Salazar, talking with his secretary, climbing the steps, shaking hands with Senhor Francisco, who didn't doff his hat or put out his cigarillo for anyone, not even the President, Professor Salazar, paying no heed to the National Guardsmen who stood at attention, stopping to admire the petunias before disappearing into the house)

and the German shepherds trampling the vegetables and the chickens, knocking over flowerpots, the tractor tearing up the rosebushes, the fleeing maids lugging their sacks on the road to Setúbal, stumbling forward as Senhor Francisco shouted

"Communists"

with a revolver tucked under his belt, pulling cartridges from his pocket, and when he noticed me he said

"Hey you"

separating me from my mother with his shotgun, grabbing my shoulder as my father, on his knees in the gravel and with the housekeeper's slipper pressed against his chest, whined

"You're not going to kill her, are you, sir?"

(and through the garden gate I caught a glimpse of Professor Salazar drinking tea in the parlor, and a plainclothesman motioned me away with his chin)

"Get lost"

the tractor going in circles inside the greenhouse and Senhor Francisco flashing his cartridges at my father

"Scram"

I heard the maids on the road, the bells of the sheep, the water overflowing the irrigation ditches, the rose stems being ripped, and Senhor Francisco grabbed my neck and led me to the stable, prodding me with his shotgun against my bottom as the dogs jumped all around and my father, still clasping the housekeeper's slipper, watched from the gate, the wind shifted again, increasing the sound of the frogs' croaking, and I tried to plead but couldn't get out the words

"Don't kill me"

in the steamy stable with hills of dung on top of the straw and urine, Senhor Francisco bent me forward against a beam where turtledoves were sleeping, and the sheet metal in the roof rattled as he poked into my dress, found me lost me tried to find me again, and I forgot him, I thought of the oranges glowing in the August calm, burning slow and steady like the oil lamps of saints, and I wasn't afraid, I felt good, I felt eternal, I felt happy, because it seemed that time had stopped forever and no one would ever die, until the oranges dimmed, death

(and, worse than death, time)

returned, the tobacco smell faded, and Senhor Francisco stepped back

"That's so you'll never forget me, you rotten commie"

and outside there were no more German shepherds, no more pigeons, no more magpies, just the decapitated rosebushes crackling in the silence and the tractor's final combustive sigh, I thought that the National Guard jeep would be waiting at the gate to take me away but there was no jeep, and the regional bus stop with its little roof against the rain was deserted as if it were Sunday, we went to my mother's cousin's apartment in Barreiro, which is where we always went on holidays, two cramped rooms behind the hospital, my father sitting on the enclosed balcony and refusing to eat, refusing to talk, still clasping the housekeeper's slipper against his chest, and my mother's cousin

"Heitor"

but my father just sitting among the shelves of Spanish dolls and miniature porcelain vases, my mother's cousin's husband offering him a shot of his favorite brandy but my father immovable, my mother taking away the slipper

"Heitor"

but my father just staring at the Tagus's rotting boats and little islands of grass without noticing the boats or islands, and soon there were fireworks, loud bangs and flashes and red streams of sparkles entered the window, the radio blared with songs of victory, cars honked their horns, the factories whistled nonstop, the café owner played his accordion on the sidewalk while dancing with his wife, my mother's cousin's husband guzzled the brandy but my father immovable, the whole neighborhood buzzing like during a Saturday fair or the Feast of St. Peter's, the town hall deserted, the police station deserted, the Lisbon-bound ships wagging their haunches in the boat station, a hubbub of workers in nearby Lavradio, and my mother's cousin gave me a bowl of soup and an apple, through the skylight I could see the hospital and the patients in pajamas, just like the ones my mother's cousin's husband wore when instead of going to work he stayed at home drinking brandy and getting surly, and since I'd already forgotten about Senhor Francisco I ate the soup, I ate the apple, and after eating the apple I went over to my father, saying

"Dad"

and he lifted his eyes to me, leaned his head against my tummy and began to cry, I'd forgotten Senhor Francisco but remembered the poor cows that hadn't been milked and had no feed in their mangers, the chickens and pigeons and peacocks without corn, and the earrings with a blue stone that I left at the farm, in the can with buttons, so that something grabbed me inside, I had to struggle not to cry too, and my mother who'd removed her shoes and was sticking her nose into her ankles to dig a thorn out of her foot with a needle

"What happened to your earrings, Odete?"

and it wasn't just rockets it was also cannons that shook the building's foundations and confounded the clock's cuckoo, which started announcing the hours without letup, flinging open the tiny door, taking a bow, peeping, retreating and shutting the door, flinging open the door, taking a bow, peeping, retreating and shutting the door, my father crying with his head against my tummy and my mother's cousin's husband still chugging brandy, ticked off at the bird

"Any minute now I'm going to twist its neck off"

my mother showing the thorn to an old woman with a black scarf huddled in a shawl too big for her, ensconced in a corner of the enclosed balcony where the winter dampness had mildewed the walls with clusters of gray mushrooms

"Look at what was stuck in my heel, Dona Fraternidade"

and the old woman, paying no attention to her, alarmed by the cuckoo's frenzy

"Holy Jesus"

the old woman, mother of my mother's cousin, grasping nothing, neither the rockets nor the cannons, neither the hubbub nor the music, grasping nothing and not caring to grasp, startled by the wooden bird's hysterical coming and going

"Holy Jesus"

there were band musicians in Lavradio, each playing his own tune, young men waving flags, a mulatto writing in blue paint on a wall, a man with a hard hat haranguing in the café from a stepladder, my mother, proud of the huge thorn and disappointed by the old woman's indifference, shaking the tweezers in front of my father's tears

"Look what I dug out of my heel Heitor"

my mother's cousin's husband so incensed by the cheeping of hours that he swung his brandy bottle at the clock

"Mother-fucking cuckoo"

the bird instantly stopped cheeping and dangled from a spring like a hung man, my mother's cousin took it down from the hook on the wall, pushed aside the dishes, gingerly laid it down

(the cuckoo, the cuckoo's dwelling, and the weighted chains)

on the plastic tablecloth like a patient recovering from back surgery, while her repentant husband, emerging from the mists of his brandy, made excuses

"I warned the bastard to shut up but he wouldn't listen"

the old woman with hands folded and fascinated by the spring

"Holy Jesus"

my mother, hurt by the lack of interest in her thorn, angling for our sympathy by announcing forlornly to the Spanish dolls

"I'll bet I come down with a blood infection"

my father to my mother's cousin's husband as if he'd just woken up from an eight-month slumber or returned from far far away

"If there's any left, I'll have a bit of that brandy to calm my nerves"

and for a week my parents slept on the floor of the living room with my mother expecting to die from poison at any moment, continually asking for the thermometer to take her temperature, I slept on the enclosed balcony with the old woman who instead of sleeping spent all night staring wide-eyed at the cuckoo, marveling at the broken clockwork spread out on the plastic tablecloth, springs, chains, weights, chips of wood, wheels and hands, the old woman who would furtively get up, shrouded in her widow's scarf, shrouded in her shawl, to touch the pieces with her finger

"Holy Jesus"

until my father found a job as a custodian at a construction site where he kept track of the machines and tools, we moved to a third-floor apartment five buildings down, next to the hospital yard where patients strolled around on their crutches or with tubes in their noses or with IV bottles suspended from iron hooks, my mother, with a slipper on her left foot because of the thorn, suspiciously running her hand over my ears

"What happened to your earrings, Odete?"

I feeling sorry for the patients, watching the sparrows on the telephone wires and the seagulls on the river

"Quit worrying, I'll put them on tomorrow"

though from where we were living you couldn't see the river, just buildings as decrepit as our own, darkened by the years and the fumes of the United Factories industrial complex, a wasteland where men stacked bricks and raised scaffolds, you couldn't see the river but you could hear the boats from Lisbon and feel the cadaverous dankness of the ebb tide, my mother worked as a cleaning lady for an architect in between complaining about her empoisoned blood and running her hand through my hair and over my ears

"What happened to your earrings Odete?"

the fumes from the United Factories blackening the clothes we hung to dry, the sheets on our beds and the casseroles in our kitchen, which was just a cubicle overlooking scrawny, leafless mulberry trees scorched by the ammonia from the smokestacks, my father fixed the cuckoo clock that my mother's cousin's husband had given us so as to be spared his mother-in-law's insomnia, when she would awaken the whole family with her astonished

"Holy Jesus"

the bird, forever befuddled by the blow from the brandy bottle, cheeped imaginary hours and boreal middays, teasing us from the clock's door, until my father sealed it shut with a dozen nails

"Mother-fucking cuckoo"

we could hear the animal peck in rage against us from inside the wood, and when it finally quit pecking, my father unnailed the door and we found the bird lying dead on a bed of screws and tiny wheels, we threw it in the trash, wrapping it in newspaper so it wouldn't smell, my mother, forgetting about the thorn, sniffled in grief before the empty box, and my father consoled her

"Don't be upset, Irene, at the end of the month I'll buy you another cuckoo"

and at the end of the month we had another cuckoo for the clock, painted red and yellow, only it didn't sing, it just opened wide its beak with a weary jerk, took a bow, looked at us with a kind of shrug, and disappeared without a sound, my father banged on the clock, took it off its hook, shook it hard

"The carpenter promised me it would sing"

the carpenter, summoned to explain, held the bird by its wings and examined its underside with a magnifying glass

"It looks like I made a female by mistake, my jackknife must have slipped, it happens with these tiny parakeets"

and my father, annoyed with the artist

"What do you mean a parakeet? I ordered a cuckoo bird"

and the artist, peremptorily brushing aside all doubts with his chisel

"For me there's no difference between a parakeet and a cuckoo, they're equally no good for eating with corn bread"

and without the squawking of hours and slamming of little doors at least we could sleep at night, at least there was no warbling to distract me from my dreams, the only sounds in the darkness, besides my father's snoring, were the kitchen faucet dripping against the enamel sink, the stray dogs hunting for table scraps, the trains switching tracks in the station, and the speeches of factory workers on the street corners, and the workers called us comrades, promised us public housing, declared that we were free, and I thought

"Free from what?"

because the poverty remained, only now with more hullabaloo, more drunks and more disorder, since there weren't any policemen, and the rockets and cannons gradually quieted, the workers got tired of smearing the walls with chalk, the café owner quit playing his accordion, the hospital patients continued their agonized procession along the fence, and my mother, returning from the architect's, running her hand through my hair and over my ears

"Don't tell me you sold your earrings, Odete"

I, pretending to be angry, curtsying in response to the cuckoo's speechless bow

"Yes, I sold them yesterday"

until I finally returned to the farm to look for them in the can with buttons, catching a bus out of Barreiro that crucified my kidneys every time we hit a bump, then another bus in Azeitão, with the radio at full blast and a stuffed bear dangling from the mirror, and when I got off at the town square in Palmela a poor people's funeral was leaving the church and proceeding up the hill amid chrysanthemums to the cemetery, with the family of the deceased pushing against the coffin to keep it from sliding off the wagon, life went on as before the rockets, cannons, the café owner's accordion, and speeches about freedom and public housing, the same retirees sat on the same benches, the same fishmongers tried in vain to sell fish, the same farm-hands still hoped for a farmer with a heart, there was the same deserted marketplace, the same chitchat among housewives, the funeral's chrysanthemums vanished around the bend, followed by a helmeted fireman with a hatchet, there was no communism in Palmela, nor singing nor flags nor charcoal writing on the walls, there was just a hapless corpse that threatened to slip off the wagon on its sad climb up to the cemetery, the ruined castle on the summit, and row after forgotten row of olive trees, and past the aviary and the restaurant for truckers with an ice-cream chest at the entrance the road curved left and came to the main gate of the farm, with its stone columns, its name inscribed on a tile, and the cypress-lined driveway that led to the house, but no dog barked, the windmill was still, the oranges in the orange grove rotted on the ground, and the tractor lay on its side on top of the ruined greenhouse, with one of its back wheels turning in silence, as it had turned for weeks and would turn forever

(the greenhouse windows shattered, the window frames crushed, the flowerpots smashed, the orchids' petals languidly hanging like huge purple lips)

and I saw a German shepherd trotting through the tomato patch and growling, the cows in the stable hopelessly licking their empty mangers, the garden statues without limbs, the pool without water, the charred remains of the burned-down barn, and not a sign of the earrings with a blue stone, not a sign of the can with buttons, I saw the pigeons' confusion and the magpies' anxiety, the chickens pecking at lettuce and hyacinths with the jerky motion of marionettes, the eucalyptus trees closing in on the garage amid a din of croaking frogs, the windows of the house wide open, the chapel with no Virgin Mary or carved candlesticks, and the chairs of the veranda in tatters, I saw the memory of the plainclothesmen copying out our ID cards and thought

"The communists carried off Senhor Francisco"

I thought

"The communists came with rockets and cannons and accordions and speeches and carried off Senhor Francisco, now there's no more shotgun, no more threats"

my mother in Barreiro, in an apartment even smaller than the first one, turning from the plastic tub with peas to run her hands over my ears

"Don't tell me you sold your earrings, Odete"

and as I crossed the thicket of beech trees that talked to themselves just like the patients who walked in circles around the hospital yard I thought

"What happened to the crows?"

because I didn't hear their mocking, I didn't see their now small now large shadows flitting across the ground, I walked around the garage and saw the car's chrome all coated with dust, I reached the laundry tanks and the clothesline with its clothespins like so many plastic finches

(a peacock in a poplar shrieked as if it had just been stabbed)

the geese murmured on the patio, wagging their tongues and stretching their dirty, irate necks in my direction, I thought

"What happened to the crows?"

my mother in Barreiro, plunging her hands back into the tub with peas as the red and yellow cuckoo gently shut the door after a soundless bow, my mother, loud enough for my father to hear

"Earrings worth at least twenty-five dollars it makes me sick just to think about it"

my father frantically rummaging in the bedroom

"Just my luck I can't find my tie"

my mother violently shucking peas as a vein in her neck twitched

"You put on a tie and drench yourself in cologne to go see your whore and don't give a damn that your daughter has sold her earrings"

I imagining that the crows had migrated to Seixal or Amora but finding them at last in the walnut tree by the well, not a hundred, not fifty, not twenty, just ten or twelve, spying at me and flapping their wings like rags, while in the old water tank a pair of May storks nested, my father looking into the tarnished piece of mirror to straighten his tie

"What whore?"

I walked into the filthy clutter of the kitchen, the refrigerator bashed in, the stove covered with greasy pots and pans, the cupboards without screens and missing cups and glasses, the stone sink filled with rinds and bones, the pots of jam coated with mold and the pantry laced with spiderwebs, the red and yellow cuckoo opening its door to take a ceremonious butler's bow, and my mother, in a caustic voice, dumping pods into the garbage and running water over the peas

"The wench that sells tickets at the boat station and paints her nails gold, you were seen with her in the park on Saturday, don't deny it you scoundrel"

the cabinets in the hallway with a thick layer of dust, the rug chewed to pieces by the dogs, the shelves bereft of books, the lampshades in shreds, and the curtains and towels in tatters on the floor, my father whistling a tune, dressed in his Sunday suit, hair combed, clean-shaven, a Band-Aid on his chin, and with a floral-print tie as big as a napkin, my father, in the clouds with joy, fishing for the shoe polish in the onion basket, dabbing the polish on his shoes

"I'm not going to see anyone I'm going to work"

and in the parlor the chair where Professor Salazar sat as the housekeeper offered him plates of cookies or toast with the pomp of an altar boy extending cruets, the flower vases tipped over, half the rug hanging off the veranda, a hole in the folding screen, the remains of a bedspread scattered on the floor, the radio without its cover, bristling with coils and lights and emitting a babble of voices, falling silent, more voices, then silent for good, inhabited by a multitude screaming for help and drowning, my mother drying the peas and lighting the stove, remembering the thorn and limping again

"One of these days I'm going to let her have it, one of these days I'll rip that braid right off her head"

the radio's voices dying and the cracked water tank dripping onto the patio where the cook beheaded chickens over a clay pot and I saw the blood and was afraid and started crying, afraid of their beady eyes staring at me, afraid of their claws, of their feathers, of the pink skin under their feathers, afraid the cook would grab me by the neck, seize the knife and slice my head off too, grab me by the neck like Senhor Francisco did in the stable, bending me forward into the cows' manger that reeked of oats and seeds, and I wanted to ask but couldn't get out the words

"You're not going to pour my blood into a clay pot, are you?"

Senhor Francisco with his belt unbuckled, his vest unbuttoned, clutching my waist with his thighs, laughing as he blew cigarillo smoke down the back of my neck

"Hold still, little girl"

I frightened by my blood dripping onto the grooves in the cement, by the cows' agitation, by the windmill's slow screeching on the south side of the farm, wanting to ask Senhor Francisco but unable to get out the words

"Don't cut my throat, please don't cut my throat, swear you won't cut my throat"

the papers from the office burned to ashes on the balcony, magazines, newspapers, photo albums, the picture of Senhor Francisco with the cardinal, of Senhor Francisco with the admiral, of Senhor Francisco with Professor Salazar, of Senhor Francisco with the pope, wearing a tuxedo with medals and kissing the Pope's ring, my father steeped in cologne, slamming the door and whistling on the stairs

"If I say I'm going to work then I'm going to work"

the desk drawers overturned, the safe wide-open and no money or jewels, a plaster bust lying on the carpet, the files ransacked in nervous haste, I thinking about the woman who sold boat tickets, thinking about the bust and whom it might be

"He went away and won't ever come back to the farm he went away"

and my mother tearing off her apron

"You'll be sorry, you liar, you'll be sorry"

a magpie calling me from the cypress trees, the daisies rattling their bony stems, the hangers swinging in the wardrobe without clothes, my mother to the woman with the braid

"You goddamn bitch"

Senhor Francisco letting me go and I shaking my dress, worried about the blood but relieved there was no clay pot or cook with a knife, I feeling happy

"I didn't die"

and then the piano started playing. It started playing not with the sound it had when you were a boy, Master João, and you'd place a book with notes above the keyboard, then twirl the stool higher with your finger, then curve and stretch your fingers, curve and stretch your fingers, tilting your head back, and the music reached the barn, it reached the road to Palmela, if we were eating supper it changed the taste of the soup and there was a sweet sadness in everything as when one has the flu or it rains on a September afternoon, it started playing not with that sound that transformed the dogs and made the oranges glow brighter at night but with the sound of a wailing cascade, of a muddy outburst, of a stagnant rush, my father separating the two women, careful not to mess up his tie or wrinkle his suit, my mother, barefoot and with the bun of her hair about to fall, entangled in the necklace of the woman who sold boat tickets,

"You goddamn bitch"

Senhor Francisco in the drawing room now without drapes, without sofas, without pictures, without the chess table, without the chandelier, without furniture, with the balcony sagging over the deserted farm, the wilted flower beds, the heap of boards that once was a dovecote, the garage where a wheelless car sat rotting, my mother to my father, on the tips of her toes and slapping the other woman

"Let me go you liar"

Senhor Francisco on the stool that went up and down, banging at random on the keys amid all the useless debris, swaying as if transported by the eighth notes, and my father, enraged because his tie got stained, shoving my mother, who fell down on her rear end

"That's enough out of you"

Senhor Francisco insisting on the music, swaying faster and hitting the keys harder, dressed in faded trousers, a shirt and socks, disheveled, emaciated, with white whiskers on his chin, much older than a month ago, incapable now of bending me forward against the manger

"Hold still, little girl"

of clutching me by the throat, of poking into my skirt, I didn't fear him or the clay pot or the knife or my blood on the cement, I felt no fear, no pity, no anger, nothing

"Hold still, little girl"

a crow passed by the window, a second crow, a third crow, their wings beating against the vines, against the columns, against the carved stone without flourishes, a German shepherd howled in the orchard but no female answered, the night grayed the tops of the beech trees and soon there were bats, a blackness with no lights, the rattling of chairs

"Hold still, little girl"

I felt no fear, no pity, no anger, nothing, the piano was suddenly quiet, and my mother rubbing her back as she bawled at my father

"So you side with the bitch and attack me, you ingrate?"

the piano was suddenly quiet and Senhor Francisco speechlessly stared at me from behind the book of notes, and he kept staring at me for the longest time, until all I could see in the drawing room were the tip of his cigarillo, the piano's candlesticks and the scarecrow of a silhouette wearing a hat and opening his arms in the form of a cross as he triumphantly sniveled:

"Tell your communist friends they can come back, little girl, tell your scummy friends they can come back, because there's nothing left for them to take from me."

Translated from the Portuguese by Richard Zenith

ALICIA VOGL SÁENZ

Blood Like a Rorschach Blot

Sometimes it is a bird's wing extended, or an oak leaf. I read the stain
like Arab coffee grounds. Oracle in membrane slick as oil. Six weeks
I waited, cramping, breasts full, nipples raw. Every time ovaries
like a fist opening, I ran to a bathroom. No stain. I held urine
soaked test, in tiny window periwinkle blue *plus sign*.

And I didn't dream about children. No interior conversations
mother to womb like Oriana or Clara. My mamá, eight years dead
that month, did not come to me, remind me: *teach your child the frog song.*
Sapito, sapón. I dreamt William and I drive up green mountains
to ancient stones where I write poetry on white sheets in charcoal and blood.

At the doctor's, sleep drips in my arm in a yoga rhythm.
I sink into the examining table, my books are pillows. Through
fog and antiseptic, I hear a woman moan while she vacuums.
I wake; a pad soaks my child, a poem is born.
William carries me to the car like an oil-drenched bird.

On the Edge of a Crater

I first feel the blueprints
of breasts in my chest
the summer on a farm
near still active,
snowcapped Cotopaxi

My cousins, Ana and Guillermo, and I
ride horseback by day through eucalyptus trees.
Thin Andean air, burning leaves, my throat
crisp, a melting glacier.

Cotopaxi shadows the landscape,
burnt orange at sundown, snow reflected
like menthol slick on skin during a fever.

Too few beds, Ana and I share,
her curly cropped hair
matted on the pillow,
alpaca wool blankets prickle my skin
through sheets.
We sleep in filtered moonlight.

Near dawn Cotopaxi peeks through the window,
erupts in moonlight.
I wake, see Guillermo in bed,
his face toward the wall.
Feel an unfamiliar rush of blood
from my toes, a sweet panic.
Time moves like molten rock,
and I lie as still as I can.
The tips of my fingers want
to run along his shoulders,
his spine,
measure his breath
by bellows of warm T-shirt
In that moment, long as Snow White's sleep,
the moon did not move.
Drifting,
I am between cinder and ash.
He moves, but it is Ana
who rolls over.

The orange light on her face.
Falling back asleep,
I feel the weight of moonlight
in my chest.

Up on The Roof

EDGARDO RODRÍGUEZ JULIÁ

Let's go up and take our picture. . . . Those rooftops hold some mysterious attraction; sooner or later virtually all Puerto Rican emigrants escape the claustrophobia of the building for that *plein aire* portrait. Despite the fact that we stand before the camera a little nervously, a little (literally) "out of place," we *have* to make it clear, in order to set down, *once and for all*, the illusion that the city has been conquered, the journey that began with the sign of the cross as the Pan Am four-engine roared to life on the runway at Isla Grande has now come to its utopian end.

Why smile so cheerily, so happily, on that inhospitable rooftop? It takes something more than innocence, naïveté, to insist on that emigrant dream. For there is a world that we never leave, that we are stubbornly determined to carry with us in our suitcases despite all U.S.D.A. regulations. At LaGuardia "they turned our bags inside out"; all the food we brought for *la parentela*—the *pasteles* wrapped in banana leaves, the leaves of *culantro*, the *morcillas*, the *gandules*—bam! into the *zafacón* under the stern and disapproving eye of some Irish customs agent irritated by the culinary ethnocentricity of "these spicks." We are "absent," here in the city perhaps just for a while, as those who frequent the Club Caborrojeño or the Yaucono are; we cling to the dream of return just as we cling to the certainty that we have brought with us to New Jersey and Chicago, the Bronx and Brooklyn, a little piece of the Island, a warm hunk of Puertorro, of longed-for *Borinquen bella*.

But just as the customs agent dumped in the trash can all the goodies we'd brought from home for the kinfolks up here, sometimes we feel that we have been stripped of our image of ourselves. The daily hustle of the big city alienates us from the utopia of memory, and at that moment there comes to us the possibility of "up on the roof." For the rooftop is not an idea that speaks only of triumph. There is too much naïveté, too much pain in the portraits for us to be able to call these snapshots simple emblems of victory. It is the Puerto Rican, all of him, that stands there; stands half-smiling, half-miserable, more inclined to survive than await defeat.

This couple proclaims their presence in *Niuyor* with the pride of two astronauts standing for the first time on the moon. The landscape is more abstract even than Anglo-Saxon efficiency—we see the outline of chimneys and the right angles of some building, all just at the level of that inclined roof constructed with horizontal and vertical panels as though in a painting by Edward Hopper. But in the midst of that desolation there stands the couple dressed up for the dance with Tito Puente at the Caborrojeño. They're trying out a cha-cha-cha step —we're back in 1956, more or less, we can sense that little breath of happiness in the pose taken just minutes before heading for the dance. *He* has gotten over the heated, excited atmosphere of the Palladium once and for all; for his forties, he prefers the Caborrojeño. *She*, younger, with that sweater embroidered with little flowers, those petticoats, puts her right foot forward a little playfully (as he does, as well)—and the moment becomes a shy gesture of triumph. That arms-around-each-other thing, though—that can't disguise the palpable fact; *her* open frankness contrasts with a certain scowling cautiousness in *him*. Let's imagine the two of them without smiles: he would be a little absent, sometimes knit-browed, while she would still (always) be open, gay.

What *is* it that they breathe in with that warm spring air? They still have their spacesuits on; in such a foreign element, just as for the astronauts, breathing is only possible when we carry a little of our own atmosphere with us—in this case, a cheeriness that still has a touch of naïveté, of innocence.

Why go up on the roof to have your picture taken? They say it's because of the light, they say it's because of the *niuyorkina* tradition of other emigrant groups. The second, maybe; the first, pretty unlikely. If it's to make sure that the pictures don't turn out too dark in the apartment interiors, then why not pose on the street? Why is the rooftop and not the subway entrance the preferred location for taking the picture that will establish my presence in New York? The subway entrance will not do, it won't do at all, as the background for a portrait of the utopia of desire—"There's no privacy here; let's go back up on the roof."

Up on the roof we avoid those indiscreet looks that recognize, stamp our not-belonging. On the street we would be reduced to the role of *foreigner*, or, worse yet, permanent tourist. Only the rooftop can offer that panoramic privacy; on the roof, open space, freedom, is harmonized with a private ceremony in which intimacy can emerge. The rooftop is the crossroads of hopes, dreams, illusions, on the one hand, and metaphor on the other; only on the rooftop can we take that step toward imagination, or, if we prefer (why not?), toward fantasy. We have to record our presence in the city, but the roof's greater freedom allows us to make ourselves slightly invisible, and to somehow become also the perfect witnesses of that dream.

This young woman recognizes that secret space; the ceremony of intimacy has begun: the zigzag of bricks, TV antenna, and cornices out of some Piranesi dream—all of that hallucinatory baroque in the background contrasts with the severe panels of the foreground. Oblivious to the contradictory and slightly hysterical architecture in the background, the young woman gives us a military salute—a gesture that seems more naive, more innocent than spontaneous. The purity of her smile would drive us slightly mad with tenderness; her beauty has something of the carnal sensuality of the Caribbean woman, but that smile—utterly free of guile—counterbalances the coquetry of posing in that squat. We should be forever grateful to this photograph, which is so perfect an example of that interiority offered to the other that is the very definition of intimacy. The rooftop provides us the forbidden space—it makes us visible only to our loved ones—but it's also where the seed of fantasy is planted. . . .

Downstairs, on maybe the fourth floor of this building, Vitín is sitting in his vinyl-upholstered chair, his bottle of bourbon by his side, in the half-light of the room. The former merchant marine has turned the lamp so its light falls on that picture over there on the wall. All of his attention (blurry, no doubt, from the bourbon) is centered on the little sailboat sailing through the magical space of the picture. There lies his every obsession. Every night he sits down before the same dream, and as the hours pass and the drinks go down, throughout the house one can hear that recurrent promise (or threat) that someday, someday, he's going to return in that boat. . . .

In the building next door that other spinner of fantasies has constructed—back in the farthest corner of the apartment, alongside the stove—a miniature tropical garden: his collection of Caribbean plants may represent the arcadian obsession of return. Nostalgia merged with the tourist's clichés. But birdcages with their budgies and their parrots aren't enough; in the background, behind the miniature palm trees, he's painted the half-moon beach at Luquillo, with El Yunque tall behind it . . . *I spend my free time back here looking at that landscape, and it gives me peace, it's my own kind of tranquilizer, ¿*sabes? *'cause I've got this nervous condition,* los nervios, *you know, but a man remembers the things back home and it's like it cures you . . . all the hassles and things just sort of go away, and like I say, even if I can't go back, I never forget, because I grew up out around Luquillo, in the little town of Palmer, and when we were kids we went all through that part out there, looking for* hicacos. . . . Your name? *José* Ruiz, me llamo *José* Ruiz.

The facades of the buildings, the chimneys and smokestacks again, the fire escapes, those bricks missing from tropical architecture, and then, as though sprung from assertiveness and self-assurance and vanity itself, two Puerto Rican women—mother and daughter, no doubt, or aunt and niece. And this photograph could well be the perfect proof that the rooftop is the place that verifies one's presence without erasing interiority. The younger woman poses proudly, regally; she guides the mother through her pose; she's been in *Niuyor* several years, and she's ready to step out with that smart look that she hints at with her left foot carefully forward and her head held high and back. But although this is a vanity that's too tense for grace or flirtatiousness, there's still that strange beauty in her determination to assert herself, reaffirm herself. The mother, perhaps just off the boat, has bought a brand-new coat to wear against the chilly autumn wind; her smile betrays a self-assertion born more of fear than of conviction—she's still a bit light-headed with the bustle of the city and the incessant rumble of the streets. The smile confirms her willingness to participate in the ritual of the rooftop, but the eyes betray the deep-seated perplexity of the recently arrived. As always, the shoes give the most perfect measure of the person . . . She's slipped her hands up inside the sleeves of the coat, but that gesture suggests as much a shyness at the still-strange taken-for-granted of life in the big city as it does cold. We must look at the shoes to understand that her smugness has already begun to turn to obedience; those high heels, so perfectly symmetrical, so solemn in their no-nonsense symmetry, assure us that despite the tension she's feeling at this moment there is a pretension to serenity, a serenity only possible in innocence. Then we see even more clearly the ultimate meaning of the photograph; the figure on the right, the young woman, strikes a pose that verges on affectation because her experience in the city demands of her such a queenly and at the same time insecure gesture. The fantasy demanded of us by vanity is moderated here by knowledge. And the mother is certainly willing to give that attitude a try; her innocence still aspires to an impossible serenity. . . . *You'll do great. It's hard at first, of course, it'll take some time to get adjusted . . .*

Here, the mother has had no need of the torturous experience of the daughter in order to strike her pose on the snowy rooftop. What's lacking is some handwritten phrase like *My first snow*, or *I finally see real snow*, or *Now this is cold!* to complete the emblematic function of the portrait. Here I am in *el Norte*; here I am in *Niuyor*; among all these buildings and all these chimneys, all these bricks and antennas, that blurry yet still smiling face seems to be saying to us. The photographer moved the camera and she pulled her cold hands up inside the sleeves of her winter coat. Once again, the high heels with the straps around the ankles . . . the entire pose, the blurred focus, the absence of the hands and the presence of the snow give the portrait a spectral quality, as though it were one of those snapshots determined to prove that ghosts exist. There she will remain, up on that rooftop, forever; she will wander with her blurry smile until she has proven that this snapshot stands at the same distance from the previous one as history stands from dreams, nightmares, madness.

This picture was taken of her up on the *rufo del bíldin* that Elsa lives in; it was cold, and again the innocence of the young woman's smile is also for the exotic landscape and the new coat. The skylight, the little wall she's sitting on, complete the portrait of "distance." The picture was taken by Myrta's boyfriend—just a friend of some relatives up there, a run-of-the-mill amateur photographer who committed the tragic faux pas of letting his own shadow get in the picture.

That summer, she went back to Puerto Rico. Her husband, Felo had found a job by then and he sent for her. . . . *He seems a lot better now, this new treatment is apparently doing him some good.* But his so-false serenity, more a breather achieved by the psychiatrists at the Hospital Rodríguez than anything else, couldn't bear the shadow in the picture . . . *Who is he? Tell me, goddammit, who the hell is that guy?—I told you, now turn me loose! And no more bugging me about it, either, do you hear? I told you he's* Myrta's novio, *keep messin' with me and I'll leave, I swear it.* . . . Felo went into the bedroom, took the revolver out of the night-table drawer, and fired three shots . . . *Why have you done this to me??! Oh my God . . . What've I ever done to you? . . . ¡Ay! . . . Don't shoot! . . . ¡Ay!, Police! He's ki-i-illing me!*

He crossed the living room and stood over the crib. He held the .38 to the *bebé*'s head and fired.

Erick, *él de ocho años*, ran out of the bedroom and was thrown against the wall by a shot to the belly.

The old she-dog ran out and started barking, almost as loud as the screaming of the neighbor-lady. *¡Jesús! ¡Ay! ¡Virgen pura! ¡Pero que ha pasao aquí! ¡Ayyy!*

Felo didn't spare the dog's life either, but by the time he took aim at *la vecina entrometía* his hand was shaking, and suddenly he was overcome with weeping.

He went out on the balcony and proclaimed to the whole neighborhood: *¡La maté por puta!* I killed her 'cause she's a whore, *puñeta!* . . . I'm a sick man, *estoy enfermo de los nervios*, but I get no respect, that filthy bitch—*¡carajo!* . . .

He killed her! He killed her! *(¡La mató, te digo! Llama a la policia*, hurry up, he's gone crazy! *¡Ay! Virgen Santa*, Felo's gone crazy, get inside, get inside, *echen pa'dentro . . . Pa' qué?* How do I know *pa'qué*. What business is it of yours anyway? *¿Pa' qué tú vas a averiguar?* The son of a bitch *se ha vuelto loco*, that's all. Go, *llama a la policía*, hurry up!

Then Felo jumped in his broken-down Impala and took off. A mob of neighbors rushed out into the street just as he turned up the hill. He came to the other barrio; he got out of the car when his best friend *de toda la vida* came over to him—*we was raised together* . . . Openmouthed, stunned, Eusebio couldn't understand the bullet Felo fired into his chest at point-blank range.

Then Myriam came out, she used to live with Felo, used to be the "other woman," she'd just come down from Boston, and she got one in the face.

Aurelito, Myriam's son with Felo, got hit in the back of the neck with another.

Felo's father, who was also "threatened by the veteran suffering from post-traumatic stress disorder," later commented with that implacable Puerto Rican logic of his that *he even killed the old bitch, although he'd never had anything to do with her before. . . .*

Felo was arrested as he was about to shoot himself.

Which was not the way the ultimate fate of the misfortune of the Borincan family generally played itself out—generally, it was "kill them all because *in our family we all sink or we're all saved—they're mine, and I can do with them what I please—right or wrong, they're mine.*" No victims of the tragedy should be left because "we're *all* guilty, and besides, *the kids ought not to be left orphans—what, so they can suffer?*" So nobody's innocent, and there won't be any pain or grief, either, because nobody will be left alive to have to suffer for the rest of their lives or (in the shooter's case) to have to have that on my conscience for the rest of my days. . . .

This logic is sterner and more mysterious than Greek tragedy: No one is innocent, let there be no victims or witnesses, let no one suffer, misfortune can be erased, done away with, through perverse compassion. There is a mysterious connection between the smiles on the rooftop of 1500 Prospect Avenue and that multiple murder in Barrio Tiburones, Yabucoa, Puerto Rico. The person that discovers it will have discovered the key to a people trapped between innocent smiles and cruel hysteria.

Translated from the Spanish by Andrew Hurley

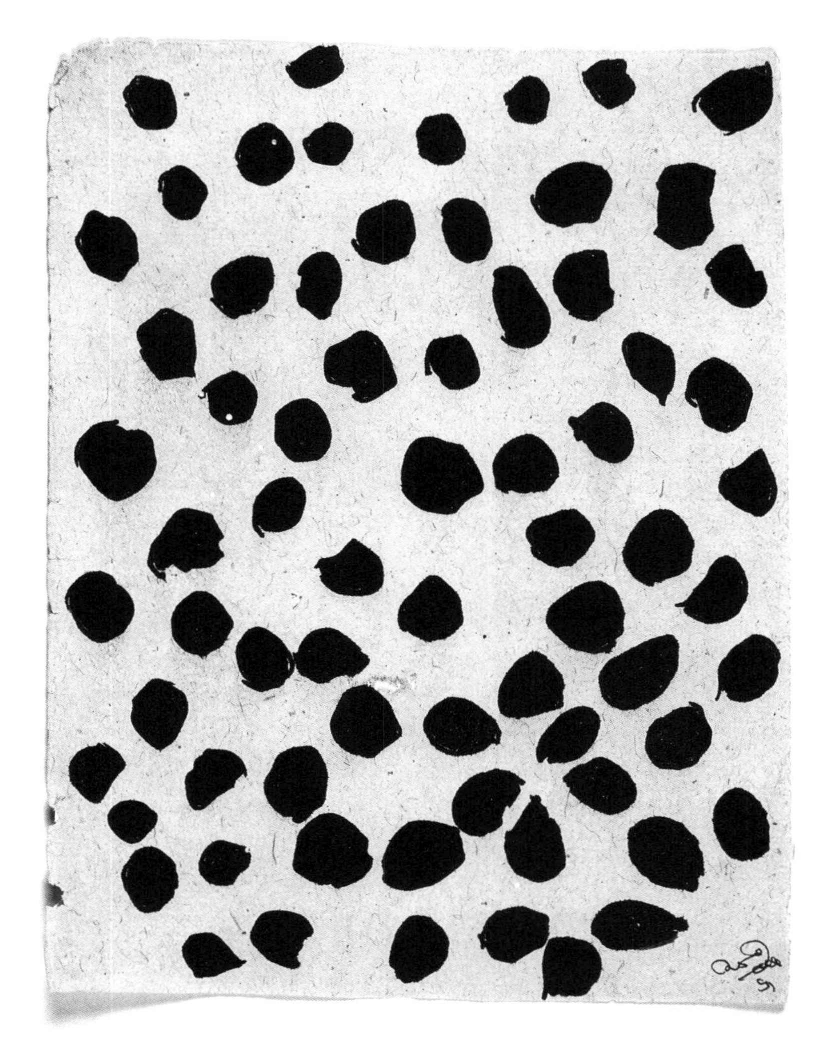

VYAKUL

PAGE 104:
Untitled, 1991.

PAGE 105:
Untitled, 1992.

BELOW:
Untitled, 1992.

OPPOSITE:
Untitled, 1996.

PAGE 108:
Untitled, 1997.

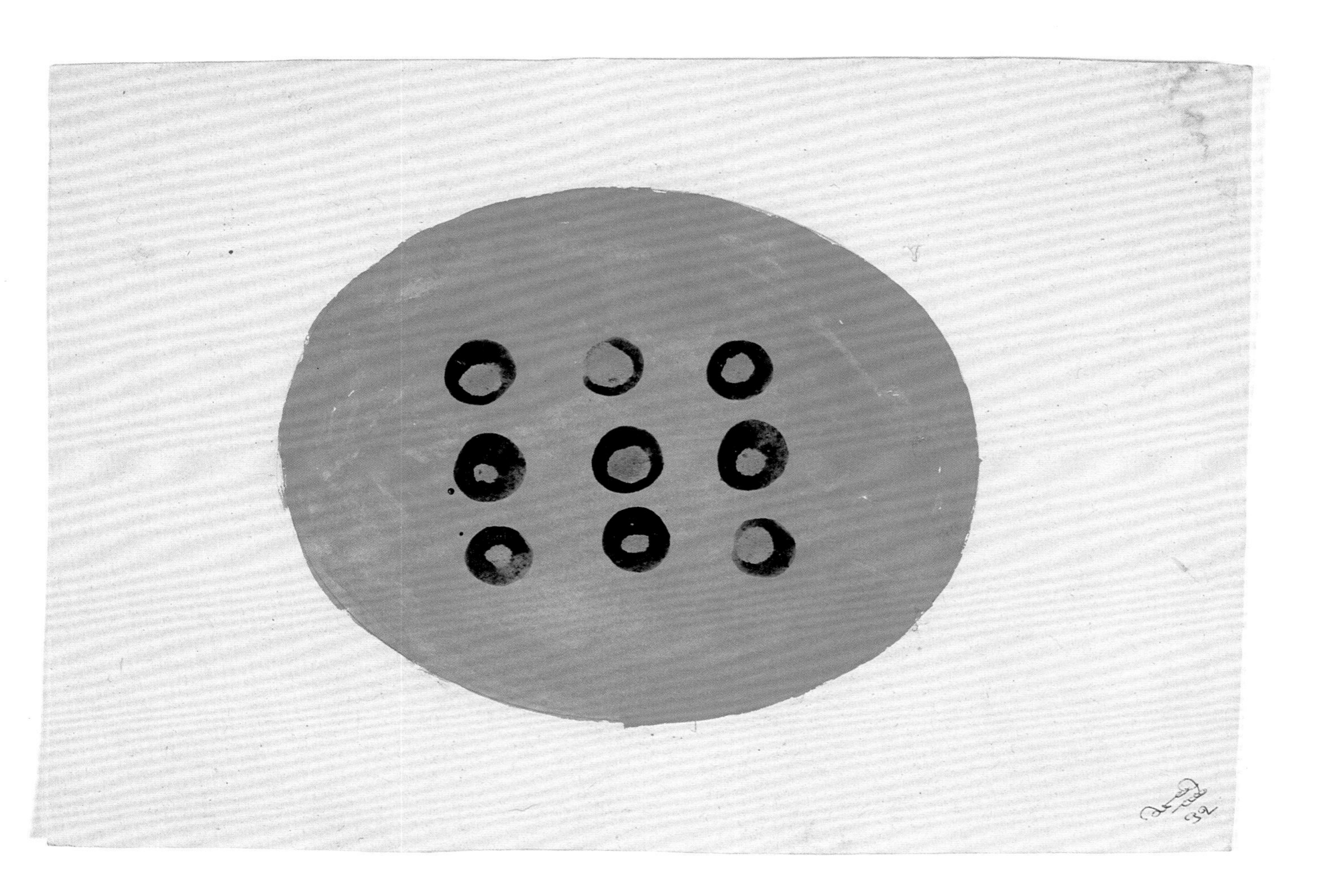

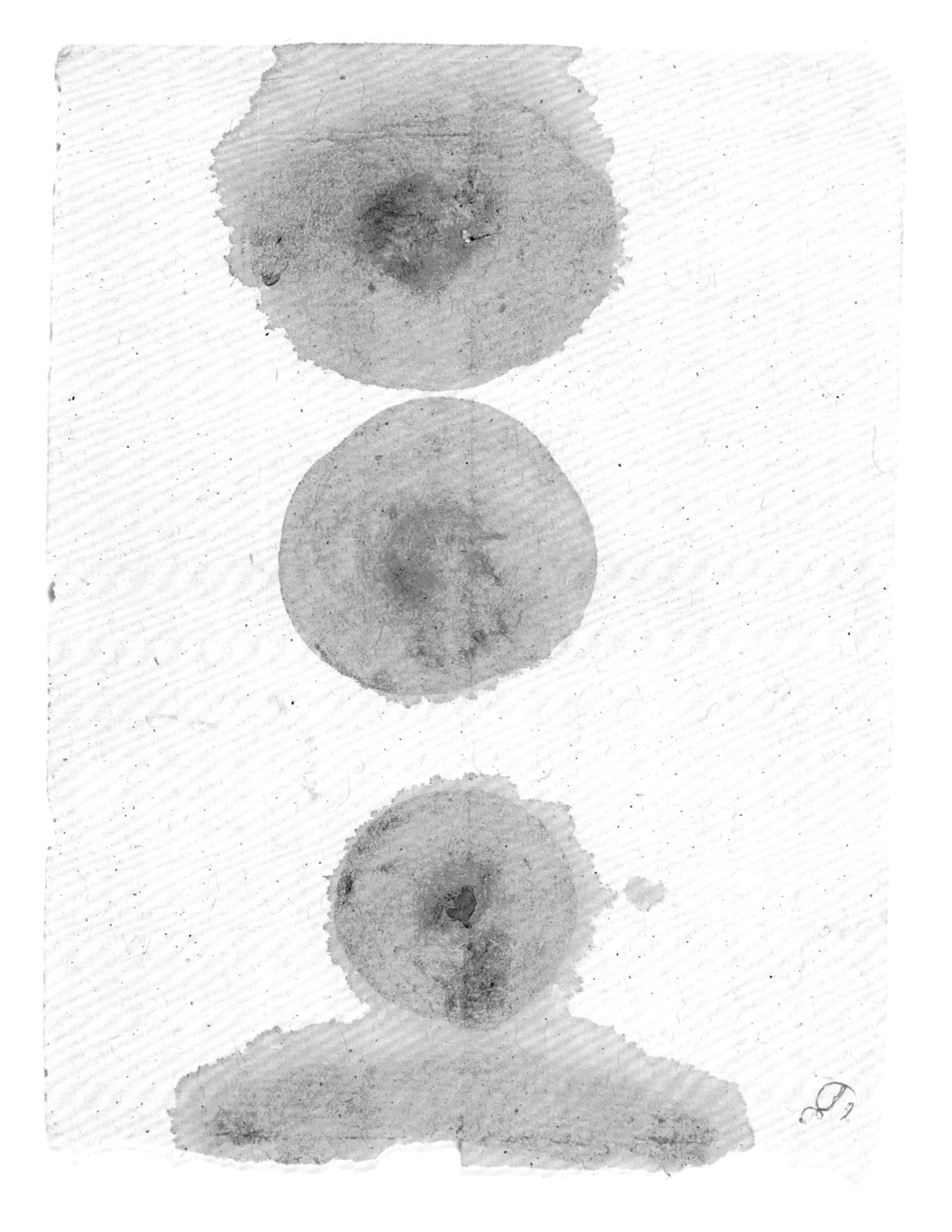

Acharaya Vyakul

Acharaya Vyakul says that the eye is such a simple planet that one must have the vigilance of a lynx. Always lying in wait.

To be able, with your hand, to choose instantly between what happens in the mind and what is based on mindless desire (with that almost instinctive wish to draw). The eye is second. That is what makes a painter.

To select or reject what arrives first in the eye, then in the mind, and then—at the blessed moment of meeting—moves from one to the other. That is what makes a spectator.

He has a strange way of doing things: "Nothing is really so important. I can even paint at night, in the dark. I prepare my paints, my brushes, and my paper. When everything is ready, I turn out the light and attack. The colors are finally at rest, they let themselves go, they are no longer afraid of being seen; they suddenly reveal all of their energy, all of their beauty."

"Nothing is really so important. Sometimes I paint with my fingers. Or with anything else I can find. Lipstick, coffee, a lump of charcoal, or sulfur. Everything is good."

He adds that it is better for life to slip suddenly into the colors and the lines, suddenly and at the moment of their arrival on the page. Still, these colors and these lines will stay forever, apparently: immobile, fixed, petrified.

Result: an open spectrum. No obstacles, no rejections. On paper, he can pass from the worst violence to the most refined delicacy. It all depends on his inner state at the exact moment of the action.

And then, finally, what he wanted to be sure to tell me that day: "You can only paint the invisible. You can only paint what you can't entirely see or show, and which, nevertheless, passes through all of us."

Franck André Jamme

CHARLES SIMIC

The Unseen Hand

in memory of Bill Matthews

It goes about its business,
Catching flies,
Letting them go as it pleases.
We do nothing.
We only note who's missing.

The bread from the table gone
And the old Italian waiter
Who brought us a new bottle of wine,
And his small white dog
Who followed him everywhere.

The bright sunny day stolen
And that long happy year
As if it were confetti
In a young girl's hair,
Someone likewise pilfered.

Five-finger discount
Is what they call it in the streets,
This short breather,
Before the final snatch.

Child Running With Scissors

Someone's calling his name
In a voice mad with love and terror.
The window is open.
The trees in the yard hang heavy
In the morning heat.

On the night table there's
A clock that has stopped,
A pitcher of ice water
And a half-empty glass
With a spider flailing in it.

My heart beating much too fast.
I can even hear the sprinkler
Turn this way and that
On the neighbor's lawn
In the returning quiet.

With These Hands

DANIEL ROTHENBERG

When we shop for produce, our actions mirror those of the migrant farmworker. Our hands stretch out in much the same way as a farmworker's hands — harvesting our nation's fruits and vegetables, piece by piece. While the produce we buy may have been mechanically sorted and packed, supercooled, chemically treated, waxed, and shipped hundreds if not thousands of miles away, often the last hand to touch the apples, lettuce, or plums we buy was that of a migrant farmworker.

Each year, over one million migrant farmworkers and their families labor in North America's fields. They earn an average of $6,500 per year and often suffer treatment that would be inconceivable in other industries. They are threatened, cheated out of their wages, housed and transported in dangerous conditions, and in the most extreme cases, held in debt peonage. Farmworkers have always been recruited from among the most vulnerable members of American society — recent immigrants, the homeless, the rural poor — and have been consistently denied the legal protections provided to other workers.

CALVIN DOUGLAS

Orlando, Florida

Over the last three decades, a number of courts have established that the conditions of debt peonage under which thousands of farmworkers live and work violate federal antislavery statutes. The farm labor contractors who ran these camps control their workers through violence and debt. This system represents the most extreme form of farmworker abuse.

For years, Calvin Douglas was a successful barber working in Tennessee. He had his own business, a house, and two cars. His wife at the time worked in the local school system and his daughter was finishing a degree in chemical engineering. Then Douglas discovered the lucrative business of dealing drugs and started selling painkillers out of his barbershop. Gradually, he expanded his business to include cocaine. After some initial success, Douglas began using his product; and within eighteen months, he'd spent all his money. Addicted to crack, he found himself living on the streets of Orlando. A "road man" met Douglas at a shelter and offered him a job, hinting at the availability of drugs and women. Later that day, Douglas and several others were transported to a labor camp in central Florida.

He was interviewed in June 1995.

The thing that astonished me most about living at the labor camp is that they didn't care about your name. You had no name. You just had a number. My number was seventy. They called you by your number. "Number seventy, come here."

Every day, we'd go to work. We worked from sunup to sundown. We'd get up in the dark and come back in the dark. The work was hard. You're out in the field and there's this long row that looks like it will never end. You think you won't finish, but finally you get there. Then, you have to turn around and come back.

After work, you'd stop by the crew leader's house. He had a real nice house with a swimming pool and all that good stuff. That's where they ran the lines. Every day you'd charge stuff—liquor, beer, cigarettes, things like that. That's also when the cocaine came into it. If you had no bad habits then they really didn't want you there. If you were the type that could save money, they found some way to get rid of you. They only wanted people with drug and alcohol problems.

They were also skeptical of white men. They'd only take a white guy if he was a real drunk. If not, they wouldn't mess with him. I heard the crew leader talking once. He said he didn't like to hire white workers because he didn't want to hire the wrong one, someone whose father or relative might come down on him.

When they figured up your paycheck, you almost

always owed them. Sometimes I got a few dollars, maybe twelve or thirteen dollars for a week's work. If you had money, he'd take you to a special store, owned by some white guy. He'd load up the bus and everybody would go to this man's store and spend their money.

I had no control over my life. I had no money. I had no clothes to speak of. With the way they talked to you and the way you were dirty all the time, I felt like a slave. If you wanted anything, you'd have to ask the crew leader and he'd tell you no. The cook wasn't allowed to feed us until the crew leader got to the camp. It didn't matter when the food was ready, we had to wait until the crew leader arrived, because he served us all himself.

Number thirty-six, number fifteen, number seventy.

He'd pile one guy's plate real high, and then I'd come next and get just a spoonful. It was like the way you'd train a dog. You're the only one that feeds your dog, so your dog is beholden to you. That's the way he felt about the people on his camp.

One day, a guy was sick. At four-thirty in the morning they started blowing the horn on the bus. The crew leader took his foot and just kicked the door in — BAM! — right off the hinges. "Get up, you going to work. You done ate my food, drank my beer, and smoked my dope. You going to work."

Another day, there was a guy who went to the fields with a hangover. He was lying halfway in and halfway out of the road. The crew leader came through and ran over the man's leg in his Bronco. I saw it with my own eyes. He wouldn't take the man to the hospital. He just left him there. The man lay there all day long. "Ain't nothing wrong with him. He'll be all right." But the man wasn't all right. There was something wrong with his leg. He never once took a worker to the doctor.

I'd seen his gun and I'd seen him reading the Bible. He said he read the Bible because somewhere in there it says that if you don't work, you shouldn't eat. I'll tell you, that crew leader is one of the worst men I've ever met. He is evil.

I wanted to get off the camp, but the only way you could leave was to run away. If you tried to get away, they'd send somebody after you. Then they'd take you back to the camp and beat you up. I saw people being beaten after they tried to escape.

Still, there was one time when I did leave.

They wanted us to pick seven bins of oranges each day as a quota. I wasn't a good orange picker, so one day I didn't get but three bins. The foreman told me that since I didn't make the quota, I wouldn't get to eat when we got back to the camp. They served everybody food except me. So the next morning, when we stopped at a store to get gas, I got off the bus and hid. After the bus left, I started walking towards Orlando. About forty minutes later, here comes the crew leader in his big Bronco.

"Hey, number seventy, come here!"

"Naw, man, I'm through."

"Come here, I want to talk to you."

"No, I'm on my way to Orlando."

"Get in, I'll take you."

"No, that's all right." I kept on walking.

He was driving and talking to me through the window. "What's wrong, number seventy, you scared? Come on, get in and talk to me."

I don't know why, but I got in his car. I was scared. I knew he wasn't going to take me to Orlando, but he said he just wanted to talk to me. "You mess with that thing, number seventy?"

"What thing?"

"You know what I'm talking about. You mess with cocaine, don't you?"

"Yeah, sometimes."

"Tell you what. Let me catch up to the bus and put you back on. You go out there and work. It don't make no difference how many bins you get. You go out there and work and when you come in tonight, you come around to the garage and I'll take care of you."

"Okay."

When we got back that night, I went around to the garage, and sure enough, he had a hundred dollars' worth of cocaine for me. He gives me the cocaine and says, "Don't worry about a thing." That's how the crew leader stopped me from leaving.

Everybody in town knew about the labor camp. The sheriff, the farmers, and the crew leader were all in cahoots. The farmers knew how we were treated. You could tell they knew by the way they'd talk. There was one farmer in particular I talked to. He owned an orange grove. Once he told me, "I know you guys are working for next to nothing, but I can't do anything about it." He said he didn't like what was going on, but then why was he using that

contractor? I didn't ask him, but I knew the answer — he got cheap labor and made more money.

This is going on today, right now. It keeps going on because of the way our society works. The farmers want cheap labor and they know they can get cheap labor with the right contractor. In order for the contractor to provide cheap labor, he's got to find people that have no hope. They capitalize on people's problems. The farmers know what's going on. They just turn their heads the other way.

When I was out there in the fields, I'd think a lot about air-conditioning. I thought about how I'd lived pretty good for a lot of years. I used to go from my air-conditioned house to my air-conditioned car to my air-conditioned barbershop. I never had to sweat. I didn't know nothing about hard work.

There I was out in the blazing sun. I'm sweating. I'm dirty. I'm nasty. I thought a lot about what I'd lost. Still, I feel lucky to have survived. There are lots of people that don't survive. I'm fifty-five now.

I'd say that living on that labor camp was the worst experience I've ever had. Most people wouldn't believe that it's true, but I know it's real because I lived through it. I guarantee you that the same things are happening right now, as we sit here, on somebody's labor camp. The road men come through here all the time and they always leave with people.

HATTIE WILSON

Fort Pierce, Florida

Before the mid-sixties, children working in the fields were completely exempt from coverage by the minimum-wage law and other protective labor legislation. Although farmworker children are now covered by federal child labor laws, they are subject to a number of special exemptions. While the minimum age for working in the United States is sixteen, children as young as fourteen can work in the fields with virtually no restrictions and children twelve and older can do farm labor with their parents' approval.

Hattie Wilson's parents separated before she can remember. Her earliest memories are of Belle Glade, Florida, an agricultural town located on the southern shore of Lake Okeechobee. Belle Glade is a farmworkers' town; recently Haitian, Latino, and West Indian immigrants have changed the ethnic composition of the town's traditionally African-American work force. It remains one of the poorest communities in the nation. Workers still go out to the same loading dock each morning looking for work and they still pay exorbitant weekly rents to live in old wooden shacks and crumbling, concrete-block housing.

Hattie Wilson was interviewed in May 1992.

As far back as I can remember is 1954. What makes that so outstanding in my mind is that it was very cold. I didn't have any shoes, so my mother put three pairs of socks on my feet.

I remember that we couldn't find a place to stay because my mother had us kids and was a single woman. None of the contractors wanted a single woman with children on any of the labor camps. I remember walking all over town looking for a place to stay. I was stepping on things and I could feel them, which reminded me that I wasn't wearing shoes.

It was getting late and we still hadn't found anywhere to sleep. We passed a house that was raised up on stilts. My mother crawled up under the house, cleared a space, and dug a little hole in the ground. She put me and my brother in the hole and told us to stay very quiet.

When she came back she took us out from under the house and told us she'd found a place to stay. It was a little room. I remember the room had kerosene lighting. It was always smoky and we coughed a lot.

There was only one narrow bed, so my mother put my brother and me on a pallet on the floor.

Every day, she'd go out to the fields to pick string beans. I can remember her bringing beans home. Oh God, we ate so many beans. I was sick to death of string beans. We lived there for a couple of years.

Then, my mother met a man, Mr. LeMar. He had the most evil eyes I've ever seen on a human being. They were like glass. There was nothing behind them, no warmth, no compassion, no nothing. They were just clear, see-through eyes. Oh, but that man could sing. He had the most beautiful voice. You couldn't imagine how such a voice could come from that man. When you looked at him, they didn't match. He sang like an angel, but the man was a demon.

Mr. LeMar came to live with us. He and my mother would work in the fields, and my brother and I would play around the house. We were only allowed to play outside so long as we could see Mama. Whenever she got out of sight we were to go inside and lock the door. I was about six years old at the time. We weren't in school and there was no preschool or day care. We just kept to ourselves and did exactly like she told us.

Then, Mr. LeMar started coming home during the day, leaving my mama in the fields. He would make my brother sit in the corner facing the wall, with his back to us. Then, he would force himself on me. I can remember seeing him spit in his hand to lubricate himself. He had no idea I was only six years old. My brother would hear me crying, but he'd be afraid to turn around and watch. I can remember hearing my brother beg Mr. LeMar to leave me alone. Then, Mr. LeMar would throw something—a cup, a bottle, a glass—and tell him to shut up.

I don't remember how many times he did that to me because for a long time I tried to forget that it ever really happened. My moods and eating habits changed. I wasn't as playful as I'd been. My mother noticed these changes. She'd ask me about it, but Mr. LeMar warned me that if I ever told my mother, he'd kill my little brother. When I started to cry after my mother questioned me, she knew something was wrong.

One day, Mr. LeMar came home early again. My brother must have been watching. I'd been hemorrhaging and my brother took my panties and threw them in a fifty-five-gallon barrel that we used to burn trash in. When my mother came in, she had my panties in her hand. Her fingers were bloody from the panties, which were still wet.

"Who did this to you?"

I didn't answer. I just knew Mr. LeMar was going to kill my brother.

When I started to cry, she didn't ask me anymore. She just went into the kitchen and started cooking up something very hot. It made my eyes water. There was a mist in the house that made me cough and sneeze. My mother told us to go outside. I didn't know what it was then, but I know now. It was a mixture of Red Devil Lye, honey, Clorox, and a few other chemicals. She put in the honey so the mixture would adhere to whatever she threw it on. When she finished cooking it up, she set it aside to cool. She used to chew snuff which came in a big tall can, Navy snuff. She poured some of the mixture into one of the cans, put the top on it, wrapped it up, and put it in her blouse.

Then, she let her hair down. That was the first time in my life that I ever saw my mother let down her hair. It fell just below her hips. Then, she dipped her fingers into the kerosene lampshade and painted her eyelids using the soot like mascara. She made up her face, put on a pretty dress, high heels, the whole works. She got all dressed up. She didn't have any stockings, but I sat and watched her lotion her legs so they looked real nice.

Then Mr. LeMar came home and she told him, "I want you to get dressed up and we'll go down to the juke."

He said, "Okay," and they went out.

When they came back, Mr. LeMar was drunk, but my mother was walking tall and straight as usual, like she hadn't had a drop of alcohol. She sat on the side of the bed. Mr. LeMar was so drunk that he fell over while he was trying to undress. Then, my mother helped him up and put him into bed. She didn't even bother to take his shoes off. In a few minutes, he was snoring.

While he slept, my mother took all of our little clothes and put them in a paper bag and stood us by the door. Then, she took this can from her bra, pulled the top off it and poured the mixture into Mr. LeMar's ear.

He started screaming.

It was the worst screaming I've ever heard. With every scream you knew that he was in absolute agony. He tried to claw at his ear and whenever he did that, pieces of meat would be slinging all over the wall. They stuck to the wall. It was burning him. She poured the stuff all over the man's ear, and it was burning.

I was crying and looking away, but my mother stood behind me and held my face towards Mr. LeMar. She said, "Do you see that? I got him! I got him! Look at that, I got him!"

Then, she grabbed my brother and we left Belle Glade that night.

Hattie Wilson continued to work as a farm laborer, eventually settling with her mother and brother in a small town in north-central Florida. When Hattie's mother died, she went to Miami where she fell in with petty criminals, but afterwards returned to rural Florida, worked in the fields and married a local businessman. Later, she divorced, went back to the fields and then remarried. Hattie still lives in a farmworker community and occasionally supplements her income picking oranges.

ALGIMIRO MORALES

Oceanside, California

Seasonal farmworkers' real wages have fallen 20 to 25 percent over the last two decades. The arrival of large numbers of Latin American immigrants, is the key reason for this drop. These new arrivals are typically the most vulnerable to abuses.

Many of these are indigenous people from Guatemala and southern Mexico, among the poorest people in Latin America. In the late 1970s and early 1980s large numbers of indigenous Mexicans — Mixtecs, Zapotecs, Triques, and others — began arriving in the Southwest, generally finding work in agriculture. There are now more than 40,000 Mixtec Indians in California. As many as 14,000 live in San Diego County, where some have built makeshift camps in uninhabited canyons near the fields where they work. Because of the informal, unregulated quality of the farm labor system, whole communities of these newly arrived workers can often exist under precarious circumstances only blocks from major highways, housing developments, and shopping centers.

Algimiro Morales first arrived in the United States in 1979. When he was an undocumented worker, he lived in a shantytown near the fields where he worked. He eventually legalized his status, sent for his family, and found a better job in a local factory. Morales is the founder of the Comite

VACUUM COOLED
UNDER REFRIGERATION
34°F 1°C

Cívico Popular Mixteco, one of a number of Mixtec community organizations that have sprung up throughout California.

He was interviewed in October 1995.

When I used to live here on this hill, life was much more difficult. Back then, very few people had papers. We couldn't live out in the open because Immigration was always looking for us. There were raids all the time. Whenever they came, people would be running everywhere. They'd catch some of us and others would get away. Usually after a raid, we'd sit around and laugh about what happened. Once Immigration caught me and about twenty others. They took us all to Tijuana. Two days later we crossed back over the border.

To avoid Immigration, we used to live in little rooms, like caves, that we built underground. The rooms were about six feet by six feet—just big enough to sleep in— and had wood roofs that we covered with dirt. Our caves were all over this hill. The ranchero built a communal kitchen, a big house with empty oil drums that he cut in half. We cooked together, making fires in the oil drums and storing our food in boxes we'd built. Our underground rooms were always set away from the kitchen so that when Immigration arrived they wouldn't find the places where we slept.

Since then, the community has changed a great deal. Now, there are no more Immigration raids because many people have papers. Instead of caves, the people build aboveground houses made out of wood, cardboard, sheets of plastic, and parts of old cars. There's no electricity or running water. The televisions here run on car batteries and water is carried in from the fields, which are quite far away. There's a spigot down below where people go to bathe. More and more people are coming to the community. All the children here go to school.

Each community elects a committee and a president to provide basic rules of conduct and make sure the place is kept clean. The president is generally an older man because, among the Mixtec, older people are always the most highly respected.

There's a rule here that since the single men drink and make noise they have to live on one side and families on the other. This community is named Kelly, in honor of the man who owns the land. Kelly allows people to live here. Other landowners call the police, who send in bulldozers to destroy the shacks. This community is illegal, but Kelly is a kind man. It costs six hundred dollars a month to rent an apartment in this area. In the fields, you earn twenty to thirty dollars a day, and in Kelly, there's no rent.

The first Mixtec immigrants to a place return to their communities and tell others to come. Now, we have Mixtecs all over California. We are very unified. We can help you find your relatives or cross the border. You might arrive in America carrying a suitcase full of letters and it's the same when you return home. It's like our own post office.

We stay in direct contact with our communities in Mexico. Wherever there are several Mixtec families from a particular town, they meet, talk, and agree on the best way to serve their community. We call this *tequio*. *Tequio* is voluntary work that a person provides as community service. Usually *tequio* is physical work, like fixing the streets or building a church. Local leaders figure out how many men they need and then each person donates one or two days of work, giving the community his *tequio*. It's an obligation. Since we're living in the United States, we send money back based on the value of a day's work.

For Mixtecs, the suffering in a place like this is nothing strange. The poverty in our land is extreme, and while here we may be poor, at least we can survive. Still, it's difficult here and sometimes dangerous. Last year, a group of skinheads began shooting at our houses. People here are cautious. We've formed a community defense group to protect ourselves from outsiders.

The worst part of all this is that we can't respond. Our words mean nothing to the Americans. Our people come here to work. It's necessity that brings us here to live through these dangers, face social rejection, and watch as families are torn apart, as fathers leave families at home, and children grow up alone. This is not the way things should be.

In the community where you were born and where you own land you're somebody. There you live day-to-day among your people. You have an opportunity to control your life, to work to become a good citizen, to be respected. Then a time comes when you have to leave your town, which these days is very common. When you leave home, you're often mistreated. This is difficult, especially if you're used to being treated with respect. People look at you as if you are beneath them. They see you as nothing, and then you begin to feel that, outside of your community, perhaps you really are worthless. You might be respected at home, but in the outside world you are nothing, nobody.

I would like Americans to understand that living like this, in huts we've built on a hillside, is not the same as being ignorant. There is a great deal of wisdom in our communities. There are rules in our culture that are often superior to those in Anglo-Saxon society. We look at the family differently. Children respect their parents. Mixtecs revere their elders.

The young people here are Mixtec. Perhaps this will change after a generation or two, but for now they identify with our people. They go to Mixtec dances and tell Mixtec tales. I'm still not used to the idea that we're leaving our communities in Mexico. Perhaps the most important thing is not that we're leaving, but that we're maintaining our unity, our identity.

A year after this interview was conducted, Kelly and another neighboring Mixtec shantytown were torn down by local authorities, who gave residents a set time to relocate and helped a number of families find rental housing. A few months later, all that was left of Kelly were pressed-dirt floors, postholes, burned mattresses, old bottles, and torn bits of clothing. Many of the Mixtecs who lived there drifted off to build new makeshift homes in other, more hidden canyons.

At Schoodic

Ocean has
no eyes

for us,
stares us

down, jumble
of rocks

& water,
a billion

syllables, an
old confusion.

•

Past the
island

dense with
pines the

lobster-
boat with

its cloud
of gulls

enters
the bay.

•

Patient, the
heron turns

sideways &
disappears.

•

Meadow by water.
Light drains away.

Many clouds marry
the one mountain.

•

Day glows
through fine rain

wave-glint
bright with spume

fog e-
rasing the

night, sea
changing rooms.

16 Songs

1
the dogwood's
rush

to surpass
itself

every surface

pressed into flower

2
gnomon
shadows the park

sundown
eases darkness from river

though facade
glow like theory

3
What he
thought were

two tiny
balls of

mercury rolling
along the

bar were
in fact

a passing
bus's reflections

in his
glasses' lenses.

4
the urinal's
fixed, ar-
chaic smile

5
sometimes the
period
is the syl-

lable: ghost
beat, the sax-
ophonist's

finger point-
ing up to
the unsound-

ed note: vow-
el, promise,
IOU

6
crane mitered like a bishop
head of the cock a

strawberry, the given world, what
could be more than it?

7
a banging
in the pipes

a cotton
sky, host to

numbers, the
syllables

counted like
seeds, tongue &

groove hidden
in the wall

8
outside the
bar the man
tugs at his

vest, soothing
himself down

on the train
the boy cups
the ball in

the socket
of his la-
crosse racquet

9
sudden, rank,
the paper-
whites burst the
green sheaths of

their blossoms,
unfold through
the declen-
sions of light

10
Both the music's
pure dream of it-
self, and the ma-
chinery of

its making: sound-
less keyboard where
David practiced
In Nomine

11
all the names
are given
names: sky,
cauldron, tun-
nel of love

12
sleep honey-
combed with dreams

a vowel
to ride on

13
The sound of
crickets pours through

the day: dry
creatures among warm

stones: one fell
asleep cupped in

my father's hand

14
the *stain*, Williams
called it: a

capillary, germinant contagion,
charged as the

air before rain:
mind sparks in

this damp, meanings
flush like desire

15
the man mending
his sidewalk, sprinkling

it down, offhand
as a priest

16
and the
sills

of
evening

Like,
my
Father

DIASTÈME

Like, my father, he knows about every kind of faucet in the world. The ones you turn, the ones you pull, the ones you lift up. The ones with red for hot, and when you turn them you freeze. He can spot them a mile off. My father, sometimes they call him from Hong Kong to put in new plumbing. A first-class ticket and a suite reserved in his name. When he gets to the hotel, he tells them what to do. You wouldn't believe the way people look at him, like he was a savior or something.

Like, my father, he knows all the provincial capitals and major towns. You tell him a *département*, any *département*, and he'll tell you how many square kilometers it has, how many people, and the best way to get there. He knows the name of the local police chief and has had dinner with him. When we go on vacation, he's gotta watch out he doesn't forget to stop and have a drink with the chief in every neighborhood. Otherwise, they get angry.

Like, my father, he's the head of the legal department at this Paris bank. Some sonofabitch doesn't pay up, he's the guy who sends out the cops. This makes some people mad, so they come after him looking to bust his chops. But they don't scare my old man. If he wanted to, he could take them all, one at a time, you better believe it. He's so good at what he does, though, he doesn't have to bust heads. I don't know how he does it, but he gets them all turned around so that by the time they leave, they're happy.

Like, my father hates paying taxes. The thought of having to pay makes him sick. It's the Arabs, my father says, the government feeds them and they steal our money. When you think about it, it's not right that we have to pay for people who don't do a damned thing. Especially since they could find work if they wanted to, those bums. As garbage men or something. My father says people who don't work should consider themselves lucky if they're allowed to pick up the garbage. No shame in picking up garbage.

Like, my father, since we got cable, he's always in front of the TV. Now, you'll be telling me he was always in front of the TV, even before we got cable. But at least before he used to take a break when the game shows were on. Now, Jesus, from eight in the morning until midnight. Sees every film at least six times. And if you try changing the channel, he'll scream bloody murder. You better make sure it's something he wants to watch. Our problems are over, though: to make sure I wouldn't piss him off anymore, he moved the TV into the bedroom.

Like, my father, he's into books. He parks his butt in his easy chair and, whoa, he's off on another planet. He's been into Balzac for a month, must be plenty there to keep him occupied. The last time he spoke to me must have been when I graduated from high school. "Good work, son," was what he said. Completely out of his mind. He also told me I ought to have a look at this book by Albert Cohen. Seems there's this awesome love story and three or four totally crazy girls. My father said he loved it. I thought it was so-so.

Like, my father, he wants me to call him François. The day I turn eighteen, he drags me into his office and tells me I'm old enough now to stop calling him papa. Papa, he says, like out of some old movie or something. Like when I hug him in front of everybody. Or when my mother calls him sweetheart. Hey, I said, really cool. I think I told him I'd always been dreaming about the day I could call him François. So I call him François. When I show up at the house for lunch, we shake hands.

Like, my father, the one thing I can't do with him is talk politics. We always end up calling each other names. My mother calls up beforehand to tell me to avoid the subject. It drives him crazy, and with his blood pressure . . . If I'm lucky, I make it to dessert. Then the sonofabitch always finds some new way to tick me off. I'm convinced he does it on purpose. So that I'll call him a Neanderthal fascist and give him an excuse to throw me out before dessert. It's been years since I had a cup of coffee at my parents' house. Not even steaming hot, right out of the pot.

Like, my father, it's with the kids that he's really too much. When I was a kid, I remember, one smart-ass word out of me and it was off to my room. But my kids, they can walk all over him and he doesn't say a thing. And my little girl, you better believe she takes advantage. Spends half of dinner pulling his hair out, and he's loving it. He takes out his comb, and he laughs. Can't get through dinner without combing his hair twenty-five times. Luckily, with the hair he's got left, it doesn't take all night.

Like, my father, it's his skin that worries me. He's starting to have these lumps on his neck and also these little freckles that just don't look normal. I beg him to go see a doctor, but it only makes him angry. So I tell him to at least stop grilling himself in the sun like a piece of meat. He tells me to mind my own business. He was born in the sun, he says, whereas you, he tells me, you were born in the city, you couldn't possibly understand. Keep it up, I tell him, and you'll wind up like Julio Iglesias. He takes that as a compliment.

Like, my father, he can't walk anymore. He can't walk, but he doesn't talk about it. Never complains or anything. When I visit, he tells me he can't get up because of last night's jog. He laughs because we both know his jogging days are over, and I laugh too. When he gets up to go to the toilet, my mother gets up too. She does something with her mouth and starts smiling. He smiles at her, too. And I also smile. It takes him half an hour to make it across the living room, and all that time everybody is looking somewhere else. At the new curtains. At the weather.

Like, my father, since he got sick, he's not the same. The last time I went to visit him at the hospital, he spent the whole time scratching his balls. It was kind of embarrassing. And then he called me *sir*. He handed me his bottle of pills and asked if I could go fill it for him. I say I'm not the nurse, I'm your son, you must have us mixed up. For a minute he sits there staring at me without saying a word, with the bottle still in his hand. Then he scratches his balls.

Like, my father, Romain said, what I'm sorry about is that I never held him in my arms. That I never hugged him tight for just a minute. More than words and all the rest, to have held him against me . . . I think he found it strange at the end because I was a head taller than he was. I wasn't the one who snuggled up anymore, he was. His cheek against my shoulder. It was strange for me too. I would bend down a little to make him seem taller. But I still towered over him.

Translated from the French by Arthur Goldhammer

The Story of a Woman Who Am I? Forgive Me

BERNADETTE MAYER

An ugly little monster is born in Connecticut
bursting out of a man's heart after dinner
it grows up housed in the spaceship's corridors
to be a combination shark, machine & Godzilla
till it destroys everybody who's looked expectantly
around the corners of the place for its forms
(including the scientist who's a robot who gets
his head knocked off and inside it's milk & wires)
except for this handsome woman who gregariously
masters and ejects the thing from the emergency
shuttle then she puts herself to sleep by freezing
till somebody will be able to pick her up later
with the cat, we watched all that & you walked
into the file cabinet again gashing your leg
which is my head and closer to your heart but
it wasn't serious and the country is so hot
and full of movies including *American Gigolo*
no real sex scenes just these shots of legs
with hands on them with a kind of tittering
music behind and between the 3 faces of the man
and woman of your body with torso—all sex-eyes
are the crooked stiles and disproportions of poems
contraptions distracting a crooked man like Stesichorus
from each human being who brings along her harpsichord
to dance on water & sing choruses with Terpsichore
muse of the way you go up and down the corner.

INCIDENT REPORT FORM CONTINUATION

INCIDENT NO.	REPORTING OFFICER	DATES AND TIMES OF OCCURRENCE

Susan Meiselas

Archives of Abuse

NOTES

PAGE_________OF___________

ICSS ENTRY BY:

SFPD 26501771

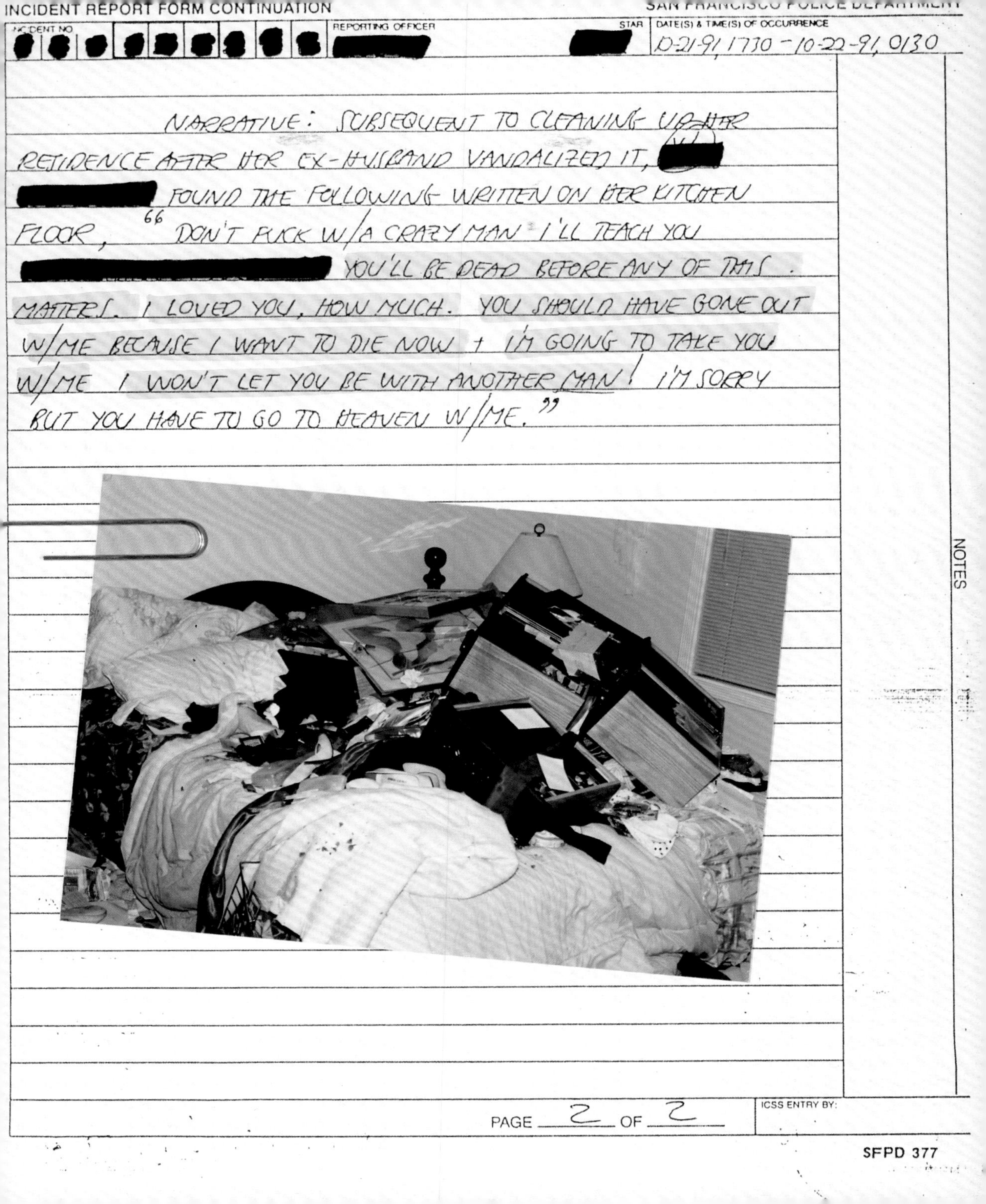

INCIDENT REPORT FORM CONTINUATION

SAN FRANCISCO POLICE DEPARTMENT

INCIDENT NO.	REPORTING OFFICER	STAR	DATE(S) & TIME(S) OF OCCURRENCE
			10-21-91, 1730 – 10-22-91, 0130

NARRATIVE: SUBSEQUENT TO CLEANING UP HER RESIDENCE AFTER HER EX-HUSBAND VANDALIZED IT, FOUND THE FOLLOWING WRITTEN ON HER KITCHEN FLOOR, "DON'T FUCK W/A CRAZY MAN I'LL TEACH YOU YOU'LL BE DEAD BEFORE ANY OF THIS MATTERS. I LOVED YOU, HOW MUCH. YOU SHOULD HAVE GONE OUT W/ME BECAUSE I WANT TO DIE NOW + I'M GOING TO TAKE YOU W/ME I WON'T LET YOU BE WITH ANOTHER MAN! I'M SORRY BUT YOU HAVE TO GO TO HEAVEN W/ME."

NOTES

PAGE 2 OF 2

ICSS ENTRY BY:

SFPD 377

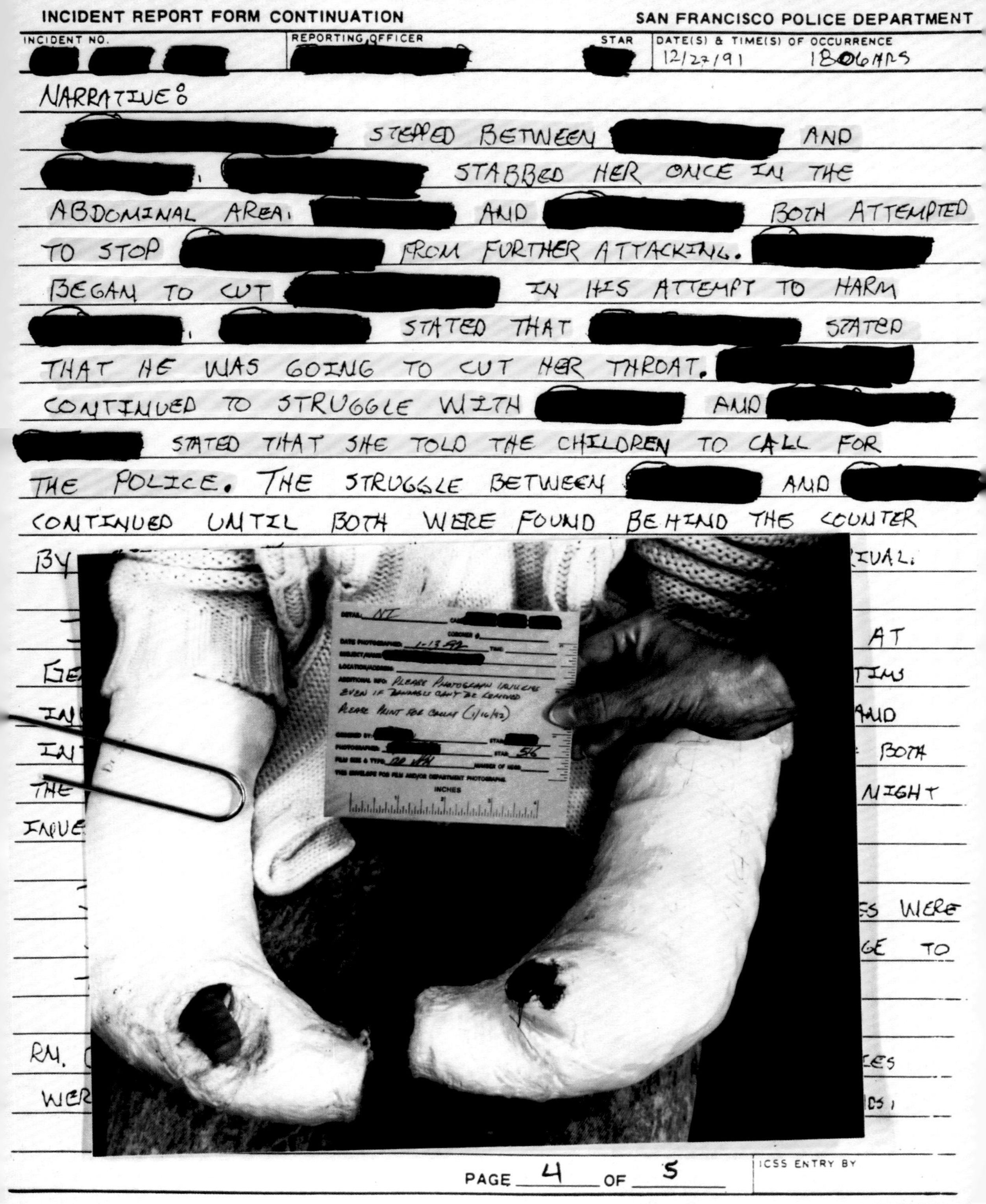

INCIDENT REPORT FORM CONTINUATION

SAN FRANCISCO POLICE DEPARTMENT

INCIDENT NO.	REPORTING OFFICER	STAR	DATE(S) & TIME(S) OF OCCURRENCE
			12/27/91 1806 HRS

NARRATIVE:

STEPPED BETWEEN AND . STABBED HER ONCE IN THE ABDOMINAL AREA. AND BOTH ATTEMPTED TO STOP FROM FURTHER ATTACKING. BEGAN TO CUT IN HIS ATTEMPT TO HARM . STATED THAT STATED THAT HE WAS GOING TO CUT HER THROAT. CONTINUED TO STRUGGLE WITH AND STATED THAT SHE TOLD THE CHILDREN TO CALL FOR THE POLICE. THE STRUGGLE BETWEEN AND CONTINUED UNTIL BOTH WERE FOUND BEHIND THE COUNTER

BY ... RIVAL.

... AT

GE... TIMS

IN... AND

IN... BOTH

THE... NIGHT

INJU...

...ES WERE

...GE TO

RM. ...CES

WER... ...DS.

PAGE 4 OF 5

ICSS ENTRY BY

INCIDENT REPORT FORM CONTINUATION

SAN FRANCISCO POLICE DEPARTMENT

INCIDENT NO	REPORTING OFFICER	STAR	DATE(S) & TIME(S) OF OCCURRENCE
			2-27-91 0030 / 2-27-91 0700

VICTIM CODES CONT ... 62

2 ... ON /

R# ... E /

R#4 ... /

NARRAT ... E TO

22 ... V.

W ... D ME

TO V, ... REAR DOOR

AND I ... FLOOR,

SHE W ... SAW

BLOOD ON ... AND

1H81 AR ...

COULD NO ...

CAME RUN ... AND SAID HIS MOM WAS

LAYING ON THE FLOOR BLEEDING. SAID SHE CALLED

THE POLICE AND THEN RAN TO 'S HOUSE.

SAID HE WOKE UP THIS MORNING AND WAS

GETTING READY FOR SCHOOL WHEN HE WENT DOWNSTAIRS AND

FOUND HIS MOTHER PASSED OUT ON THE FLOOR AND BLEEDING FROM

THE HEAD. TOLD ME HE RAN TO

HOUSE TO CALL THE POLICE BECAUSE THE PHONE LINES IN HIS HOUSE

WERE CUT. STATED THE PHONE WAS WORKING AND THE

LINES WERE FINE WHEN HE WENT TO BED LAST NIGHT.

TOLD ME SHE CONVERSED WITH VIA PHONE LAST NIGHT

AT APPROXIMATELY 0001 HRS.

NOTES

ICSS ENTRY BY:

SFPD 377

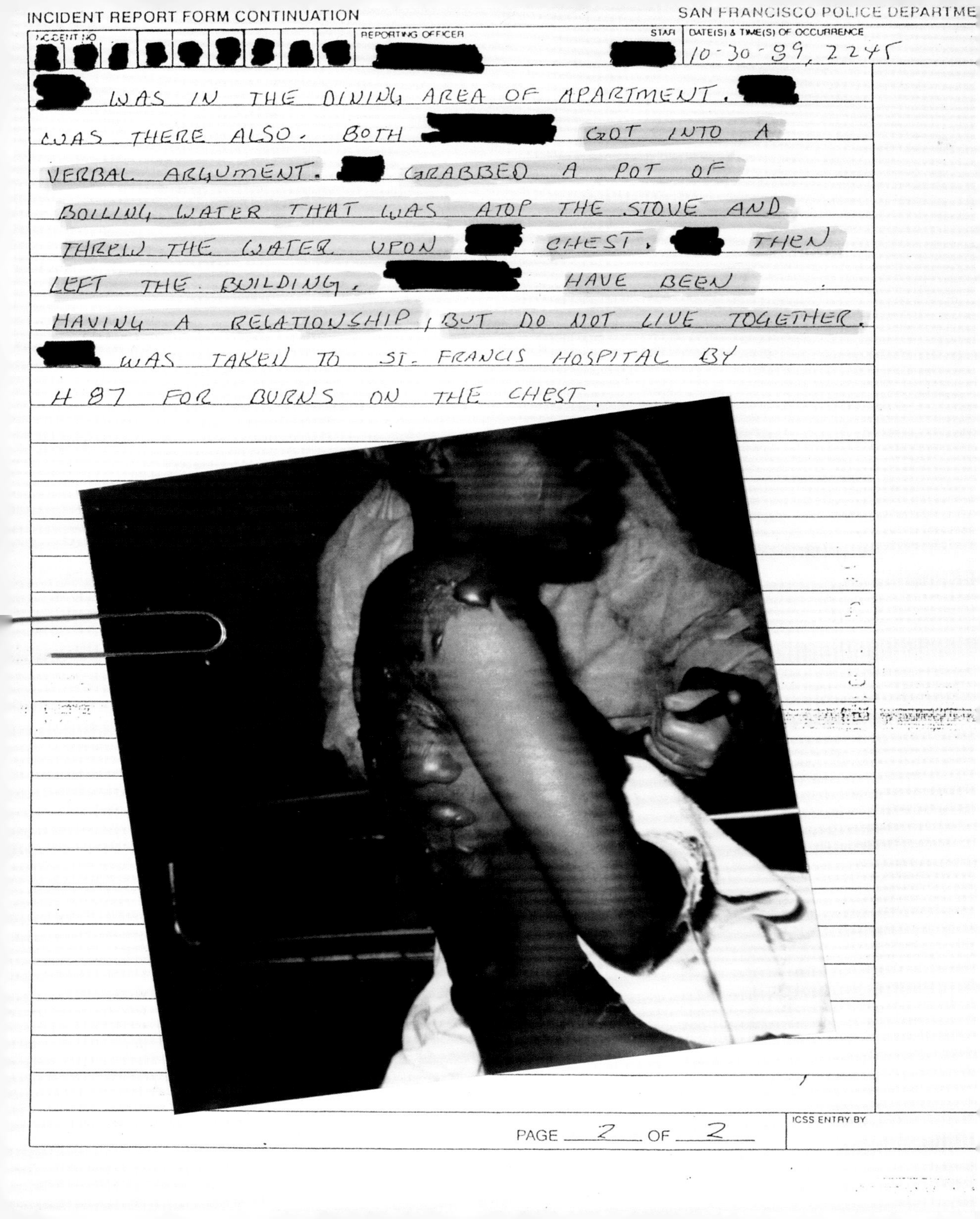

INCIDENT REPORT FORM CONTINUATION

SAN FRANCISCO POLICE DEPARTME

INCIDENT NO	REPORTING OFFICER	STAR	DATE(S) & TIME(S) OF OCCURRENCE
[redacted]	[redacted]	[redacted]	10-30-99, 2245

[redacted] WAS IN THE DINING AREA OF APARTMENT. [redacted] WAS THERE ALSO. BOTH [redacted] GOT INTO A VERBAL ARGUMENT. [redacted] GRABBED A POT OF BOILING WATER THAT WAS ATOP THE STOVE AND THREW THE WATER UPON [redacted] CHEST. [redacted] THEN LEFT THE BUILDING. [redacted] HAVE BEEN HAVING A RELATIONSHIP, BUT DO NOT LIVE TOGETHER. [redacted] WAS TAKEN TO ST. FRANCIS HOSPITAL BY H 87 FOR BURNS ON THE CHEST.

PAGE 2 OF 2

ICSS ENTRY BY

The following is taken from interviews conducted by Susan Meiselas on May 6 and May 8, 1998.

Susan Breall, Assistant District Attorney
San Francisco District Attorney's Office

I've prosecuted domestic violence cases for more than eight years, and in that time I've seen women who have been beaten and raped. I've seen women who have been burned, I've seen women who have tried to jump out of fourth-floor windows to escape their batterers. I've seen women who've had men leave marks on their bodies in places that most people will never see. And I've seen these same women have the courage somehow to come to court, and talk about what happened to them. The only thing you have going for you when you are in court is the emotional impact of the stories. I tell each woman it's going to be your word against his word, and we need to take this crime and stretch it out in slow motion. You have to make this come alive for me so I can make it come alive for the jury. We have to take this frame by frame by frame. How many times did he threaten you? What did you think the first time, or the second time, or the third time he threatened you? How did the windshield get broken? When he stabbed you in the stomach, is that when he twisted the knife? What was he saying as he twisted the knife? What were you feeling? And I need to know whether you had anything to drink. I need to know everything they are going to know, because believe me, he's going to tell his attorney anything that can make you look bad.

Eighty-five percent of our victims, in one way or another, don't want to participate in the prosecution of their cases. But I believe that under the surface, most of those women are ready to cooperate, and you need to talk to them. When they really care about the person who has beaten them, you have to care about the person who has beaten them, too. You can't objectify and vilify the defendant. A lot of counties brag about their success rate in proving cases without victims, and that's better than having the case dismissed, but I think you are far more successful when you work with a victim—if you spend months with her, and educate her, and don't take no for an answer; and you don't get angry and always treat her with respect—so that even if she doesn't cooperate this time, she'll come back the next time.

In my experience, domestic violence is a pattern offense. The literature talks about the "cycle of violence," and about "battered women's syndrome." There may or may not be a typical battered woman, but in my experience, there is a cycle and it happens over and over again. There's the honeymoon stage when things are really wonderful, and there's the stage when the tension builds, and then there's the eruption of the violence and then you make up. Usually that's right at the time you're about to go to trial, and he's calling her from jail, and then they're getting married in the holding cell by the judge who's about to be the presiding judge on the case .

The majority of cases get worse at the trial stage. Money is running out for the victim while her partner is in jail. The children are starting to miss their father, and she starts having second, or third, or fourth thoughts about actually showing up in court and being the one to point the finger at him. Usually it's a lot better if you can hold him accountable without going to trial.

Abusive men are very controlling individuals, and they know how to get to these particular women. They know just how to give them the look which means that they're going to get it. Sometimes when the victim gets up on that witness stand it's the first time ever that she has been able to look him in the eye, and articulate all the things he's done without being hit. She can get up on that stand and say exactly what he's been putting her through, and he will be forced to listen. I've had women who've said, "You hit me, you beat me, you know you did." And I've had a guy say, "No I didn't, you fucking bitch." The judge was pounding the gavel—before that case, I never saw a judge use a gavel.

When you get a conviction, it's not like you go out and whoop it up. There's this sadness that you have had to go through all this, just to get one word: guilty. It means punishment, incarceration. Here's this young man, in his twenties, he's going to spend his life in state prison. Here's this young woman, and she'll have physical and emotional scars for the rest of her life. The conviction is a validation of what she went through, but it's not some wonderful thing for her. I am very satisified when I get one. I feel it is fair but I do not feel like celebrating

Amy

Family members that I had been close to my whole life were very reluctant to help me when I needed a place to stay after the shooting. They were afraid for themselves and their families. A lot of people asked, "How did you get involved with someone so controlling?" because I was always outspoken in life. It was a shock to everybody who knew me. The relationship evolved very quickly—it consumed and overwhelmed me. I let it overwhelm me. I didn't have all that much self-esteem at the time. We met at a gas station. I was pumping my gas and he came over and helped. He called me later on that night, and we went out, and we started seeing each other every day. Two months later he moved in with me, and then I found out I was pregnant. Things happened very quickly. One night I questioned him after he showed up from work four hours later than usual, and he got very defensive. When I tried to leave he grabbed me and dragged me back into the apartment. I was kicking and screaming—people's doors opened, people looked out from their windows, but no one called the police. I was four months pregnant at the time. I went to a pay phone, called the police, and filed a report. They said there was no physical evidence that he had harmed me. I'd never been in a situation like that. I went and stayed with relatives.

We spoke later, and he wanted me to go away with him for a day. We went to Reno and I think I was lucky to come back alive. He didn't harm me in any way, but in my opinion he was a time bomb waiting to explode, and it just amazes me that nothing happened that weekend to set him off. I came home and I was even more confused than I had been before—I didn't know what I was supposed to do. A baby on the way—how was I going to support a child?

I decided it was over. I needed to get my things back from him so I reluctantly agreed to meet him in a well-lit parking lot. When I got there, he came over to my truck and got in on the passenger's side. I asked him, "Where's your car?" He said, "It broke down." He wanted to talk. I just wanted my stuff. He talked me into giving him a ride to his car. He started getting more and more angry. He had two other children and he said, "A.J.'s mom fucked me over. Tyrell's mom fucked me over." That's it. I saw him reach over to his right side, into his jacket, and he pulls out this gun, and puts it in my side. I immediately slammed on the brakes and he wasn't wearing his seat belt, thank God. He went flying forward and the gun got knocked away. I put my hand on the barrel of the gun, and I was trying to honk the horn with my elbow. He backed out of the truck. The truck was in third gear, so when I took off, it lugged. I'm trying to get it into first gear, and he's out of the truck now, and he's shooting at me. I get hit, and I'm screaming and yelling and Lord knows what's going through my mind at that time. *Get out. Go.* The first shot was my face. The second was my arm. There were five shots total. One of the last shots was the shoulder. When I'm taking off, the driver's side window shatters, I know I'm bleeding and I feel like I have no jaw left. I have no idea what my face looks like. My hand gets really cold and I can feel the warm blood on my hand. Creepy feeling. I put that hand up on the steering wheel, because I had to shift with the other one in order to drive. There was a gas station but it was closed. Up on the other side of the freeway, I knew there was a 7-Eleven. So I run all the red lights, honking my horn. It's a very busy area, thank God I didn't cause an accident. I pulled into the 7-Eleven, and there happened to be a couple walking out of the store. There was someone else walking out who just kept on walking—looked at me and just kept on walking. The couple came over, the girl went to call 911 and the guy said, "What happened to you?" I told him, "My boyfriend shot me." My arm is shattered and I take my jacket off and I say, "You have to wrap a tourniquet on my arm." He didn't know first aid. So I'm teaching him first aid and I tell him, "Keep talking to me—don't let me pass out." I told him my name, who shot me, that I was pregnant. Then I finally heard the sirens, and my eyes closed. I was very aware of everything that was going on, and my biggest fear was that my ex was going to come running down the hill and finish me off. I went through childbirth, and that was nothing compared to this. It was an atrocious amount of pain. It was just amazing—I could feel the bones rubbing against each other.

This happened on a Sunday night, and they didn't catch him until the following Friday afternoon. I don't understand why he was not arrested before that. He wasn't running, he was going to work all week. They arrested him Friday afternoon at work, as he was walking out. It just gave him time to get rid of the evidence. I wanted him put away for good. I took a criminal-law class, which actually helped me a lot with the trial. Instead of attempted murder, he got voluntary attempted manslaughter. He got sentenced to fifteen-and-a-half years. I have a private attorney who keeps me up-to-date, if I ask her, on where he is. Personally, it gives me a big fear if I don't know anything about him. I want to know where he is, what state of mind he's in. I want to keep tabs on him. I still have the desire to ask him, "What were you thinking? Why did you do this? What on God's earth were you thinking?" Just recently I heard that he got moved to Vacaville, that he's in a mental institution. It's hard to think about my life fifteen years from now. Where will I be? What will I do? What kind of person is he going to be? Is he ever going to get out? He has a terrible temper. Sometimes I keep my fingers crossed that he doesn't make it out.

Noline

You are almost not the victim, you are almost the cause of the crime. There are a lot of games society plays with you. The person who stabbed me, because he had three strikes, he got one of the best lawyers in San Francisco, pro bono. His lawyer was an ex-policeman, a very, very good lawyer, and they didn't think what was done to me was serious. The defense investigator used to come over to my house and talk to me, ask me not to press charges. The things that I had to go through until the day that person was sentenced were humiliating. The police would ask me, if I was afraid of this person, why did I allow him around me? They investigate your personal background—where I met him, the length of time the relationship went on—and they let you know that that's what they're doing. You cannot be intimidated.

In the beginning, I believed in the law, but I didn't know how the law worked, and it was really surprising. I got stabbed in August 1992, I think. It took a year for the police to find cause that he had actually stabbed me. I had been going to court that whole time. I felt that he had more rights than I did, even though he was locked up. His lawyer tried to break me down. They wanted to know what I did wrong to have him do something like that to me. I mean, what do you do wrong to be stabbed six times in your car?

I didn't know that he had raped somebody, and then he beat his wife up really bad with a telephone, almost killed her. He had a drug arrest, then he stabbed me. I met his family, his sisters, they were all really down to earth, and nobody told me that he was violent until after. They knew and they didn't tell me. If he had been arrested for violating his parole—he was on parole when I met him—this would not have happened to me. The system has a lot of loopholes in it. There's a lot of people out there that have been hurt because there's an overload on the system. It's just by the grace of God that I'm alive. He didn't fool around—he missed my heart by a quarter inch and my lung by half an inch. He meant to kill me.

I had post-traumatic stress disorder. I was actually seeing him. He would walk into my work, he'd be in my car, he'd be sitting on the end of my bed. He'd be following me places. I'd be driving down the street, and he'd be on every corner. I don't take my car to work anymore because on more than one occasion, he was in it. Most people they'd say, "Well, she's really nuts." But fortunately, I got to talk to psychologists.

For a long time I fought with the idea of why he did it. I didn't want to think that I was living in denial, thinking that I didn't do anything wrong. Obviously I did something wrong by not paying attention, but nothing so wrong that he should have done what he did to me. Everyone said, "Oh, you must hate him." But I didn't wish him any harm at all. I felt that if I wished him a lot of harm, then there would be no closure. I never really wanted to see him again. It makes me feel good that he can't walk away and no other women will get hurt by him.

I've always been in abusive relationships. Always. It seems like they all ended up with some kind of violence. And one day I was thinking to myself, I never picked one of these relationships. It was them attracted to me. Even though their personalities were different, they were all basically the same man. I have learned not to find that person again.

Irma

He got fifteen years, but he'll be out in the year 2000 because they only serve half the time, right? I'm very scared about that. But I was able to stand on my own after he left. I joined the Start Your Own Business with the Homeless Project. I think I am the only one who survived from that project. I got a loan from the mayor's office, I got a loan from the Y., and I was able to pay it off. I was able to expand my business through hard work. I was able to send my children to private school. With Ray, I didn't even have a phone. I remarried and I have a nice husband. It scares me a lot to think about when Ray gets out of prison. What's going to happen? Two years ago he was saying that when he got out, he was going to finish us off, me and my children.

Archives of Abuse

In 1992, the Liz Claiborne Foundation invited me and five other artists to work on billboard and bus shelter ads for a campaign in San Francisco to raise public awareness about domestic violence. As a documentary photographer, my instinct was to find a way to work with the police. Essentially, I hit a brick wall. I was hanging around the police station, trying to get information. I saw their reports were accumulating in folders on their desks and I began to read them and ask questions.

I had been paired up with a specialized investigative team that goes back to the domestic violence crime scenes and tries to gather additional information from witnesses. I asked permission to go out with them to get a sense of what they were up against.

I remember arriving with them at the scene of a homicide in a small hotel downtown and watching the police photographer at work. I was frustrated at not being permitted to take pictures myself. But I was given permission to select the reports that I found most interesting and to look at the photographic evidence that accompanied them. I decided to work with what already existed, instead of generating my own photographs. Then I agreed to go back to the victims and get their permission to use this material for my collages. Susan Breall, at the San Francisco D.A.'s office, contacted the women and arranged for me to go to their homes and talk to them.

I always intended to return to this project. Several months ago, I began to interview the women I had met in 1992. I was somewhat intimidated to go back to the survivors and ask them to speak again about these experiences which have been so painful for them. I went cautiously and took it quite slowly. It's taken time to be comfortable with what it means to open up scar tissue.

Susan Meiselas

TERESE SVOBODA

Sleeping Apart

Beyond the door
he says and she
believes him.
On an evening like this,
she waits in the dark.

She knows about hurt.
She will sleep apart.
The blinds spell
the I prone and awake
over and over.

She never tries the door
or even looks out.
She sleeps and the moon
in its fashion
lights them both.

Islam Extremist

A train full of fire
and people
travels the horizon.

They say
Allah laughed
when he made this country.

A train full of fire
travels the horizon
to its vanishing,
the very blue
I stand under.

Say it is as persistent
as a dream: I wake
and it's gone and it's not

Africa where flat earth theory
runs to hell—you can see
the curve, how the clouds
suck over, where the mind teeters.

A whole trainful burnt.
Hear His laugh?
Hear the soldiers'?

The land is bare now,
nothing to interrupt the sky,
nothing, not even dunes,
not even death.

QUESTIONS OF LEGACY

CHARLES MEREWETHER

What future does the archive hold? Why do we care about piles of musty old papers, other people's letters, records and documents of a long-gone past, files of people we never knew, of the dead? What is an archive but a repository of traces that represent histories, histories of which, for many reasons, we are no longer aware? There are many kinds of archives, some that appear benign, and others a record full of horrors committed against humanity. And there are many ways in which the archive can be used, yielding information that seemed to have no value until it was placed within another context, or pieced together as one might a collage. In such instances we may wonder how and for what purpose something becomes an archival object.

The existence of archives created by repressive regimes or collections that document genocide and acts of great violence pose other questions that we are only beginning to comprehend and answer. What uses can be made of them in the aftermath of a violent regime or civil conflict? Can they enable us to repossess a history that has been forgotten, untold, banished, or repressed? Can they help people to overcome actual experiences that have passed into history? Is there an obligation to the past? A responsibility to the dead to keep whatever records there are of their lives? We can begin to find answers to these questions in the work of certain historians, writers, artists, and filmmakers who have sought to use or to reconceive the archive. Their work with the archive is an effort to locate the truth or acknowledge past abuses, by filling in what is missing or written out of the record, matching names and lives to the traces, statistics, and objects.

For many people, the archive remains an essential resource and critical tool for the future of democracy no less than a history of the recent past, just as control over the archive is essential to political power. Dmitrii Iurasov, a founding member of the nongovernmental Russian association Memorial, speaks of the need to join the "restoration" of the country's memory in the present to the issue of the country's future development so that the Soviet past need not be repeated. When it was founded in 1987, Memorial's purpose was to use the records recovered from Soviet archives in order to build a monument in honor of those who disappeared under Stalin and the succeeding regimes. But a monument was not enough to restore "the stolen truth" and recall the "names of those who lived, worked and died in the misguided utopia. . . ." The project increased its scope to gather not only documents but also testimonies so that the "right of memory . . . be returned to the people. . . ."

In Latin America, organizations such as the Mothers of the Disappeared insist on a moral right to know what happened to family members who remain among the disappeared. It is a question of finally giving names to the dead, of resolving how they died and honoring them: the uncertain status of "disappeared" prevents the survivors from ever doing this. From this ethical imperative, however, emerged a choice between accountability or acknowledgment of the truth without reprisal. In some countries, the end of civil conflict came at too great a cost: a quick amnesty for the former military regimes, protecting those who committed crimes against their own people, or sometimes leaving the archives of the state inaccessible and their truth thereby undisclosed. The demand of *nunca mas* (never again) voiced by popular movements in Argentina, Chile, Uruguay, and Brazil expresses a hope that the telling of history will expose past crimes and thus be a reminder to future generations of what they themselves are capable of and must prevent.

This hope, like the goals of clemency and reconciliation expressed by various (though not all) truth commissions, derives from the idea that the telling of history can be a redemptive act. In South Africa, for example, the truth commissions could enable better access to restricted information held in archives and thus allow for the possibility of finally establishing an accurate record. Although we can never be certain that such disclosure will not, in fact, cause adverse reactions, according to Juan Mendez of the Inter-American Institute on Human Rights, "official acknowledgment at least begins to heal the wounds."

On the other hand, the historian Michael Ignatieff asks, in his book *The Warrior's Honor*, how much truth can societies stand? All nations have a need to forge "myths of unity and identity that allow a society to forget its founding crimes, its hidden injuries and divisions, its unhealed wounds." As Ignatieff notes, there is a difference between factual and moral truth, with the latter being necessary for social reconciliation, but ultimately far more difficult to achieve. In Germany the silence concerning the country's Nazi past that characterized the Adenauer years of the 1950s may well have led to the restoration of democracy, and yet not to an amelioration or end of the memory of those years. Opening the archive raises all manner of dangers in connection with who has access and for what purpose, what should be made public, and what kept private. The archive's contents can provide evidence that permits an orderly prosecution of past crimes or that triggers spontaneous acts of revenge.

It is instructive to observe the way in which the legacy of communism is now being addressed in East Germany, through the establishment of the Gauck Authority. Since 1990 this office has been overseeing the opening up of approximately one-hundred miles of shelved files of the East German Stasi to those individuals who are themselves subjects of the files. However, some commentators suggest that the process has been wreaking havoc with people's ideals and breeding a need for revenge accompanied by bitter cynicism. In fact, for these reasons some of the Stasi files were destroyed, especially those incriminating politicians and state officials. Then, in 1990, the East German parliament voted to destroy the hard disk of Stasi's central records. As Lawrence Weschler wrote in *A Miracle, a Universe: Settling Accounts with Torturers*, the opening of the files proved to be a "toxic dump at the core of the new democratic order, and the frenzy of truth-telling suddenly seemed decidedly problematic."

From this perspective, the question becomes twofold. Can opening the archive be sufficient as a means of answering or consoling those who suffered? Is it better that a nation's archival secrets remain hidden or do they then linger to haunt future generations as the unspoken, troubling both those who wish to forget and those who live without history. How much truth can a fragile new democracy bear, how many untold secrets can be recounted without opening old wounds that may never be healed? In Argentina, the setting up of a truth commission led to a series of small military revolts in army barracks and military academies. This resulted in a reversal of governmental efforts to prosecute those who had committed human rights abuses. It is possible to argue that only amnesty by way of collective amnesia will allow the immediate period of recovery in places where there have been repressive regimes or traumatic events of violence.

But the memory of the experience never just goes away. In some countries, like Germany, the past has erupted many years later as if experienced belatedly, both by survivors and by later generations. The disclosure alters the conventional meaning of the archive: disclosed, it becomes no longer a source for

essential truths about the past but, rather, a present constantly being constructed and reconstructed, open to being deciphered and used by its new proprietors. As Michael Ignatieff points out, "the past has none of the fixed and stable identity of a document." It is rather an argument, open always to interpretation. Only those with direct experience can know the past, bound up as it is with myths of identity and fictions that a concept of truth is never sufficient to account for. All this adds up to a crisis of legitimacy, a gulf between official, public lies and private truth. But perhaps Ignatieff gives too much credit to the idea that the document has a fixed and stable identity. A recent case in point is the vitriolic debate surrounding Daniel Goldhagen's book *Hitler's Willing Executioners: Ordinary Germans and the Holocaust* and its interpretation of documents about the Reserve Police Battalion 101.

The archive is thought of as a repository of history, its keepers entrusted with the responsibility of remembering. Yet, the concept of the archival document as neutral is fallacious. It is insufficient alone to count as evidence of what has passed. Disinformation was invented by the very informants and spies who provided eyes and ears to regimes. Furthermore, the construction of the archive is dependent on various technologies of inscription and transmission. In the face of the ever-increasing power of technologies to not only capture but manipulate the record of each and every passing event, questions about what is fact and what is fabrication, and of the interrelation between the event and its telling, become more and more complicated—and therefore more pressing to address.

Some historians argue that new technologies of recording and reproduction are so ubiquitous that collective memory has suffered a decline, and we have become more and more dependent on history as a way of relating to and accounting for the past. The French historian Pierre Nora, who for more than fifteen years as editor has overseen a collaborative history of French collective memory, *Les lieux de memoire*, is profoundly skeptical of the obsessive reliance on what he calls "lieux de memoire" or places of memory such as archives, museums, and monuments. Nora is overwhelmed by the evidence, by the documents that surround him, like the mountains of files waiting on the desk of K. in Kafka's *The Castle*. He argues that relying on such institutions and technologies of remembrance has produced a fatal schism between history and memory. For Nora, there is no discrimination in the archive. It retains everything that may have been or may best be forgotten, thereby breaking a natural law surrounding the need to forget. He writes of institutional archives as "the deliberate and calculated secretion of lost memory . . . a prosthesis memory." Our relation with the past is no longer that of "retrospective continuity" but the "illumination of discontinuity." And yet, while personal memories may be distinguished as a form of resistance and truth-telling from the collective histories constructed by the state such memories are also open to manipulation self-censorship, forgetting and may therefore be unreliable. The task is to recognize that memory has a double valence, and it is the use to which such testimony is put that remains critical for periods of transition and the possibility of democracy.

Nevertheless, the function of conventional archives in totalitarian regimes teaches how powerful they can be. Think of the twenty-four tons of Iraqi government documents cataloging the detention and execution of Iraqi Kurds, as well as the endless files resulting from Iraq's program of domestic surveillance and persecution. Or the Khmer Rouge archive captured by the Vietnamese when they took control of Cambodia at the end of 1978, which constituted an extraordinarily detailed history of the Cambodian people and record of Khmer Rouge atrocities. According to Craig Etcheson, the former program manager of Yale University's Cambodian Genocide Program, the Pol Pot regime required its literate citizens to produce autobiographies that detailed their work and family background, to be cross-checked with other records and used against them when the regime so desired. Alongside these individual histories were found records of the killings of hundreds of thousands of Cambodian civilians, including a daily execution log that listed the name, age, occupation, and village of origin of each "enemy," and served as a form for authorizing and witnessing his or her execution. Beyond this grim utility, these examples also show how archives may be used to control the past, present, and future. By elevating its own historical record the group in power destabilizes and threatens to extinguish the value of individual memory. Excluded from official history, the unofficial account is known only in its absence, a secret whose historical status is tightly controlled. And the differences between fact and fiction, between document and account, can all be manipulated so as to consolidate power in the hands of repressive state regimes. Record keeping was reserved for the state and helped to confirm the rulers' claim to legal authority. It laid the groundwork for forging a new order. And in the Khmer Rouge case the archive was not only a portrait of the Cambodian people, but a record of the government's achievement.

Then there is the matter of secrecy. While there is something terrifying about such obsessive and clinical documentation, we can better understand the apparent compulsion of those in power to keep such detailed records of their own crimes if we recognize the role of secrecy (and by extension, the archive) in maintaining social control. At its core, state power is an intertwining of privileged knowledge, both secrets and truths, which the archive protects. The secret file and informant become central components in a totalitarian society. However, the secret record may contain only lies, hence a reason for its being kept secret in the first place. This produces an epistemological instability, which the state tries to resolve through an ever-increasing exercise of the archival function, a more stringent and extensive gathering of information, and revision in forms of classification that enhance the archive's comprehensiveness and the sense of imperial expansion and control over its subject.

But the sheer enormity of the archives kept by the Soviet Union or East Germany's Stasi, or those of the successive Brazilian military governments between 1964 and 1979, show the degree to which, in those cases, secrecy engulfed the very concept of national security. The sheer volume of the files produced simply overwhelmed any efforts that might have been made to completely destroy them as the military period came to an end. In Brazil, even before the first open elections were announced in 1979, a number of individuals were secretly at work to preserve the military archive's contents as a record of the junta's crimes against the Brazilian people. Sometimes the greatest challenge facing those who would confront the record an archive contains is dealing with the sheer volume of material, as if the archive has been accumulated precisely in order to drain their will and energy.

How then to deal with the legacy or heritage that the archive presents to us? In redefining the claims made for the archive by the society that inherits it, claims that mimic the authority conferred on it by totalitarian regimes, it must be understood that the names, dates, and details in a secret file are ultimately unreliable and produce only a kind of palimpsest of the real. In his book *The File: A Personal History*, Timothy Garton Ash notes that while his own Stasi file sought to record events and encounters of his everyday life, it was actually full of misinformation, inaccuracies, and was without context. Caught between history and memory, the archive offers what can only be a radically imperfect account of the past. Yet, as Garton Ash observes in *The File*: "a file opens a door to a vast sunken labyrinth of a forgotten past, [and] the very act of opening the door itself changes the buried artifacts." At such times our sense of memory and truth becomes uncertain. To account for the past in this way means coming to terms with this uncertainty. Archives, like documents or the notion of heritage, do not have a fixed and stable meaning

but, rather, constitute a collection of traces, of fragments, shards that stand in a metonymic relation to what they are meant to record. They are neither sufficient nor adequate to the truth nor to what we think of as the real. For that very reason, they always contain both the promise of reconciliation or the threat of revenge. Their unstable relation to the real means they are always open to misuse. Writing about history was for Nietzsche, in the words of Michel Foucault, not "an acquisition, a possession that grows and solidifies; rather, it is an unstable assemblage of faults, fissures, and heterogeneous layers that threaten the fragile inheritor from within or from underneath."

Uses of the archive, after the fact of its existence, can take many forms. The Russian project Memorial appropriates the official archive to disturb its authority. In recovering the names of the dead, project researchers use small index cards as a way to consciously expose the incompleteness of the record, and the partiality of the information given. In their brevity, the use of the cards emphasizes the discrepancies, the silences and erasures, the divergences and omissions that undermine the consistency and coherence usually associated with the archive. The photographer Susan Meiselas brought together a team of researchers who collaborated with her to produce *Kurdistan: In the Shadow of History*—a history in photographs and documents that account for the history of the Kurdish people and their fate under successive Iraqi, Iranian, and Turkish regimes. The book itself became a form of archive, combining material found in archives, state documents, and newspaper reports with testimonies, stories, and photographs of the Kurdish people themselves.

In the wake of the Khmer Rouge genocide, different kinds of archives have been established. Four years after Pol Pot's government was driven from power, the Tuol Sleng Genocide Museum and Documentation Center were established in Phnom Penh. Once a torture and execution prison, Tuol Sleng is now filled with several thousand confessions extracted from prisoners while being tortured as spies and traitors. Also on display are photographs taken by Khmer Rouge cadres of those whom they subsequently executed. Meanwhile, Yale University has established the Cambodian Genocide Program that, with funding from the U.S. government, will eventually employ a web site and database, allowing people to put names to photographs and to read documents and records from the camps. The aim of these projects is twofold. They provide a means for survivors to learn the truth of what happened to their families and friends and perhaps begin to make sense of their past, and also a means for gathering information that might be used as evidence in war-crime trials of Khmer Rouge leaders. Alternatively, Yale University's Video Archive for Holocaust Testimonies or the similarly conceived Shoah Project endowed by Steven Spielberg are at work recording the memories of survivors—both projects expose the fault lines in conventional recorded history.

All such testimonies reveal the vulnerability of memory to the pressure of time as much as they reveal the limits of history. But these efforts to create new forms of archives assume dissonance and discontinuity as preconditions. In his 1993 film *Prime Time in the Camps*, Chris Marker recorded the words of a Bosnian refugee, "We want to hold on to this moment. How can we keep hold of a moment for a time yet to come. So many things we've seen have not been recorded."

This witness to the atrocities of the Bosnian war points to the gap between the technologies of representation and unmediated experience, a disruption of the power to represent the past. She makes a claim for a memory that is prior to any archive, a moment that by definition distinguishes a memorial from a monument. Something has occurred that cannot be named, that has been witnessed and persists, but remains at present impossible to speak of, to record. As the French theorist Jean-Francois Lyotard notes, writing becomes the memory that "never forgets that there is the forgotten and never stops writing its failure to remember and to fashion itself according to memory."

In the wake of periods of violence and extreme repression, the reconstruction of the past often assumes not only a personal but a public urgency: there is a responsibility to acknowledge the right to memory and to restore memory. The opening of the past regime's archives reveals the ways in which people and events were erased from history and from consciousness so as to replace the past with an enforced collective cultural amnesia. In this sense the issue of overcoming amnesia must be separated from that of amnesty. Amnesty of former perpetrators may be necessary, but it should not be confused with the destruction of the records that remain. The archive constitutes the repository of these histories, and free access to such content is a democratic right. To permit its destruction is to endorse the powers of secrecy and erasure that repressive regimes have exercised over their citizens.

The task of historians and artists is to intervene and appropriate the records not only in order to expose the falsifications and erasures they embodied but to offer a re-elaboration, a working through. Access to the archive and the critical dissemination of its contents are ethical actions. By working with and around the archive, artists,

writers, and filmmakers may offer ways to reclaim the names and lives of people whose entrance into the archive meant the loss of identity and often foreshadowed the destruction of their lives. The work of these artists is about the recovery of traces—that is, the residue of the original subjects and of that which has occurred. At the same time, it seeks to acknowledge the power of the trace to erase its subject. *Counter-archival* may be the best way to describe the practice of certain contemporary artists whose work is concerned with mnemonic traces. The contents of counter-archival art, like the objects in archaeological collections, begin to yield information about a culture whose people have disappeared, who have become nameless. By using objects and images associated with the particularity of individual lives—the "private"—the artist implicitly recovers a world where privacy itself was at stake, as well as the private and personal lives of citizens. Again, as Timothy Garton Ash suggested in *The File*, a distinction must be made between his Stasi file and his life as lived. To recover this dimension is to work against the grain of conventional archives.

These counter-archival practices are to a certain extent empathetic rather than critical or objective. They may contain as many omissions and silencings as an archive produced by a repressive regime, and therefore require an equally critical view of their contents and aims. In this sense they are no different from other types of archives. Nonetheless, there is a crucial difference in the originating purpose of art that embraces or addresses archival practice—its use is already given as historical, a condition of being after the fact. Such work represents a corrective to history as it is constructed by conventional archives, a corrective that however partial remains necessary.

In many countries, it appears that now is a time of listening, of testimony, of the belated witness to past events. Listening to the accounts of others, we may recall the words of Paul Celan who spoke of an attunement whereby art becomes a turning toward the other that is an openness rather than a containment, an opening onto an outside where the breath of speaking and freedom meet.

The installations of the French artist Christian Boltanski mimic the archive, but also produce a certain distance from its customary effect. The use of photographed portraits emphasizes the disappearance of the individual subjects and their representation as object. Throughout his work, Boltanski returns to these same faces, over and over again revisiting anonymous people neither he nor we have ever met, people we never will meet. Who are these people? What response is possible or appropriate? What is it that they want as we stand before them in silent contemplation, as they come to us from out of the past, from elsewhere. The work has to do with death but it is also about the loss of identity and the entry into the archive. It is a witness to this passage.

C.M.

BERTOLT BRECHT

A Visit to the Banished Poets

When, in a dream, he entered the hut of the banished
Poets—which you'll find alongside the hut
Where the banished teachers live (from there he heard
Disputation and laughter)—at the entrance
Ovid approached, and said to him quietly:
"Better not sit down yet. You're not yet dead. Who can know
If you won't one day go back? Even if nothing has changed
Except yourself." But then, solace in his eyes
Po-chu-yi came over and smiled: "This is a rigor
Earned by anyone who even once called injustice by its name."
And his friend Tu-fu said softly: "You understand, banishment
Is not the place to unlearn arrogance." But, more worldly
Shabby old Villon joined them and asked: "How many
Doors has the house where you live?" And Dante took him aside
And, grasping him hard by the arm, he murmured: "Your verses
Are teeming with error, friend, just think
What manner of men are gathered against you!" Voltaire called over:
"Keep an eye on the pennies, they'll starve you out else!"
"And mix a few jokes in!" cried Heine. "That won't help"
Growled Shakespeare, "when James arrived
Even I was prevented from writing."—"If your case comes to trial
Take a rogue for your lawyer!" counseled Euripides.
"He'll know all the holes in the mesh of the law." The laughter
Was echoing still, when, from the darkest corner
Came a cry: "Hey you, do they know
Your verses by heart? And those who know them
Will they prevail and escape persecution?"—"Those
Are the forgotten ones," Dante said quietly.
"In their case, not only their bodies, their works too were destroyed."
The laughter broke off. No one dared look over. The newcomer
Had turned pale.

Translated from the German by Tom Kuhn

Besuch bei den verbannten Dichtern

Als er im Traum die Hütte betrat der verbannten
Dichter, die neben der Hütte gelegen ist
Wo die verbannten Lehrer wohnen (er hörte von dort
Streit und Gelächter), kam ihm zum Eingang
Ovid entgegen und sagte ihm halblaut:
"Besser, du setzt dich noch nicht. Du bist noch nicht gestorben. Wer weiß da
Ob du nicht doch noch zurückkehrst? Und ohne daß andres sich ändert
Als du selber. "Doch, Trost in Augen
Näherte Po Chü-yi sich und sagte lächelnd: "Die Strenge
Hat sich jeder verdient, der nur einmal das Unrecht benannte."
Und sein Freund Tu-Fu sagte still: "Du verstehst, die Verbannung
Ist nicht der Ort, wo der Hochmut verlernt wird." Aber irdischer
Stellte sich der zerlumpte Villon zu ihnen und fragte: "Wie viele
Türen hat das Haus, wo du wohnst?" Und es nahm ihn der Dante bei Seite
Und ihn am Ärmel fassend, murmelte er: "Deine Verse
Wimmeln von Fehlern, Freund, bedenk doch
Wer alles gegen dich ist!" Und Voltaire rief hinüber:
"Gib auf den Sou acht, sie hungern dich aus sonst!"
"Und misch Späße hinein!" schrie Heine. "Das hilft nicht"
Schimpfte der Shakespeare, "als Jakob kam
Durfte auch ich nicht mehr schreiben." — "Wenn's zum Prozeß kommt
Nimm einen Schurken zum Anwalt!" riet der Euripides
"Denn der kennt die Löcher im Netz des Gezetzes." Das Gelächter
Dauerte noch, da, aus der dunkelsten Ecke
Kam ein Ruf: "Du, wissen sie auch
Deine Verse auswendig? Und die sie wissen
Werden sie der Verfolgung entrinnen?" — "Das
Sind die Vergessenen," sagte der Dante leise
"Ihnen wurden nicht nur die Körper, auch die Werke vernichtet."
Das Gelächter brach ab. Keiner wagter hinüberzublicken. Der Ankömmling
War erblaßt.

HEAD UP
HEAD DOWN
HAND UP
HEAD UPSIDE DOWN

HAND UP
HEAD FACING DOWN

HEAD ON TOP
HEAD ON BOTTOM
HEAD TO HEAD

HEAD FACING FRONT
HEAD FACING BACK

STAINED FACE
FACING STAINED
FINGER
STAINED FINGER
FACING STAINED
FACE
STAINED ARMS
BALANCING STAINED
HEADS

WASH FACE
WASH HANDS
WASH HEADS

HEAD FACE UP
HEAD FACE DOWN

FACE WALL
FACE FLOOR

THOMAS SAYERS ELLIS

HEADS (All Caps)
1989

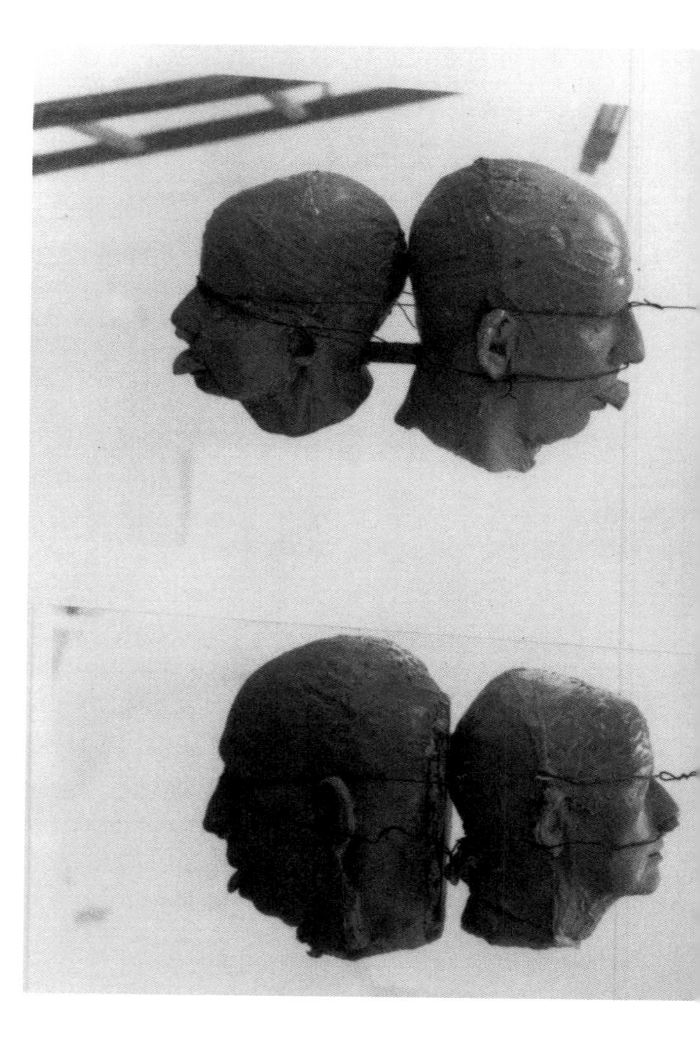

FACE TORTURE
FACE HEAD
ON FINGERS

FACE HEAD
ON HEAD
FACE FINGERS

FACE TONGUE
ON NOSE
FACE DOUBLE SIZE HEADS

FACE SCALP
FACING SCALP

BALANCE HEAD
ON HEAD
BALANCE HEAD
ON HAND

BALANCE TWO HEADS
ON TWO HANDS

NAIL HANDS
HANG HEADS
BREAK ARMS

BALANCE PENCIL
ON PAPER
BUY CATALOG

FACE DEATH
HEAD ON
FACE DOWN

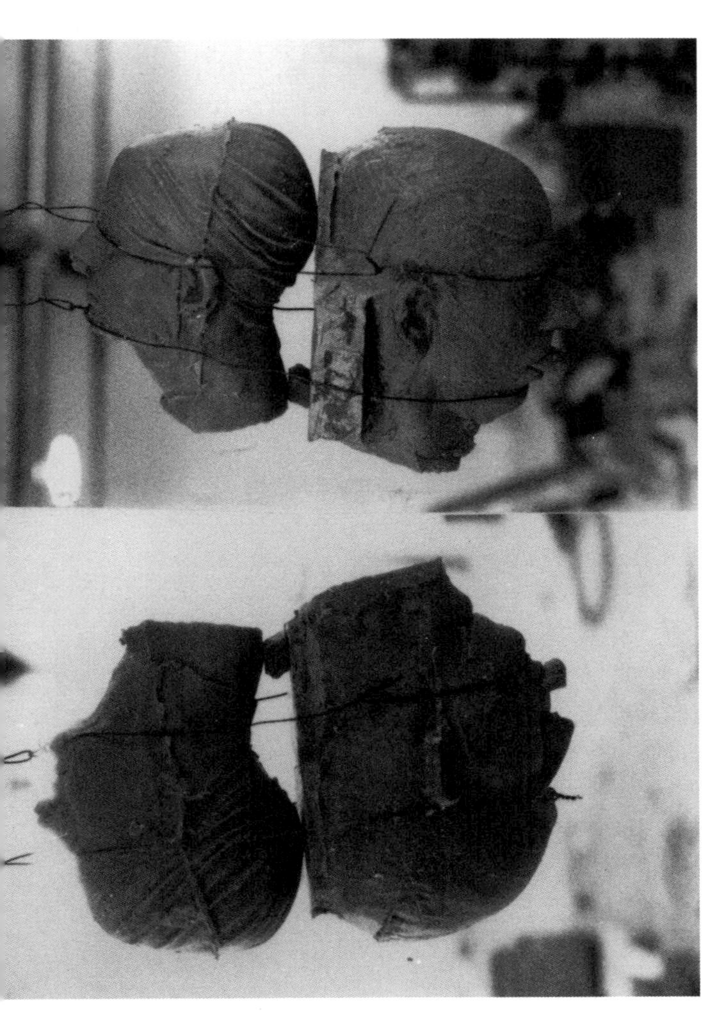

Bruce Nauman, *Four Pairs of Heads*, 1991.

Cowboy Minimalism

for Michelle Weinberg

About 12 in
-ches or seconds
of pure

pencil is
all any outlaw
needs to draw

both hand
& gun. Most
need less

when the saloon
is cactus
dry

—the whole
town covered
wagon

-dependent, young
& old guns,
for hire,

dying of
thirst but still a
posse—& an

insider, what
every white
male artist

wants. To be
ridden. To be
horse-like this way,

hung. Why
else go
West—hot on

the pictorial trail
of a woman
known for

never cleaning
her brushes
—when all

of New York
is making
pictures artificial as

REALISM?
Gold Rush. Enough
of false risk

in this Age or
any other.
This is

how to draw & how
to show
off. Over-

emphasized gentles. Sex
exposed. Before
& after the

opening Bruce
& Susan
take turns in

the saddle,
improvising dripping.
Revolver.

Holster. Revolver.
Barrel &
hole.

Eye shot
point blank with
envy.

PAGES 164–165:
Bruce Nauman,
Video Still from *Green Horses*, 1988.

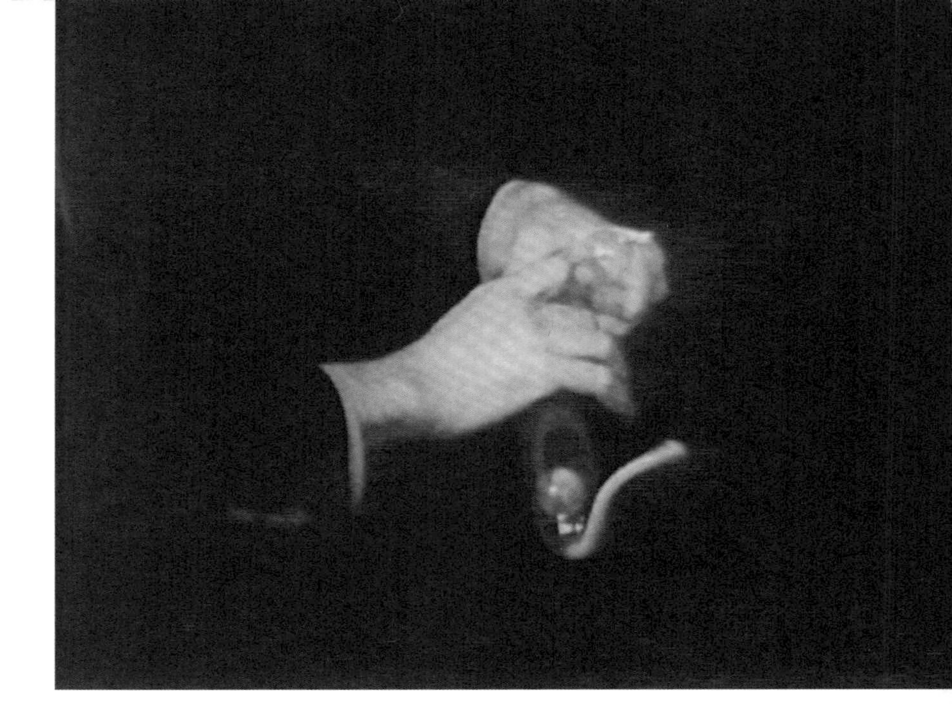

Balloon Dog (1993)

for Janeen Moore

Snap. Blow.
Twist. Squeak.
So this is

how—fenced
in by camera
& nightness

—you
got born,
both you

and the cube
coming
into life,

in the white
hands of
some even whiter

face clown.
Auguste
aka dumb

-dumb. The
only one capable
of seriously

loving old air & rubber.
Little balloon
dog, totem

-billed one
monitor above
Coffee Spilled,

are you any-
body's best
friend? Your parents

were hands,
co-signers
& you are

you because
your balloon
bones

know you,
ON AIR
& OFF. I paused

when I noticed
your skin had
already

started to
lose its shine, the
air inside

your sausage-
linked tubes
escaping

the way poetry escapes
poems that
contain more

ego than
feeling. I feel sorry
for

you. Worse off
than the boy-
in-the-plastic

bubble, you are
bubbles, all fragmen
-tation & some-

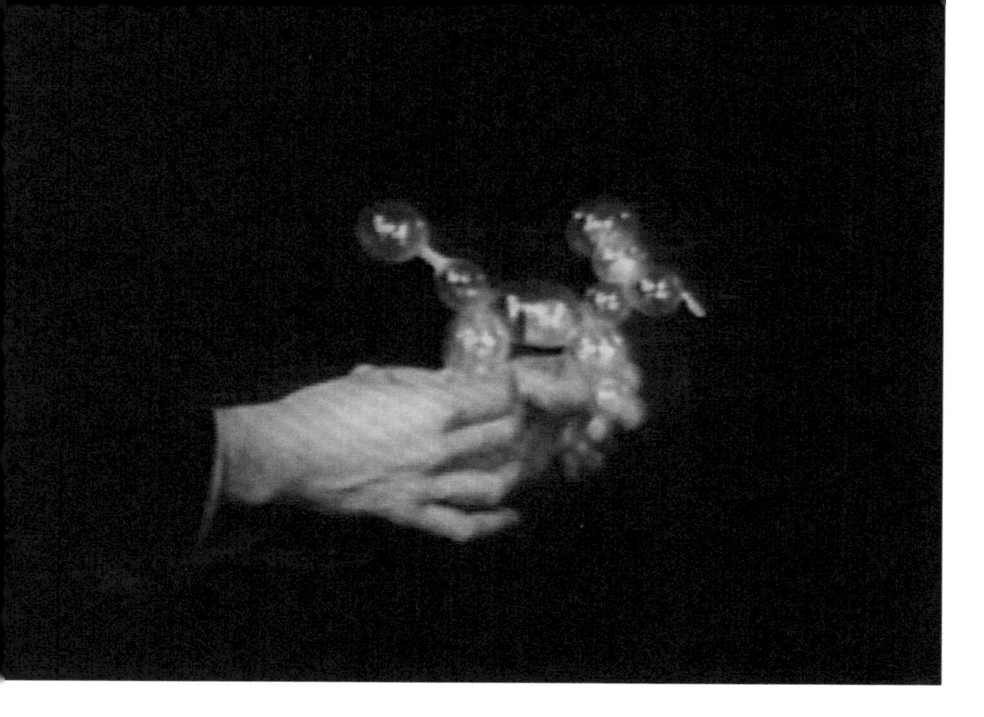

PAGES 168, 169, AND 170:
Bruce Nauman, Video Stills from *Coffee Spilled and Balloon Dog*, 1993.

body else's
breath, Romanti
-cism, in

slow motion the way
love scenes
hatch.

ASSEMBLAGE
is female. No
-thing, not even

love, should
have to live up
to, or as long

as sculpture's
attempted
permanence. Little

balloon dog, the
best your
little balloon heart

can hope
for is silence,
the invisibility

surrounding
the struggle
between

what goes
Pop &
Art.

These poems were written at the Cleveland Center for Contemporary Art during the exhibition Bruce Nauman: 1985–1996, Drawings, Prints and Related Works.

I am indebted to the Cleveland Center for Contemporary Art, especially to Jill Snyder and Noelle Celeste for welcoming me into their workplace and homes; to the Baker-Nord Center for the Humanities at Case Western Reserve University; and to Bruce Nauman without whose work these poems would not have been possible.

SKY LUBRICATION

C.A.A. DELLSCHAU

HOUSTON, TEXAS, WEDNESDAY, AUGUST 2, 1916.

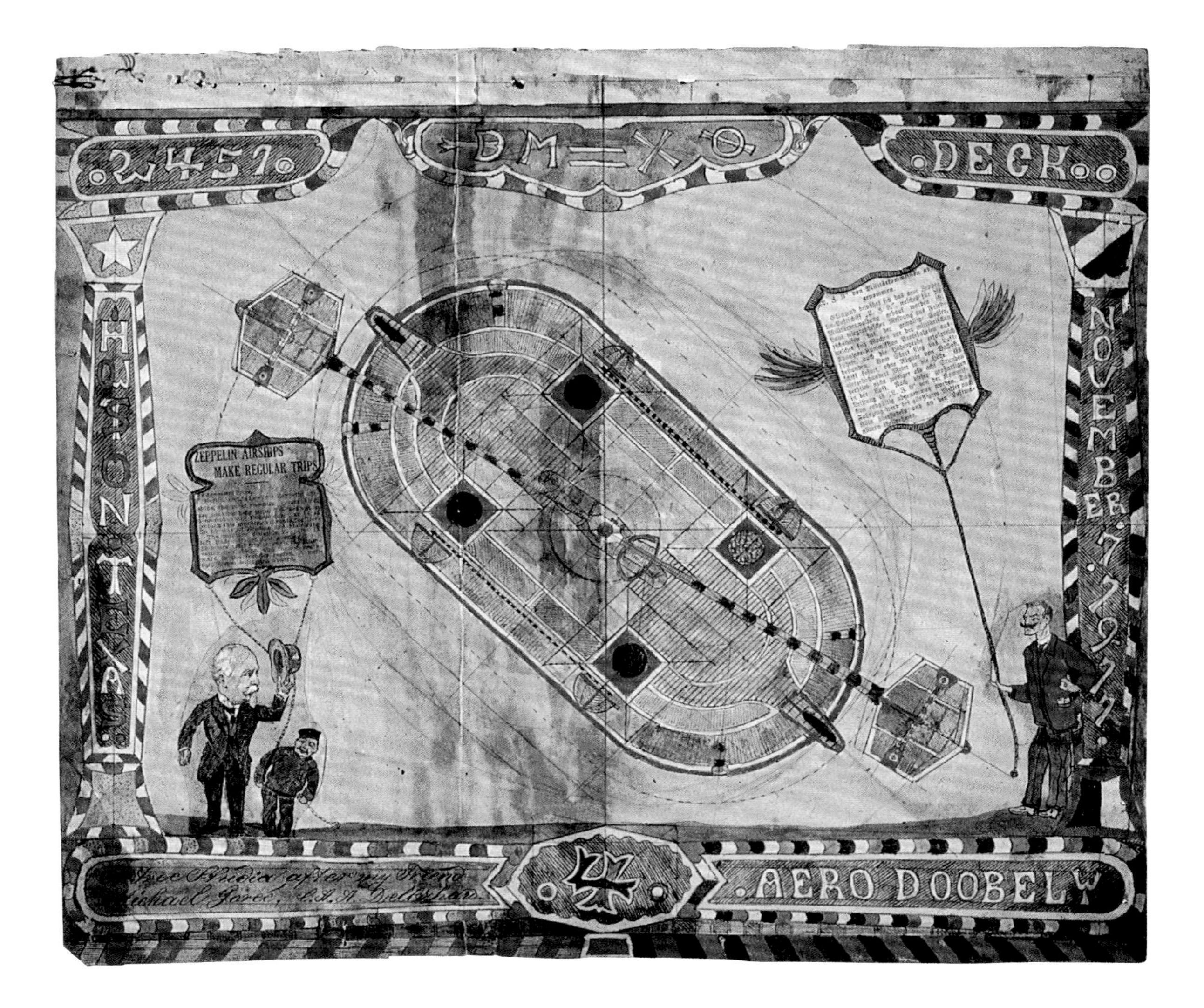

PAGE 173:
Plate 3584, August 2, 1916.

ABOVE:
Plate 2451, November 7, 1911.

PAGE 175:
Plate 1608, February 8, 1908.

AFLYING
HOUSTON
TEXAS
TRE BLA

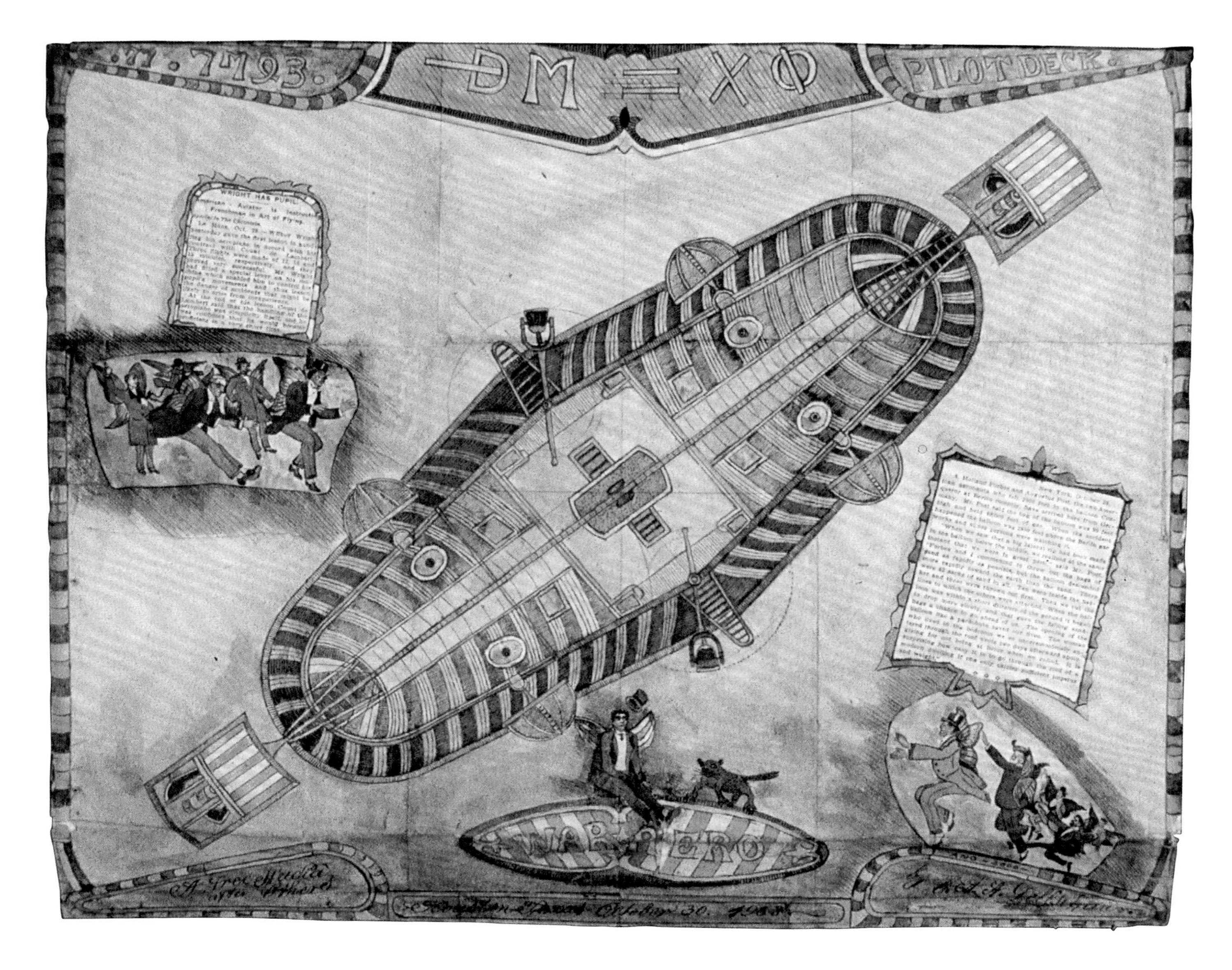

Plate 1793, October 30, 1908.

C.A.A. Dellschau

"Bringing the idea in lines on paper,
what would the good old soul say to it.
Yes, yes, earth covers him too."

C.A.A. DELLSCHAU

In the early years of this century, Charles August Albert Dellschau, a retired butcher, re-created himself as an inventor and scientist. In a series of aeronautical notebooks Dellschau documented his association in the late 1850s with a California flying society known as the Sonora Aero Club. According to Dellschau, this secret fraternity, active fifty years before the Wright Brothers, was dedicated to designing and constructing navigable aircraft; and his visionary journals purport to illustrate their hitherto unrecorded exploits. He marveled at the fierce competition during club meetings, as the members, each trying to outdo the other, argued over the merits of newly presented designs. By 1859 the club had disbanded, and Dellschau moved to Texas to raise a family.

Forty years later, news reports of the latest experiments in powered flight in Europe and America inspired Dellschau to create his first notebooks. By the time of his death in 1923, he had created a phenomenal oeuvre of more than five thousand renderings of elaborate flying machines which eventually filled at least twelve bound volumes. It is likely that Dellschau never thought of himself as an artist but rather as an historian, documenting his friends' overlooked achievements with a promise: "You are not forgotten."

Dellschau carefully constructed his notebooks page by page, ingeniously layering readily available materials such as butcher paper, paper bags, newsprint, and thick stencil paper. He used pencils, a ruler and compass, gouache, and watercolors to reproduce the innovative airships designed by club members. These renderings bear titles such as Aero Mio, Aero Trump, Aero Meta, Aero Schnabel, Aero London, and Aero Jourdon: personalized names the "proposers" gave to their flying machines. Dellschau, refusing to accept credit for the creations of others, would humbly inscribe a drawing "a free studia from recollections of old friends, by C.A.A. Dellschau."

The "aero" is usually portrayed in the center of the design, viewed from different positions ("above deck," "central crosscut," and "flank") on successive pages. Although few look as if they could actually get off the ground, the array of technological innovations evidenced in the aeros include retractable landing gear, gliding keels, revolving generators that operate by means of chemical action, bendable rubber joints, revolving shear blades, fluid collecting electrodes, and "aero ramm or sucker kickers."

As actual aviation achievements took place, Dellschau incorporated them into his notebooks in what he termed "press blooms." Perusing newspapers and magazines such as *Scientific American*, Dellschau clipped, collaged, and painted decorative designs sometimes celebrating but frequently deriding the latest advances.

The aeros are resplendent objects with ornamental striped surfaces invariably poised against a vast expanse of blue sky. These contraptions hover between imagination and technology, permutating from page to page, all alike and yet uniquely different. Dellschau, creator and sole witness to his creation, acknowledges their ambiguous reality at times, annotating his drawings with statements like "Dream Yarn" and "Dream and Real."

Dellschau plays with the embellished borders of the pages, using them to surround and isolate his metaphysical realm from the real world. At the same time, these borders operate as informative marquees, providing details such as the aero title, drawing number, date, place of creation, and proposer. Dellschau deepened the mystery of his notebooks with an encoded alphabet of forty as-yet-undeciphered symbols. This encrypted writing has been the source of much speculation linking Dellschau and his aeros to aliens and UFO groups.

At age ninety, because of failing eyesight or an unsteady hand, or simply because his work was done, Dellschau stopped making his notebooks. Three years later, he died. During Dellschau's life only his immediate family was aware of his eccentric preoccupation. When asked about the strange activities of the old recluse living in a backroom of their Victorian home, they replied, "he knows things about the future."

William Steen

DON BOGEN

Cardinals

Just before daybreak
   tweezering at the cold edge
for a disk of sun.

Whipping, whipping air
   out from the poplar in waves:
Here I am, here, here.

Common, loud, garish,
   a pinup in the field guide,
amateurs' first crush.

Flitting jerky-hop
   from twig to twig on the limb–
never the right spot.

A shopkeeper's eye,
   relentless, shutter-quick, honed
on the day's small gains.

Perched on the phonelines
   calling sunset, hooked around
the black rope of talk.

Demons and Childhood Secrets:

An Interview

INGMAR BERGMAN | JÖRN DONNER

The following interview was filmed in Stockholm during three days in November, 1997.

Jörn Donner: Sometimes you talk about yourself in the third person.

Ingmar Bergman: I'm usually a stranger to myself, someone I'm not especially acquainted with. I've nothing against that person, but don't know much about him. Just as when I read books or things written about me, there's always that stranger there.

Jörn Donner: But haven't you ever had the experience of watching yourself doing something, as if another person were doing it? As if you're somehow divided?

Ingmar Bergman: Yes, maybe.

Jörn Donner: Anger, or . . .

Ingmar Bergman: No, no, not that, but myself—or the person there—is probably quite together. To a large extent, I'm all of a piece. There are huge antagonisms in this composition, a lot of chaos and enormously complicated situations.

It's probably always been a problem I've tried to tackle: Who am I and where do I come from? And why have I become what I am?

Jörn Donner: Do you understand it any better now?

Ingmar Bergman: *[long silence]* No, no, it's worse, or rather not worse, but I probably know even less about myself now than I did ten years ago.

Jörn Donner: But as you yourself say, you've taken over certain characteristics, behavior patterns, from your father, for instance, authoritarianism.

Ingmar Bergman: But when you say "taken over," that's quite conscious. There's nothing conscious about it, but something that's just become that way. I don't think I'm all that much like my father. On the other hand, I think, especially now that I've read my mother's diaries, I recognize an awful lot . . . that I'm tremendously like her. I'm perhaps like my father in looks, but I'm probably most like my mother. Anyway, as far as my artistic talent is concerned—if you can call it that; such a silly expression—but I've probably inherited that from my mother.

Ingmar Bergman, Stockholm, November 1997.

My brother, Dag, you see, became in many ways a person who was damaged, finally and for good, because of his upbringing. I was brought up in exactly the same way as my brother, but I managed to cope better than he did. He reacted with aggressiveness and attempts to defend himself. I did the same with lies and dissimulation.

Jörn Donner: Escaping?

Ingmar Bergman: I escaped and found myself an identity that might be acceptable to my parents, and tried to find out how my parents would react. I was also an arch liar. I lied quite happily and uninhibitedly, and occasionally I was caught and severely punished for lying. Then after a while I went on lying just as uninhibitedly. It was a sin, too, and punishable, so of course I saw myself as a shit and a coward. But on the other hand it was a good way of protecting myself, the only way I was able to cope.

My parents never did anything out of malice or cruelty, nor from any desire to punish me, as I imagined when I was exposed to it, but they did it because they were horrified by their children's behavior, especially us boys.

Jörn Donner: You must have had an amazing sense of freedom when you left home.

Ingmar Bergman: Yes, but by then I was extremely damaged and that stayed with me for a very long time, and I also noticed how that damage affected me in my work. So for a terribly long time in my life, I've had to work on cleaning up after my upbringing, trying to keep what was good in it. You see—perhaps the wrong impression has often been given—our home wasn't hell.

I mean, we had fun, too, and things were all right for us. There was lots of imagination and joy and music and lots of people. We could bring friends home, and there was the theater. I mean, when Father was in a good mood and not . . . He was a manic-depressive and made huge demands on himself. When he was happy, no one could be happier—he shone with it. And Mother was very loving and tenderhearted, compassionate, too, and clear-sighted, so you see, they did their very best. My parents were people of goodwill, but our upbringing, especially for my brother and me, that was hell, there's no doubt about it. It was much the same for many of my generation.

Jörn Donner: Only they didn't become artists. [*laughter*] They just suffered.

Ingmar Bergman: Yes, then hurried to oppress others.

DIALOGUE WITH CHILDHOOD

Ingmar Bergman: When I am going to sleep at night, I can walk through my grandmother's apartment, room by room, and remember everything in the most minute detail, where different things were, what they looked like, what color they were. I can also remember the light, winter light or summer light, through the windows, the pictures on the walls. The apartment was furnished before the turn of the century and contained a huge number of things. That was the bourgeois style of the day, not a millimeter was to remain uncovered; there had to be things everywhere. It's really strange. My grandmother died when I was twelve and I haven't been there since I was about perhaps ten or eleven. But I remember it in detail. The things there in the apartment, they still have a magical content and significance to me. I made a lot of use of that in *Fanny and Alexander*. If any conclusions are to be drawn from that, Jörn, then it may well be that in that way, the whole of my creativity is really tremendously childish, all based on my childhood. In less than a second, I can take myself back into my childhood. I think everything I've done in general, anything of any value, has its roots there. Or dialectically, it is a dialogue with childhood.

PERSECUTION IN SWEDEN & SELF-PRESERVATION

Ingmar Bergman: I was a faithful social-democrat up to when I discovered that they were trying to take my life with that tax affair* and they tried to kill me.

Jörn Donner: Do you see it as a social-democratic plot, or was it the Swedish bureaucracy?

Ingmar Bergman: No, I see it as an offshoot of the reckless claims to power by the new social-democrats. They allowed themselves practically anything, and were allowed anything. But they went on for four years. After that, I couldn't stay in a party that wanted to finish me off.

Then I was affected by a reality that I couldn't do anything about. I couldn't manipulate it or control it, and then life became unbearable. . . . It's happened several times in my life. I couldn't go on living.

Jörn Donner: What did the doctors say to you in a situation like that?

Ingmar Bergman: Oh, doctors! They say, "Let him have eight 10-milligram Valiums a day, and if he needs any more, give him two more and he can have two Mogadon at night. I asked one of those shrinks once—a good friend of mine—if he had ever cured anyone at all. He was an old man, a clever man, and he stared sorrowfully at me and said: "Ingmar, *cure* is a big word." He was famous, a guru to lots of people. He's dead now. The only problem with him was that he hung on to his patients for eighteen to twenty years.

Jörn Donner: In your wildest imagination, could you see yourself submitting yourself to some kind of psychoanalysis in any other way apart from writing?

Ingmar Bergman: No, I don't think so. The only time was in connection with that tax business, when I was in the nuthouse for three weeks. I didn't want anything except to jump off the balcony, and I thought that was a poor solution, too, so I agreed to be locked up. And then the tremendously heavy medication they gave me—which actually removed the torment itself, the actual suffering—also changed my identity bit by bit. I no longer recognized Bergman. I couldn't recognize myself. I went there so meekly and I read books, slept a lot, and walked along corridors talking to the other nutcases, and we had quite a good time together, sitting and watching an old faulty television set in the evenings. [*laughter*]

Jörn Donner: So you didn't become terrified that you might sink permanently into a state of passivity or despair?

* On January 30, 1976, in the middle of a theater rehearsal, Bergman was taken by the police for interrogation about alleged tax offenses. He was later acquitted on all charges.

Ingmar Bergman: It wasn't even thinking, just an instinct for self-preservation. If we take that further, it was quite simply my aggressiveness that saved me. Because when the tax people didn't find anything in the way they first set about it, they took to new tactics and blackmail, everything they could think up. I was so damned angry, I decided I would leave Sweden—and then I recovered. So in a way, for once my anger came to my rescue. Anger; I was utterly, simply furiously angry, and that cured me.

Jörn Donner: Can you remember what you were thinking when your exile began? Did you imagine that the rest of your working life in film would be abroad?

Ingmar Bergman: I couldn't stay in a country where judgment would take my life. Where it would kill me. So, then my wife and I went to Copenhagen. And I became so fearfully homesick for Sweden. It was summer then, you see. So one evening I chartered a plane and Ingrid and I flew home to Fårö. We drove that evening up to Fårö and sat on the steps gazing at the lilac hedge that had just come out. We sat on the steps in the twilight on a mild, light summer's night. Then the next day we drove down again and went to Munich. I was abroad for eight years and I didn't work in Sweden for a long time.

Jörn Donner: So it wasn't just the Swedish language, but also the lilac hedge in Sweden.

Ingmar Bergman: Yes, it was the amazing feeling of coming home and working in Swedish again. It was an incredible feeling, being able to use the Swedish language again. A great sensual pleasure. Unforgettable.

Jörn Donner: And you've never had any more of those introspective spells?

Ingmar Bergman: I've had something like it, but not in the same way. Of course—my wife's death, that was a mortal blow to my will to live in general, to my whole existence, my reality.* A disaster in every respect, but my grief has never had anything to do with anger or bitterness or cynicism, or anything like that. But I've been living in my grief as if in a room and regarding myself as an invalid, and I just get by—I mean, I'm now in my eightieth year. I get by from day-to-day. It's rather trivial. There are things that are boring, and some that are fun.

WRITING

Jörn Donner: Quite often, you've been considerably more experimental in films than in the theater.

Ingmar Bergman: Films demand their form, and staged plays theirs. I've never simply decided that now I shall experiment, but everything has just been given the form I've thought it ought to have. I'm not at all interested in whether I'm experimenting or not.

Jörn Donner: But is it some kind of intuition? Who the hell would be crazy enough to write a script such as *Cries and Whispers*?

Ingmar Bergman: [*laughter*] It's like this: it was necessary to write it in that way, or *Persona*, or the one I've just written, *Faithless*. They've found their

* In November 1971, Ingmar Bergman married Ingrid von Rosen. It was his fourth marriage. They lived together for twenty-four years until her death in 1995.

form simply because it was necessary to write them in that way—to do them in that way.

Jörn Donner: You didn't think about the drama . . .

Ingmar Bergman: No, in general I wasn't thinking about anything.

Jörn Donner: That's not what I meant. But to go back in time, to *Sawdust and Tinsel* or *Prison*. Didn't you think them out either?

Ingmar Bergman: No, I didn't. Well, not *Sawdust and Tinsel*, but *Prison*—I suppose that was the first time I wrote my own script. I was quite crazy with delight and had to get everything that I had been walking around and thinking about into it. Without my really making any effort, it became . . . peculiar.

Jörn Donner: I suppose you don't want to say you're an intuitive writer.

Ingmar Bergman: But wasn't it you who said that when you begin writing, you don't know how it will turn out?

Jörn Donner: That's right, of course, yes.

Ingmar Bergman: It's just intuition, and it's the same when I start writing, I have a kind of basic scene, a beginning. I usually say that in *Cries and Whispers* I went on for very long, and had a scene with four women in white in a red room.

Jörn Donner: And that was all, generally speaking.

Ingmar Bergman: Yes, it was only that. And then I started thinking about why they were there and what they said to each other, that kind of thing. It was mysterious. It kept coming back again and again, and I couldn't get that scene to come out right.

Jörn Donner: A kind of dream image.

Ingmar Bergman: Yes, you know what it's like. Then you begin winding in a long thread that appears from somewhere or other, and the thread can suddenly snap. That's the end of that, but then all of a sudden, it's a whole ball.

Jörn Donner: Have threads often snapped for you?

Ingmar Bergman: Yes, lots of times.

Jörn Donner: But not the kind of threads you've spent weeks working on, or in manuscript form.

Ingmar Bergman: No, not once I've started writing. By then I've already done my working books. In them, I've written endless things, masses of stuff, but once I've started on the script, then I know what I'm doing.

Jörn Donner: What are your working books about?

Ingmar Bergman: Absolutely everything.

Jörn Donner: So the script grows out of the working book?

Ingmar Bergman: Exactly. Well, it's unfinished, completely. Keeping working books is fun.

Jörn Donner: Have you always done that?

Ingmar Bergman: Yes, always. At first, I didn't really have the time. But when I did have the time, yes. Often when I was younger and had to earn money for all my wives and children, then I had to begin on the script, so to speak, bang, directly, I mean. But now I can lie on the sofa and play about with my thoughts and have fun with them, looking at images, doing research and so on. All that's great fun. My working books are also quite illegible to anyone else but me. But then the actual writing begins out of these notebooks.

Jörn Donner: And it goes quickly?

Ingmar Bergman: Relatively quickly because it's so boring. It's hellishly boring, just like when you do a theater performance and sit there sketching out the scenes, how the actors are to move and stand, when they're to say what, and all that—hellishly dreary. When I'm writing the script, I write a certain number of pages a day.

Jörn Donner: Would you consider writing in any other way but by hand?

Ingmar Bergman: No, never.

Jörn Donner: Why not?

Ingmar Bergman: I can't type. [*laughter*] I've tried.

Jörn Donner: Is it a physical thing?

Ingmar Bergman: Yes, it's a physical thing, profoundly unsatisfactory. I use a sort of notepad to write on. They existed when I was employed as a slave scriptwriter at Svensk Filmindustri in 1942. You were given a kind of lined yellow notepad. Then you had to write by hand and with a broad-nibbed fountain pen. Since then, I've always written on that yellow paper and those notepads.

Jörn Donner: Where do you get them?

Ingmar Bergman: About twenty or so years ago it turned out that they weren't making them anymore, so I had them make eight-hundred pads especially for me. And I've still got a few left. I think they'll just about last me out.

Jörn Donner: I should damned well think so.

Ingmar Bergman: I write with a ballpoint pen nowadays, but not just any old damned pen. It has to be a very special ballpoint with a very fat tip. It's the actual writing, although my handwriting is so difficult to read, that gives me pleasure. I like writing by hand. It is very satisfying. In that I always write on the same kind of pad, I know how much I've written, you see. And I never write for more than three hours. When the three hours are up, even if I'm in the middle of a scene or wherever the hell I am, I stop working. I stop for the day. Because it's so boring. But the working book is fun. That's the actual creative process. Writing the script is just the arranging process.

Jörn Donner: Do you think you have some sort of ritualistic superstition about these notepads and pens, where you work, and those three hours, or is it just a routine?

Ingmar Bergman: No, it's a ritual. I have very precise rituals. Get up early and eat breakfast, go for a walk, don't read the paper, don't talk on the telephone with anyone. Sit down at the desk.

My desk has to be tidy, nothing lying about in a mess on it. I am maniacally pedantic when it comes to what it has to look like if I'm to be able to sit working at it. Then when I've been writing for about three quarters of an hour, I take a break. I've usually got a backache by then, so I walk all through my house, or go and look at the sea, or something like that for a quarter of an hour. Writing scripts is a *Pflichtbüng.**

Jörn Donner: A kind of battle? Against . . .

Ingmar Bergman: Against disorder, sloppiness, lack of discipline.

Jörn Donner: You never lacked that.

Ingmar Bergman: Well, no, I've never lacked discipline, but if I had, things would have really fallen apart, I assure you. Because I'm constantly battling against my lack of discipline. You just can't be undisciplined in my profession, you just can't. That's why I've become so frightfully pedantic, so trying to so many people.

DEMONS

Jörn Donner: There's a strange contrast between two things: in both your films and your autobiography you describe your demons with a capital D, while on the other hand in all the pictures of you at work in the theater and on films, you always seem to be in a good mood.

Ingmar Bergman: I think it's part of a director's duty to be in a good mood at work. To create a kind of cheerful atmosphere around the actual exercising of the profession. In the workroom, too.

Jörn Donner: A sense of comfort?

Ingmar Bergman: Yes, and security. It's terribly important. When I was young, I didn't understand that at all, and took it all with me into my working life, my hangovers and troubles with women, all my shortcomings and stupidities. I dragged them with me into the studio or on stage and raced around like a demon creating hideously unpleasant and uncomfortable situations.

But there's also something called the educational outburst, that you sometimes have to make use of. These are enormously premeditated attacks of rage. And they are a precision bombing, because that is what's needed. Things mustn't be lovely and cozy in a studio, or on stage. And the people we work with, they're so often tremendously ambitious, so tremendously sensitive, that although we're playing a game, although it looks like fun—we're joking and telling funny stories and we relax and so on—they still feel it's a matter of life and death. And when I say life and death, I actually mean just that.

Jörn Donner: Is it also a matter of keeping up a certain tempo?

Ingmar Bergman: Yes, to a tremendous degree. For instance, when you start in the film studio, at nine in the morning, then you start at nine in the morning. The first scene is to be shot at ten. Somehow you have to start punctually. A day shouldn't start with endless discussion. To me, chatter is largely an abomination, because then there are one or two people, perhaps more involved, while a whole lot of others are standing around,

* A compulsory exercise.

Ingmar Bergman and Jörn Donner, Stockholm, November 1997.

fed up and thinking it's all a terrible bore. I think all such discussions—it applies to theater, too, even more in the theater—should be outside of rehearsals and outside the studio.

Jörn Donner: How have you managed to create a distance between what you yourself call your demons and a film studio or a theater?

Ingmar Bergman: My demons . . . well, they've somehow got to be harnessed. They have to be there, because I suffer from, for instance—how shall I put it—the demon of suspicion. I am an immensely suspicious person.

Jörn Donner: And a hypochondriac, too, perhaps?

Ingmar Bergman: Let's not keep on counting my demons, for Christ's sake, but I think they ought to be present. They have to stand at attention, on parade, so that I can convey to the actors how suspicion functions and how hypochondria functions, in gestures, tone of voice or in movements. Obviously the demons have to be brought into it. It would be tremendously risky not to have them with you, but they have to be kept very much under control.

You see, as long as I'm inside the studio, or in the theater, then that's a universe controlled by me. Then the demons are also under control. Everything's under control. But the moment all the lights go off and the camera stops, and I leave by the stage door, or the rehearsal is over, then I no longer have control over the demons. Then it is no longer my universe, so to speak, but the often unpredictable universe that I try to control, but which has constantly bedevilled my efforts.

LIVING IN SORROW

Jörn Donner: I can't get away from the fact that not only your films but you yourself have rather unusually been surrounded by illness and death.

Ingmar Bergman: Yes, the two . . . since Ingrid died. I thought, in fact was convinced, that when Ingrid fell ill, my creative activities would be totally at an end. But as long Ingrid was still alive, she was terribly keen that I should keep going, so I did two productions. . . .

Jörn Donner: While she was ill?

Ingmar Bergman: Yes, and then I went on. After Ingrid's death, I simply couldn't write anything. My writing was totally paralyzed. I could sit for hours at the desk, and nothing got written. But, you see, it's another matter sitting alone and writing. These are two quite separate things: if ten actors are in front of me saying, "Do something with me," then I get moving. They're demanding me to do something. I must tell you it's been a great relief, with this dreadful loss I've been through, going to the theater and facing the actors and forcing myself into some form of activity. Meanwhile my writing has been totally dead. Not until this last summer have I been able to resume writing.

Jörn Donner: Has your desire to write come back?

Ingmar Bergman: I thought something had to be done. I was in Fårö at the beginning of April this year and sat down at my desk. And just to get my hand going I decided I would write five pages a day —on anything. That's how it started. Then I could gradually ease myself into the actual story, but it took a hell of a long time. Then it became five, eight, ten pages a day. About all kinds of things. It was rock-blasting work. Everything had gone rusty and turned to stone. I was really in a bad way.

Jörn Donner: But living with grief, thinking about your father dying, then your mother and your brother. That wasn't the same thing?

Ingmar Bergman: No, not at all. It wasn't that at all. It's sort of like becoming an invalid. Ingrid and I had lived together for twenty-four years. We were very close, in a very good relationship, good comradeship. I can't call it anything else but becoming an invalid. I could say it's like losing part of your body: it hurts all the time. But I've taught myself a technique that means I can live with it, more or less.

Jörn Donner: What kind of technique. Working?

Ingmar Bergman: That's one of the ways; living a strictly humdrum life. Having something to do every hour. I follow a tremendously constructed routine.

Jörn Donner: But you've done that for ages.

Ingmar Bergman: Much more than before, so as not to fall apart.

Jörn Donner: Is this why you don't want to meet other people? You've become a bit more of a hermit.

Ingmar Bergman: Yes, to a very great extent.

Jörn Donner: Don't you want to see new people?

Ingmar Bergman: No, I find that difficult. I like talking on the phone. I think the telephone is a wonderful instrument. You can find great delight in being good friends on the phone. But nowadays I live mainly alone, quite alone. And I like it very much. It means life is bearable.

Jörn Donner: Predictability, is that what does it? The fact that you know the times of the day when you do this or that?

Ingmar Bergman: Exactly. Shakespeare says somewhere that sleep is "the chief nourisher in life's feast, the death of each day's life." I take a soporific at night and can then sleep for six hours.

Jörn Donner: I think there's a Bergman quote, if I remember correctly, "The trouble with death is that you don't know what happens afterward." It's so unpredictable.

Ingmar Bergman: That's quite right. When I was young, I lived with a great fear of death. It was really through *The Seventh Seal* that I more or less overcame that fear, for I wrote about it then, about the Black Death. I once had an operation—a minor one—in which I was given too much anesthetic so they couldn't bring me round again. A minor operation, and I was out for eight hours! The interesting thing was that for me those eight hours weren't hours at all, nor minutes, nor a second. I was completely out, extinguished. So eight hours were completely out of my life. It felt wonderfully safe when I thought, so this is what death is. At first you're something, then you're no longer anything. You're nonexistent. You're like a candle blown out. That gave me a sense of security.

What's complicated is this sense of security and then the total extinction that is Ingrid's death. I find it immensely difficult to imagine that I'll never see her again, an unbearable thought. So those two lines of thought are in great conflict with each other. I've tried to write about it, but I can't yet, and no doubt it'll be some time before I can. And also, I often experience Ingrid's presence.

Jörn Donner: In the room?

Ingmar Bergman: Yes. Yes, not as a ghost, but I somehow feel her quite close to me. Whether that's a projection from inside me or a reality doesn't really matter. If you live very much alone, you start talking to yourself. Then I have conversations that I carry on with Ingrid, and I think she answers me, and sometimes I think she gives me good advice and opinions on what I'm doing or not doing. That's some consolation. That brings great relief.

CONCLUSION

Jörn Donner: When you finished *The Magic Lantern*, I had a letter from you. In it you said: "I'm now on my way out of everything with no bitterness, and with a great sense of peace and satisfaction. All I have to do now is to organize the epilogue so that it becomes more or less decent. You simply have to have something other than theater between yourself and death." So over that period of years, you produced numerous books, scripts, films for television—you can't just call that an epilogue.

Ingmar Bergman: Well, it surprises me that I'd already begun talking about the epilogue, for I do that nowadays a great deal and with great empathy.

I think a reason why so much got done could be that I stopped making films, and filming is both physically and mentally such an effort—the actual working on films is such a strain. When that was gone, I suddenly had a whole lot of time and plenty of strength left, and the desire.

Jörn Donner: I was just wondering whether it got easier or more difficult over the years. If you think about when you were doing *Fanny and Alexander*, you had been making films for almost—how long was it?—about forty years. If you include *Crisis*, it's an awfully long time, so it should have been easier once you knew the job.

Ingmar Bergman: No, it grew harder. It grew more and more difficult. When you're young and making films, you know this, you see it when you see the rushes and accept them, and you're so pleased the actors are moving roughly as they should. But then when you get older and have been doing it for so long, you actually feel that there's only one solution to this scene, and you sincerely hope you've found it.

Jörn Donner: What would you like to be said about Bergman in twenty years time? Or thirty years? Or what would Bergman himself say?

Ingmar Bergman: That's something I've never really thought about because, as I said before, I'm so one-hundred–percent convinced that I make useful things, both in the theater and on film, and if they survive me or not—or what people say—I'm totally indifferent to. You must believe that.

Jörn Donner: You must remember you're already part of everyday language. For instance, when you read a novel by V.S. Naipaul, and two people are talking in the African night, and one of them says to the other that this is a Bergman landscape. [*laughter*]

Ingmar Bergman: Well, as I say, all that seems to be about someone else. Somehow or other it has nothing to do with me. I start rehearsing a play, I start on a production. I begin on a Tuesday and with the terror I feel—it's preceded by a sleepless night and great terror—then it's no use saying to myself that I've done this or that and that it's succeeded. And although I'm world famous and written about and people are immensely nice to me, that doesn't help, because I go to that rehearsal thinking only one thing: "Please may this rehearsal go well, please may it be meaningful, and please may it be alive." I think that when I go into the studio as well, like with these television films, or films I make, the only thing that means anything when I'm working is that the work has to be meaningful to those who are carrying it out, and that it has be alive. That's the only thing I'm afraid of, and God knows, I'm dead scared of it—that my ability to make things come alive and be effective is taken away from me, or that I might lose it, that I suddenly don't know how to do it. Or that time leaves me or I'm left with people doing what I say, out of politeness. But most of all, I think, I surprise myself when I'm thinking about this on Tuesday morning at five A.M. and I know the anguish will continue until I go into the rehearsal and then five minutes later it'll vanish. But I know before that the terror is total. And it's always been like that. Maybe you don't believe me, but it is so. I mean, every filming day of my life, every rehearsal day of my life, I've always had—naturally in varying degrees—this terror, this anxiety that what I am doing won't come alive, that it will be stone dead. And I've had many stone-dead days. It's the most frightful thing in the world. That's the kind of thing that I still dream about.

You know I don't have so many nightmares, but that's my recurring nightmare: me, doing things that are stone dead. That I can't put any life into what I'm doing.

Translated from the Swedish by Joan Tate

CHRISTIAN WIMAN

The Last Hour

Lean and sane
in the last hour
of a long fast
or fiercer discipline
he could touch dust
into a sudden
surge of limbs
and speak leaves
in the night air
above him, inhabit
quiet so wholly
he heard roots
inch into the unfeeling
earth, rings increasing
inside of that tree.
Without moving,
hardly breathing,
he could call
out of the long darkness
walls around him,
a house whose each room
he knew, its hoard
of silences, solitudes,
doors opening
onto the wide fields
through which he moved,

breathing deeply,
unbewildered by the dead
with their hands of wind,
their faces of cloud.
Stilled and gifted
in the last hour
before the first light,
in the dark place
of his own making,
he could feel rocks
relax alive
beside him, gather
from a moon-raveled
river the pearl
curves and blue
fluency of a girl
his hands once knew.

He could let her go.
He let it all go,
desire and grief
and raw need
going out of him
moment by moment
into the mild
immaculate dark,
love by love
into a last
passion of pure
attention, nerves,
readiness...

Light carves
out of the darkness
a muscled trunk,
each clenched limb
and the difficult tips
of a plain mesquite
taking shape
over the hard ground
where he lies,
his eyes wide
and his whole body
hungering upward,
as if he could hear
and bear the bird
singing unseen
deep in those leaves.

MANUEL
BAUER
THE SINICIZATION OF TIBET

PAGE 196:
Ruins of the 14th century Shide Tratsang Temple, Lhasa, Tibet (Tibet Autonomous Region, China).* Before and during the cultural revolution, the Chinese suppression of Buddhism in Tibet resulted in the deaths of thousands of monks and nuns and the destruction of some 6,000 monasteries and temples.

ABOVE:
Erlang Pass, Kham province, Tibet (Szechuan, China). The People's Liberation Army built and maintains this road, which is one of the two main routes from China to Tibet.

LEFT:
Potash extraction at the Dabsan Hu salt lake, Qarhan, Amdo, Tibet (Qinghai, China). This plant, owned by the Chinese Qinghai Potash Company, has 4,000 employees (mostly Chinese) and an annual output of 200,000 tons of potash.

*Names in parentheses are the current Chinese designations for areas of Tibet.

PAGE 198–199:
Tibetan pilgrim making a traditional religious encirclement (Khora) of the Chamdo monastery, Chamdo, Kham, Tibet (T.A.R., China). The new Chinese city of Chamdo is behind her.

RIGHT:
Tibetans selling their traditional goods to tourists in front of the Potala (the Dalai Lama's Winter Palace), Lhasa, Tibet (T.A.R., China). The Dalai Lama, Tibet's spiritual leader, has lived in exile in India since 1959.

BELOW:
Khampas, Manigango, Kham, Tibet (Szechuan, China). The Khampas of eastern Tibet come to the cities to find work, but employment opportunities for Tibetans are virtually nonexistent.

Manuel Bauer

I met Manuel Bauer at a dinner party before I had seen any of his photographs. He had just come down from Dharmsala and regaled us with stories of his adventures in Tibet. He had repeatedly put himself in great danger there to record the effects of the Chinese occupation. To reach areas forbidden to tourists, Bauer would feign illness to get his tour bus to stop and then run off into the countryside. He hid his exposed rolls of film in streams and wells, protected by water-tight bags. Bauer had recently been arrested by the Chinese military, but escaped and was taken in by nomadic Tibetans; despite all this he was eager to return and continue with his project.

Then there are the photographs themselves. Bauer is pointing his camera at the result of five decades of Chinese occupation. In that period, sixty-five percent of Tibet's forests have been cleared by the Chinese, resulting in an estimated profit for them of more than fifty-four billion U.S. dollars. Seventy to eighty percent of young Tibetans in Lhasa are unemployed. Before and during the cultural revolution, over one million Tibetans died and some six thousand monasteries and public buildings were destroyed. China has initiated an aggressive resettlement program which threatens to make Tibetans a minority in their own country; in some towns only one percent of the population is native Tibetan. Large areas of the city of Lhasa have been destroyed and rebuilt; the Chinese plan to completely "modernize" it by the year 2000. While China sees itself as having liberated the Tibetans from feudalism, some Tibetans blame the Buddhist rulers who demilitarized the nation and created conditions for the takeover.

China's prize is the natural resources of the Tibetan plateau, which include the world's largest deposits of uranium as well as coal, mineral ores, tin, petroleum, salt, and gold. Potash, used as a fertilizer, is a particularly valuable commodity. While one factory produces two-hundred thousand tons of potash each year, a second one, four times as large, is being planned as a joint venture with Israel. Another potentially lucrative industry is tourism. To create the sweeping new square in front of the Potala palace, the Chinese destroyed the Tibetan village of Shöl.

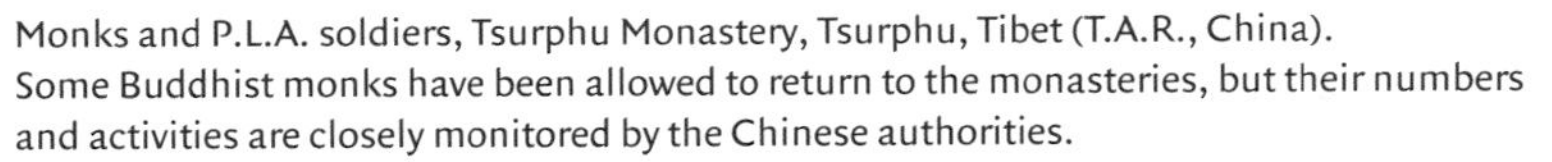

Monks and P.L.A. soldiers, Tsurphu Monastery, Tsurphu, Tibet (T.A.R., China).
Some Buddhist monks have been allowed to return to the monasteries, but their numbers and activities are closely monitored by the Chinese authorities.

Prostrating pilgrims and P.L.A. soldiers, Lhasa, Tibet (T.A.R., China). Pilgrims follow the eight-kilometer-long Linkhor, the outermost of the three ring roads which encircle the old part of the city and the Jokhang, Tibet's most sacred temple. They continue to follow traditional routes, regardless of new obstacles in their way.

Where did the Chinese find the model for their manifest destiny? Is our instinctive disgust at these images partly a product of our own complicity? America seems to be waging its own cultural revolution by way of satellite broadcasts, videotapes and Happy Meals.

I am fascinated by Bauer's photograph of a Tibetan deity figure staring agape in the ruins of the Shide Temple. The picture has an obvious sadness, of course, but also something avant-garde, resembling the experiments of Rei Kawakubo, Zaha Hadid, or Cady Noland. Bauer's work records a moment of chaos: the Hindus believe that we are living during the Kaliyuga, the Age of Kali, a chaotic endtime; the Dalai Lama has consulted with rabbinical scholars for possible insights into how the Jews retained their identity throughout their own centuries of exile. Perhaps there is an equilibrium to be found among these horrifying images, a divine meaning—albeit perverse—that we are unable to grasp. I choose to see the convulsive beauty of the ruined Shide Temple as an image of transformation and possibility, a symbol that Tibetan culture will survive the forces that have changed it utterly.

Peter Nagy

night lessons

LATIFE TEKIN

I was a fresh bud of eighteen years. Besides, my name was Gülfidan*.
I mixed with the forty women huddled in the small night shelter on the street with the old open-air cinema and the row of firewood sellers. When they asked who I was, I hung the picture of a sensitive bird before the eyes of forty women. Slowly I tilted the bird's neck. "I come from a house of lonely women," I sighed. It was afternoon on a spring day when the warm breeze rustled the leaves. Possessed by the inquisitive gaze of forty women, I brought to sunlight the illicit phantasm hidden in my mind. Those huddled sitting in the night shelter leaned over the pale image of a young woman sobbing, staring at her bleeding finger in a stone kitchen. I told how my coal-black-haired mother cut and bled her fingers with knives all her life, how, while sobbing, she wrapped her fingers with colored paisley swatches, holding one end between her teeth.

* * *

On that spring afternoon, the innocent mold into which I poured my delicate girlish voice was crushed to pieces by the first seminar's magic reality.
The problem: since time immemorial, women gathered fruit and men hunted.
The problem: icebergs floated toward warmer regions. The problem: it rained incessantly in the warmer regions. The problem: the progress of the means of production led to the creation of the Cro-Magnon race. The problem:
I imagined my novice face smeared with the black mud of ignorance.

---

* Rosebud.

A sense of shame, three coughs and four teardrops spotted me. I moved a little sideways. When nervous twitches swarmed through my body, I fought back. Scarred and wounded I hid in the snowy nights when my father went out rabbit hunting on his tractor. I curled up on the snow, panting, and horsemen charged, galloping toward me; I ran toward the september afternoons when my mother gathered young shoots in our fruit garden. On the bank of a scarlet river, I encountered the Cerementine giant. I crawled and pressed my mouth to her breast lying on the ground. My tongue wet with her milk, I climbed her hair up to her lips in the sky. Swinging from the branches of palms sprouting off tuberous clouds, I realized I'd fall, break into pieces and disappear. "Something must be done . . . something must be done . . ." vibrated the vocal chords of the forty women; with all my heart I reached out to those chords, and wearing flames like rings around my neck I stood panting inside the sentence, "Write me in the organization book, too!"

* * *

Ah, souls! I couldn't even recover the broken pieces of my life, the lighthouse of dark oceans. Autumn splish-splashed across my face with its icy yellow color. I couldn't even find the strength to protect the irises in my eyes or the curves on my lips drawing deep smiles like dark blue wells. Sitting in the tattered armchair, I tensed my lungs and, looking like a slip cover, I whispered, "My code name is Secretary Wind; I was abandoned at a young age, on the ground floor of a gigantic complex. My life's dream, tumbling, turned its face away from the memory of our people in me. I still haven't recovered from the shock. I was no different from the afflicted one who years and years later searched for herself in the house where she was born. I am experiencing difficulty recalling my name and who I am; I am being forced into a deep, impenetrable sleep."

* * *

Oh the brigade of crimson-winged vanguard women,

Outside, the streets have been displaced, factory gates broken, the night shelters' ceilings collapsed, I am afraid. But don't expect any good from me. I'm not about to accept your offer and fight death with my hurt body. Tell me, what am I to make of your idea that I should enlist in a small thread factory? Keep your hearts' gaze away from me. Becoming a worker doesn't suit my dreams. I've chased the hope of capturing a life much fresher than the one I've had since my breath smelled of milk. But pain pierced my spleen. My throat and rib cage became the stage for inconsolable sobs. Now I stare at distant faded phantoms and can't even form a single feeling.

* * *

Gülfidan, illegality's fairy-tale writer,

While we were crushed under the grave duties piled on our shoulders, you always went for revelry. You fancied as many dreams as stars in the sky and trees in the forest. The star pastries served in strike tents, the solidarity saplings planted in factory yards were contrivances of your perverse heart. One day you showed up bearing the cheerful signs of imagination in your face and suggested that we walk up to one of the grand avenues and leave our white scarves on the asphalt. A Dajjal* you were. You influenced our leader with your screams resonant with touching words, whispers and faith that lasted until morning and convinced her to organize the children. You brought countless misfortunes upon us. And now you belittle the duty to work in a thread factory, to fight like a soldier, to keep our cause alive.

* A messianic deceiver in Islamic eschatology.

* * *

My rose,

Don't presume I'm unwilling to devote my inner organs to our people's sunny future. Remember how I sang the most beautiful marches, breathing through my abdomen, tearing my heart's membrane. It's not the thread dust and shuttles that blacken my two faces. Here, while I sat in this tattered armchair and counted the rain drops falling off the iron bars to the soil, I heard certain things that distressed my ears. All the swarthy and dark-haired pioneer women had turned blonde to go incognito. Prettied their foreheads with tiny curls and big waves . . . Covered their noses with glasses like butterfly wings outlined by three pairs of shiny stones. The wardrobes and maquillage bags of certain wealthy relatives had been pillaged. And our Leader, who protected me from countless threats, unfair criticism, and calmed my heart with her love, had vanished from the face of the earth.

* * *

Secretary Wind,

Clara Zetkin's soul dressed in artist's clothes assumed flesh, bone, and our Leader's countenance, and, walking along Baghdad Avenue, she protected her.

* * *

My darlings,

Your fiery provocations caught me in a moment of weakness. At the risk of tiring my body flickering like a dying candle, I couldn't help reviving my sad face reflected in the rear window of a public bus on Baghdad Avenue. Seeing her walk coquettishly on the edge of the sidewalk, my eyes opened wide like amulets. I also felt strange. I heard that they made her wash all the dishes in the house where she was hiding. That's why, they said, her lips always drooped and she sulked. I attempted to throw myself in the cool waters of a very long prayer, and I rolled around on the ground laughing so hard that my face was all torn.

With my most clandestine regards and love,

* * *

Mukoshka, ah, Mukoshka . . . my beautiful sister, my daisy, my curly dove . . . I want to kiss under your wings, why? Won't we ever delight in love, you and I, tell me . . . I know, you'll paint the white of your eyes rose and say, "I don't know, perhaps we will love, in honor of the staired street we walked down in the mornings, weeping . . ." For god's sake, tell me, what's there for us to miss from the past? Why do I keep wandering among the bits and pieces of time, all the pictures of madness. Look at this one: after a beating, the two of us in a laughing contest. Tell me, wasn't ours a brutal life! These old broken objects, the dusty tiles, the dirty bed in the backroom; when I see myself being dragged around the house, I want to cry from hatred. Do I need so much anger in order to obtain time that won't break or corrode? I know, "To us," you'll say, "kisses never came rushing . . . ." Time and again we turned to the past and derived vengeful feelings from those pictures of madness and chased them with wild greedy bulls . . . I know very well, Mukoshka, my dear sister . . .

* * *

The water was deeper than I could touch, warm as blood, it spread rippling through my skin; this is where I encountered the first ferocious monster. Suspense. I acted quite calmly. Slowly I parted my lips, inhaled a sharp whisper that formed curved dimples on my cheeks, and, hurling it, I struck her right in the middle of her forehead. Overjoyed, I approached her. Leaned over her face. My fingers touched the hair draping her eyebrows, "Pink rouge," I said, "goes well with your lips . . ." A delicate smile appeared and quickly broke across her face, and all of a sudden she handed me her womanhood. Outside the city, on that remote street curving discreetly toward deceit, the forty-year old fugitive, this crumbled woman, became human and young again on account of a pitiful phrase like, "goes well with your lips"; the experience sunk in and touched my heart's ventricles with love . . . She anxiously chased away the swooning look forming on her face and quickly took back the only glimmer she had offered me throughout the hours we walked side by side, slightly touching each other . . . She frowned, puckered her beautiful face, small as the palm of a hand, tarnished my eyes; she accused me, silenced me with the voice my ear knew so well, her voice that gave her exuberance as she spoke . . . Didn't I see the birds flapping their wings? I did and wanted so badly to fly with them, to wander among the icy white clouds, to wash my eyes slowly, slowly . . . And if those very birds had turned into one of the symbols of our cause . . . Why, why, then, did I not want to become a worker!

* * *

I remember my whole being wrapped in a feeling of secrecy, estranged from myself, shaken with a dizzying nausea. When we got to the courtyard of that small mosque on the seashore that always evoked unruly joy, I was facing the twisting waves. I dreamed of horses pulling small wooden carts, spurting froth off the strait's cool waters. My primitive, so-called sensitive jinns, why did they want hundreds of horses running across the sea, sinking and rising, in this icy cold weather? What did they expect to gain by reenacting, in this clear daylight, the night when I was only nine and had seen for the first time this city, these waters, under the lights, and had left on the sea's surface the wooden carts and horses I had hidden in my mind? Surrounded by an insidious silence, I was clearly provoked to load on those small wooden carts the burden I could not carry . . . The dark-blue path traversed by the poor passenger ferries, the seagull's feeding grounds would have been almost plundered by the horses of a small village girl . . . Thankfully, "Hook, claw, what have they to do with me." I said, "I'm not a conspirator, neither are you . . ." I turned to wave at her, and the wind beating my face didn't make me sob . . . .

* * *

Twenty or so years ago, I was alone, kneeling by the tray and eating breakfast. My six siblings made of thighbone and clay were playing ball among the mulberry trees. My father was off to his Friday prayer and those two sitting at the bay window were my mother and my brother's godfather . . . I had my back to them. A breeze gently touched my cheek, turned my head back. Toward fire and gunpowder. All at once, my mother's hand disappeared in the shimmer of sun dust. Like ladlefish in warm murky ponds disappearing among shimmers . . . The charming smile that came upon her face quickly turned into a tempest, circled her lips, and, whirling, rose to her eyes. Her hand was smitten, twisted on the cheek of my brother's godfather, her fingers draped the light gravely, caressed it. His eyes skewed, his mouth opened. Flames shot through his white teeth. The tulip sofa cover, the rug, the tray, the bread, the sip of tea, the brief hot dampness between trembling lips, the door, the stairs, the street, all caught fire. My eyelashes and hair were singed. My nose blistered. My head spun from the rush of my footsteps. The tempest that circled my mother's lips and, whirling, rose to her eyes, chased after me, caught me helpless, panting, bewildered, in the decrepit mansion's garden in the neighborhood below. It sucked my stomach inside its cyclone. My eyes spewing terror, I began to throw up out of jealousy and, upset that my mother was in love, I cried quick tears.

Love was a distinguished visitor who came from the land of silk, ate roasted chickpeas and drank red wine. Yes, it was so. I remember very well.

* * *

Mother dear, if anyone asked, what would I say? Laundry soap. I'd walk closely by the walls, pitter-patter in one breath, go to the grocer and come back. I would not break love's wine or spill his chickpeas. I secretly cut my singed eyelashes. Trimmed the burned ends of my hair. Peeled the skin off my blistered nose and became a militant like the wind.

Autumn arrived with whispers and I got caught. Nothing came out of my paper bag. I was locked in the back room of our house. Held inside for a month with no news about my mother. My older sister was the chief warden. I begged her to let me see my mother. She told me mother had left. Showed me an old letter that my brother's godfather had written, and beat me for denying my guilt. I was surprised my mother had garnered no love in my sister after so many years. I remember well, I was surprised. While being dragged on the floor, the moment I realized my mother and I were victims of a thrashing tale, I fell apart, grieving. Amidst the sounds of creaking stairways, footsteps and water, I split in two. Tumbled in the middle of jingling spoons, laughter, shouts. I fainted while searching for my mother's cough, her warm breath, the shiny gold tooth in the very back of her mouth.

The evidence was a wet towel, I think. (It had dried by the time they laid it on my knee.) I never grasped its meaning. What does a wet towel have to do with love, what does it tell people . . .

* * *

How many nights we spent dreaming, how many days longing, I don't know. In the end, they also set my mother free. She returned the luminous shadows of her flowing hair to our house. She killed all her voices, buried them inside inscrutable graves in her soul. After the massacre she began walking from room to room with her head down. I followed her for days and finally discovered the site of the mass graves. Writhing with pain behind doors, she'd put her hand on her forehead and disappear through the traces of colors reflecting off her face. I was certain her fingers burrowed through her forehead, and she slipped through a secret door all by herself. I was afraid thinking that one of these days she wouldn't return from the memorial service she performed at the site of her dead voices, so I wanted to talk to her. Perhaps she'd hold my hand, take me through the door she opened in the middle of her forehead and bring me along to her voices. One morning, by intent, my accomplice and I came face-to-face in the bathroom of our house. She saw my eyes soaked in sweat, tired of watching her, and she couldn't leave me behind. Slowly, her hand reached out and caressed my cheek. She took a deep breath, stepped back, leaned her head back, thought briefly; then, acting for both of us, she invited one of her voices' souls into our bathroom and waited reverently. A voice near us—but whose resonance suggested it had traveled a long way—graced me and her, and said, "I am very happy you didn't tell." I was embarrassed and so excited that I couldn't hold my head straight. I bent my neck on her gently heaving chest, buried my nose in her belly. She held my head in her hands. "Where in me have you been all this time, Gülfidan," she whispered, "where in me, dear daughter!"

* * *

She tightly held the end of the rope she had tied around my wrists. And I kept turning around her, drawing rings. I was there. Right beside her. I was being tossed about on the wooden floor, now this way now that. I was staring at the ceiling. Tip-tap descending the stairs. Playing nine stones, running. Falling, hitting my head on the stone. My cheeks burning, I was drenched in sweat, palpitations, dirt, and darkness. Holding on to the wall, I was climbing back up the stairs. Secretly eating ice. Always eating ice. Crump, crump . . . Turning cold as cut stone. She was spanking me, taking me to the doctor. Finger-length stalactites inside my mouth, ice-blossoms in my irises, I was lying on her lap. My head hanging loose was banging, now right now left. Apparently she was hearing none of the noise. Neither was she seeing me. That is, until she fell in love.

* * *

My closest friends want me to distract myself by fighting. They even object to me expressing their wishes in these words. None of them thinks I should collaborate with the dead one, who is less experienced than I. They say they fear she'd hurt me, that they want to protect my future. I wish I could believe them. But it's too late already . . . Her bulldog courage enchanted me . . .

* * *

The strange relationship between her and her mother—her husband always objected to calling it a relationship—started on the twelfth morning of september [*] when radio static and extremely cinematographic glints of fire burned the clouds—sound, sassy, steamy, eye-watering, nose-itching sizzles that made Gülfidan pluck from her singular bud her ten-year-old fruit of life. The resin-smelling smoke that made a person lose her sense of space and twisted her joints, met Gülfidan's lungs, inside the small room where syndicalists had gathered. Gülfidan's tender voice tittered in the syndicalists' faces—almost a bleating—and then grasped the seriousness of the situation. And slowly sliding through froth, her voice managed to hide behind her spleen.

* * *

I want to add one more thing, a creeping numbness that's like old habits visiting a person. In those days when our friendship deepened, do you remember I always walked with a sheet inside the house, and, every chance I got, pulled the sheet over me and curled up with sadness underneath? Never mind, Mukoshka . . . Take a deep breath and just smile . . . Our friends who rack their brains to untangle our relationship want to pull that end of the yarn which demands so much, my dear. This little is all I can ask from you. Because I who am quarrelsome, violent, vulgar; according to them, I always found a way to save my life. And at the same time intentionally caused you to become an introvert, tongue-tied, cold creature . . . I have too many sins, Mukoshka .. . You see, I hold the right to assault . . . Besides, you can't actively participate in these discussions. Because I pacified you. (Made you smell chloroform, it's as bad as saying I raped you, goddamn it!) So far as I can remember, in the fifth term you didn't enroll in the A-level staff training either. Since you are a petty clerk who works eight hours every day and supports the household, I assign you the duty to smile silently. No, we won't be able to arm wrestle. We have no arm-wrestling skills. We are robots living on definitions.

[*] September 12, 1980, the last military coup in Turkey.

What I want from you is: stay awake and allow me my voice a little. I'll grab a bullhorn. During those election campaigns, there used to be a public square behind Shishli . . . *Abide-i* . . . There, on the wooden podium of that public square, imagine the wing of a young woman arched toward the sky. Send the security guards after those who think I intend to solve my sexual problems in front of the masses. Issue a military order to oust them from the rows. This is the only way to put an end to gossip . . . No, Mukoshka, no, dear, take my wing down from there, hold my arm, protect my eyes frightened like a child's heart, keep my head on your shoulder. Let's return home. All homes are tarnished, what does it mean? You want to tell me that we are classless? Drop those sentimental theories now and speak openly. Your sister is a bolt that's been stripped by every theory, it's time you accept this. Tell the sherbet-sweet street-smart one with bruised kneecaps: We'll travel throughout the night, guided by the stars. We'll stay hungry because there's no money in our pockets. Whether or not we'll be able to find an attic tomorrow or any day after, it's not certain.

* * *

With their signet rings, navy-blue suits, and white socks, the syndicalists were a big crowd. I was the only woman in the room, a sister-in-law to all. Among them was a small man, slight as an apple tree, whom I didn't recognize. Was it his tattered look that reminded me of the apple tree I'm used to seeing in the small yards of night shelters and counting among the symbols of poverty? Or was it because his cheeks were round and red like apples? My husband said that the man was the custodian of a chapter formed in the southern region. A whisper that belonged to no one passed from mouth to mouth like a sacred object while he remained staring ahead. With rhythmic tilts and measured hand gestures, he approved of the speeches; his head kept nodding, as if heeding the call of a primitive beat. My attention was entirely focused on him because when he had come to our house, he had refused to shake my hand and caused my fingers to bob in the air and sadly fall to my waist. Who was this man? Was he one of the Shafi'i[*] chiefs?

---

[*] One of the four schools of religious law in Sunni Islam.

He was the last speaker.

Each in his turn would whisper some things, extend his hands and restore silence, then clear his throat, swing his torso back and forth as if chanting a sacred prayer, string words like *Kerensky*, *Winter Palace*, *imperialism*, one after another, and, lowering his eyes, resting them at his feet, he'd pass out of elation and take refuge in calm.

As a child I had watched in fear through wooden fences, understood that it was passed from hand to hand, the lock of the holy prophet's beard, although I never got to see it. I steeled myself as if he'd pull the holy relic from a pouch in his pocket and push it up to my nose. Oh how, after each political comment, he rubbed his eyes on the shag carpet, polished them and fixed them on my face, hoping he'd win my heart . . . How he flung against my soul the body language of clandestine activity . . . Finally I couldn't contain my anger, I leaped with fury and caught one of his glances in midair, right in the middle of the room. I clenched my teeth. Between my fingers, I squashed the light in his eyes. Staggering, I went outside. I struggled to catch my breath ebbing in warm waves into the depths. The doleful wheezing of diphtheria rose and sunk in my throat. My husband's hand slid from my forehead to my cheek. With his shoulders' help, I managed to pull my breath up. "You want me to take you to bed?" I nodded. I nodded repeatedly. My body trembling, trembling under the blanket, cast me outside itself. I remained trapped between the warmth of my skin and the dark face of the blanket. Raging tremors underneath, the weight of darkness . . . "Horsemen, horsemen with hoofbeats sweet..." I rambled endlessly. "Get me out of here, get me out . . ."

The horsemen didn't hear. Perhaps I saw not horsemen but birds with fur caps and whips. Flying the wind toward a scarlet dawn. Who was this man spreading the wormwood smell around our house like poison from his green mirrored vial? Was he the shoemaker involved in party work in Cossack villages? The one who knocked on our door, on the vanishing night of that morning when I, emerging perfunctorily from the pages of a novel, had just bid sad farewell to ten years of my life . . .

* * *

I heard the voice I expected. Ringing through earth and sky, it was the voice of the giant mother. I knew there was no choice besides sneaking under her legs and begging her to adopt me as her child again. In a hurry I prepared the touching words I'd string one after another, poking my head from between her hips. "*Niva niva sare militan.*"* Just then, I was left with no reason to poke my sad face from between her hips or to beg and plead. A black Murat-brand automobile entered my field of vision at full speed and came to a screeching stop right at nose level. My mother came out, lifting her black veil. "I know very well what you're up to, perfidious child, I've followed you all along," she said. Even though the syndicalists saw no reason that I should be scared, I was very scared. I jumped out of my nest—between my skin and the blanket's dark face—with such a jolt that my mother and the blanket were both thrust onto the ceiling. The black Murat automobile rolled down into my dream abyss. Burst into flames, then to pieces on the linoleum tiles. My body was squashed whimpering under the pressure created by my soul. My mother's black veil fell over my eyes. I thought my body and soul would never come together.

"What's there, what's there to be so afraid of?" Poor dear mother, weary as if a rabid jackal was about to pounce on her, but trying not to let on, she was consoling me. "God willing, you'll fall in love with a boy all green under his brows, and come out of these dark waters, Gülfidan . . ." If I knew where my head was, I'd come near it, touch its face, part its lips and make them say, "Who in the world issued you the license, woman . . . Why this obsession with black, little slut!"

* A variation on a Kurdish phrase that the author recalls hearing in one of her mother's fairy tales, and associates with solitude.

* * *

The Murat automobile, the black veils as well, I was the one who gave them to her as gifts. A mean-hearted angel must have issued her the license. We were at my mother's funeral. Away from everyone else, I leaned against a tree and stared in front of me. Welling up, anger constantly welling up inside me, I could no longer bear the solitude of being her only faithless child, and, turning around, I started walking away. "Stop that savage!" my father shouted. "*Ashadu anna*."* That's when I learned that *ashadu anna* meant ass-son-of-an-ass. "Let go of me. I'm going nowhere . . ." Pressing my arms against my belly, I began to writhe. My older sister coiled around my neck, dragged me to the grave. Was she thinking that not once I opened my hands like two lemon leaves, that I cheated mother of prayers? She was gazing at my face through her tears, full of sadness. She approached, wishing to share my solitude; she gently took my arm and said, "If mother could see all these cars arriving at her funeral, how happy she'd be!" Grief leaped off its seat in my heart as shame singed my brain.

Of course, if they were arriving, just as they had arrived in the city, wearing their clogs, if they had rejoiced the day my mother taught their feet how to wear shoes, and if my older sister tells me that we were the ones who plucked their lice one by one, as sure as if she held their heads, and above all, if I am being included in this delousing operation even though I wasn't even born then, it was certainly my vital duty to offer my mother one of those cars as a gift. I looked around and the first car that caught my eye I buried in the grave of my beloved one with the blue scarf with marred sequins. My nails digging the fresh soil again. Then I turned and ran without looking back. Ran where I thought neither the clogs chasing me, the lice, nor the relatives or the humiliated hirelings could ever catch me . . .

I could have never turned back. The stones of the staired street Mukoshka and I had walked in the mornings, weeping, could have remained where traces

* The opening of the Shahada, the Muslim confession of faith, here mispronounced, as it often is in the colloquial; it sounds very close to, and is at times used instead of, *eshhe'oglueshhek*, a common insult, meaning, literally, as translated above.

remain, like those of floral prints on a fluttering paisley robe, aided by time's fading light. If I wanted to. I could have left the place where, in my father's words, people were kicked around like shit is kicked around,
I could have walked away, collecting shards of colored glass along the way. And no one better than myself could have offered me the chance. But I rejected myself. Because there in that place one person alone looked ridiculous for watching the world through a mirror. And that was me. Once, seeing my mother's love affair as my chance, I managed to step outside the "luckless" place—as I knew it because father had called it that—outside its reality. I climbed on her shoulders hardened by love and jumped atop the luckless wall. I flung myself off into the distance. I landed, I shook the dust off, straightened myself, yearned to tell her one last thing, and ran back at mad speed. The windblown straw from september roofs rained down on her head like bright yellow ashes. Her fingers, her face covered in blood, she was struggling all alone. Suddenly she caught the sound of my breathing. Flailing her arms, she kept me from getting closer. Made furious signs telling me to leave. "Go away, go, don't ever come back to these parts . . ." I couldn't go. I came back. I squandered the first political position my mother offered me. Acting out of fear, I convinced myself that I'd best fight by putting on costumes at night and making them laugh. Mine was a storytelling of sorts. After I told the tales I concocted, they did not object that I danced stark naked and worked up a sweat to collect money. They repealed all prohibitions and shames for me. They began showcasing me to guests, dragging me to the center of the room. I was free to curse people, tear their clothes, spit on their faces, stab them with pins, say unspeakable things out in public. During the day, some opportunists would whisper their innermost secrets into my ear. I did everything they asked me to do without even thinking of extorting money. I enjoyed making them laugh, making them happy. One day—perhaps they laughed at me more than usual—I began to pity them intensely . . . The feeling of pity charged into my boundless world like a wild ram. I trembled with fear while it noisily chomped down my paper stars and wasn't poisoned. From where I lay cowering, I began to pray and plead that it would get struck by the moon's electricity. A fear so immense it twisted my tongue back, inward. It pierced through my trachea. It opened the trail of fire that coursed down my mouth to my abdominal cavity, the trail I had kept concealed all my

life. It turned me into a strange creature that quietly smoldered within and was terrified by the sudden flare-ups of her lips and eyes. It invaded our room, our sofas, my mother's loose-weave bridal kilim—with small red roses against a black backdrop—that I likened to a poisonous veil cast over all of us, it invaded time inside the four walls and outside. I took a sheet in my hand, walked quietly to the southeast corner of our house. I pulled the sheet over my head. Stayed curled up.

* * *

Calves with black wet forelocks stabbing each other, when you played their part, your guttural snarls and bellows never left our ears. We recalled sadly your eyes melting like butter, oozing across your face, your hands holding the bloody knives like toys. On nights when I buried my head in the pillow, the male woodcock fluttering on top of the stairs would appear before my eyes, the one who grabbed his mother from her ankles and thrashed her on the floor. You'd push your arms between your legs and flail them behind you like a pair of wings. How you'd fold your head slowly against your belly and roll like a ball of feathers . . . You'd proudly shake the dirt and dust off you, tossing them at our faces . . . If you hadn't been defeated by shame, you'd have surely become a great folk artist. We wish you remained hanging for years as a warped mirror on our wall, reflecting your hip joints. But you couldn't bear losing your silver, flake after flake. You fell in love. You began feeling shame which quickly blunted your talent. Our room was tiny. You hid your eyes behind the stove pipe for a long time, to avoid looking at him. But your hands, your eyes, your feet would leave your body, slide along the surface of scalding water, and float toward him. You got very scared. You anxiously retrieved your hands, your feet, your eyes, gathered them on your belly, stirred quietly, then took a sheet in your hand and hid under it. For exactly seven years . . . You spent your first youth like the turtle who reluctantly extends its slender neck outside its shell from time to time. Under that sheet, the color of your eyes deepened. Your bones hardened. Your hair flowed down past your waist. We knew you often went to the back room—crawling with the sheet over you—and smelled his sweater at nights.

But we couldn't bring ourselves to ask how, under that sheet, you bore the love that blighted your youth for so many years. He'd slowly lift the sheet off your head, kneel beside you and weep. Seeing his tears, your face would turn pale, your lips would tense . . . He got scared and went far away . . .

* * *

By the time I was eighteen, my knowledge about life was a dead monster. Under that sheet, I angrily cut its ears and the tip of its nose. I pierced bloody holes all over its body on account of love, to take revenge on that grasshopper which jumped off my mother's hand and landed on me. I was like a sad murderer who walked around with pieces of ears and half of a monster's nose inside her pocket. My fingers would often rub against the remains of dead knowledge. My foot would stumble. I feared that the smell of blood would draw me back. That the monster would rise from the grave in white sheets, shriek and thrust itself upon me . . . I'd be whitewashed like a terrified girl. My breath wouldn't find a place to hide. I'd watch it fly away in dejected arcs. My mouth agape, hatred would fill me. "Ah, life, you were never mine . . ."

Seen from the inside, I resembled a sorry villager living through a second sexual awakening with a fairy maiden. In the end, my history turned out to be artificial like nylon flowers. Though I wasn't naive enough to die for this improper relationship either. I mounted the camel I made of fleas. In the small night shelter, I brought it out on stage as a marvel of class and human love.

"Honorable ladies," I said, "I swear on the sheet, the shield of my stray heart, that I knew you'd descend on earth one day and touch me with your enchanted fingers. Once I sent off the woman who brought back your news—she spoke in broken Turkish, had black veins in her eyes and long lashes—I realized I needed the sheet no more. Recalling my promise to myself, I went down to the pomegranate tree in our garden. I held the sheet to the sun and burnt it. It was a simple ceremony, not worth describing. What I mean to say is: out of the smoke and burnt swatches emerged this diamond fragment who wants to devote her being to the destitute . . ."

And how this lie changed the course of my life that once flowed like a quiet stream. My sweet dear camel I made of fleas stared and stared at my face and fell ill of grief. "Ah Gülfidan, miserable child . . . An artificial history can only be borne without lies . . ." She died deeply hurt. And took with her the piece of diamond in whose brilliance I had concealed a terrific secret.

* * *

Years later, your devastating light from the house of the dead hits our ceiling: in its glow, I am looking for this piece of diamond, mother . . . Don't think I'm greedy. I want to reunite with my terrific secret, the anger and disaffection I feel against my class. " Faked love . . ." I concocted this phrase so you understand me better. Now I know very well why I was unhappy during those ten years when I was forced to love everything I hated. What's called science cheapened my dignity, you understand. I was obliged to smash my obstinate horns with my own hammer. That's why I cried, every night for ten years, when all the hands and feet retreated to their rooms. I poisoned my lungs with remorse . . . Because I was a bad child who hated her glorious class. What a sad childhood whose hemorrhage can't be cured, this, your little daughter's . . . How I let the feeling of guilt overtake my heart . . . "Ah, gods of revolution, I'm ready to be cast in front of the wolves, for your forgiveness . . ."

* * *

If I say I resemble a poor crippled rat caught in the red glow of this science, addicted to mental strategy and tactic, and say it without concealing I've been a sly militant, an ingrate child who roused her mother from the sleep of death, what sort of mayhem would follow? Mukoshka, why shouldn't we stay away from the scales of gods, my beautiful introvert friend. What if we attack the horses, the people, the trees, with our bats, if just once . . . Look, for God's sake: as if it's not a place but some foreboding ruin long lost in an eastern legend. Neither a yellow illusion nor a faded piece of paper. Don't mistake this bizarre sight for a marvel of photography. It's real as ice: the dead one on the ceiling. Shouting, "Today, no later, learn to cry with one eye! . . ." Those in the inner room: the faithful vanguards of the revolution. Thrust your breath into the air and pray for your sister. So she can retrieve from the chimera's mouth the hatred stone she made into a star for her soul . . .

* * *

She said: The unimaginative pessimism of a simpleton operative is very depressing. Those who think the soul is made of rectangular wooden boxes —when our cause is unfortunately forced into a dark tunnel—can't resist jumping back on stage with posing magicians. To attempt a colorful spectacle while using their solid knowledge smothered inside those wooden boxes is the mark of obsessive fools only . . .

I said: Your face clear as the dew drop is full of rage, Dear Leader! It's not possible to speak with you about ghosts of knowledge, hurt camels gone to the great beyond, the diamond mass that is nothing but the word, hate. Because we've begun understanding each other.

She said: You were a rosy laughter fairy, and, inside the small night shelter, we plucked your wings' dappled plumage, pulled your gleaming teeth mercilessly. So you turned into a pesky bird of revenge? You're right, we often criticized you for laughing too much, court-martialed you in the end. "My lips are free and will remain free, comrades!" Where, in what regulation is it written that those who claim, with a mocking face, to have left a fairy-tale world to come into the small night shelter should be treated with kindness, Secretary Wind?

I said: Why did you think I've been looking for my hatred stone, Mamzelle! Obviously I don't intend to aim its glow in my eyes, to blind and cripple myself. Of course I'll taunt you with my pretty diamond. Regulations! Chilling, terrifying handbooks. Those thinly sooted articles on white glowing marbles don't get written in the inner voices of children born of adversity.

She said: Then graciously remove that fancy hair clip. Turn it over to the guardians of the revolution. Workers don't like fancy hair clips. Nasty rhymester! Now embrace me cheerfully, then go and make some coffee . . .

> A little suitcase in my hand
> I came to be your friend la la la

Still, I find the most comfort around you.

I said: Hope to god, Muawia's men didn't follow you. They alone are missing amid these ruins. Not even bat shadows are absent from our ceiling. Your red lace gloves are in the refrigerator. Your words invisible, penned with milk. The waxed paper, the glass and the India ink for printing are buried in the backyard . . .

She said: Give up comparing me to nostalgic generals after a battle. Bat shadows and Muawia's men can't intimidate me any more. Because my nerves are loose like cheese from washing dishes. And my fingers have grown supple like rubber. Sadly, those days when I took you under my arm belong to a time now undone . . . Now little concerns me . . .

I said: I understand, sir.

* * *

When I climbed to the top of our class outlook and gazed at our love—secret, circumspect, scientific—I resolved to fight to explain what I had understood. My hands feeling the void I was falling through, I only succeeded in tracing some odd shapes. The painful stirring of my body, word crumbs falling between my teeth, and sweat running down my hair to my face, ushered a mute worker to my mind.

Translated from the Turkish by Aron R. Aji

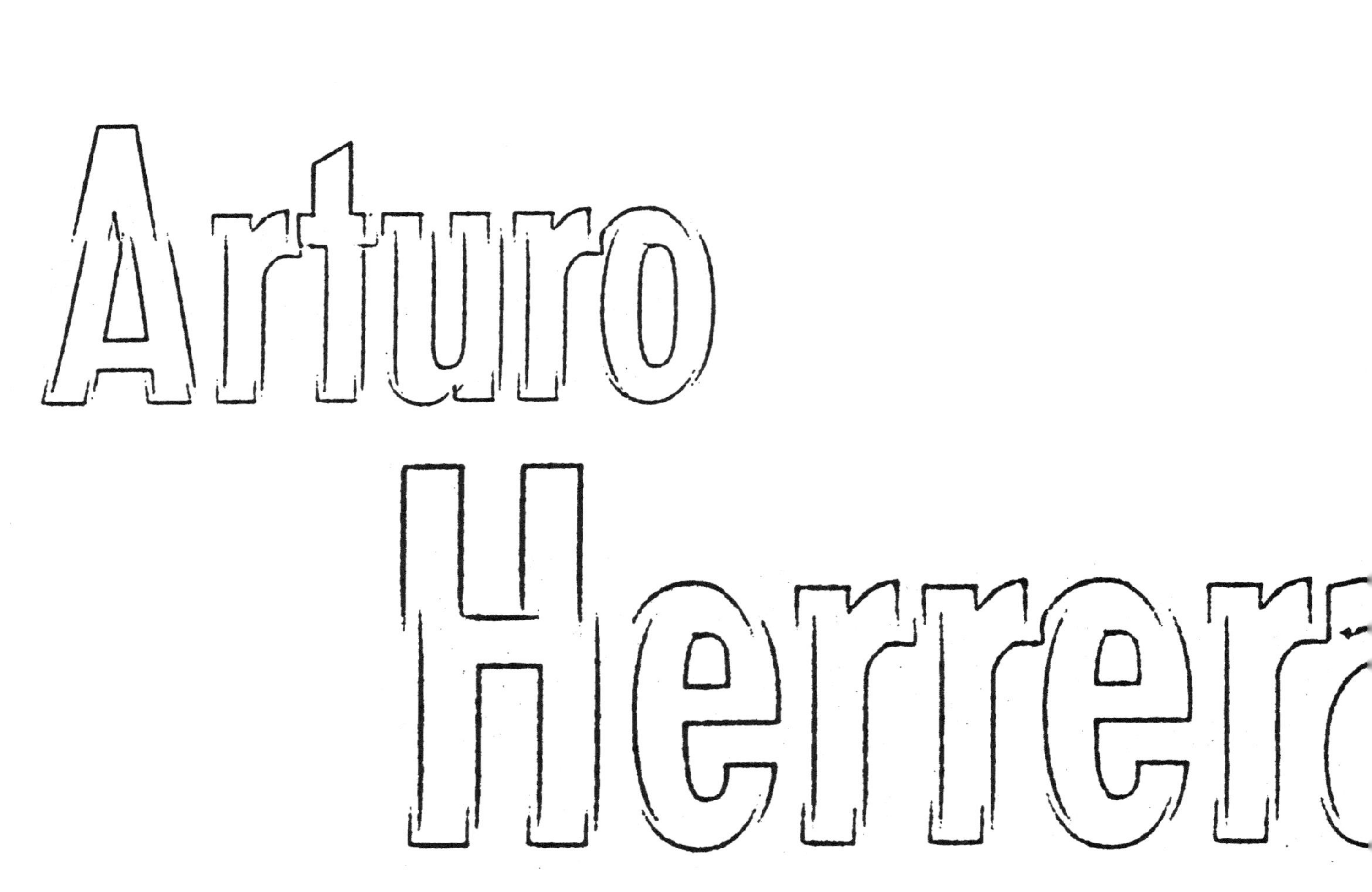
Arturo
Herrera

WONDER
NET WT 16 OZ (1 LB)

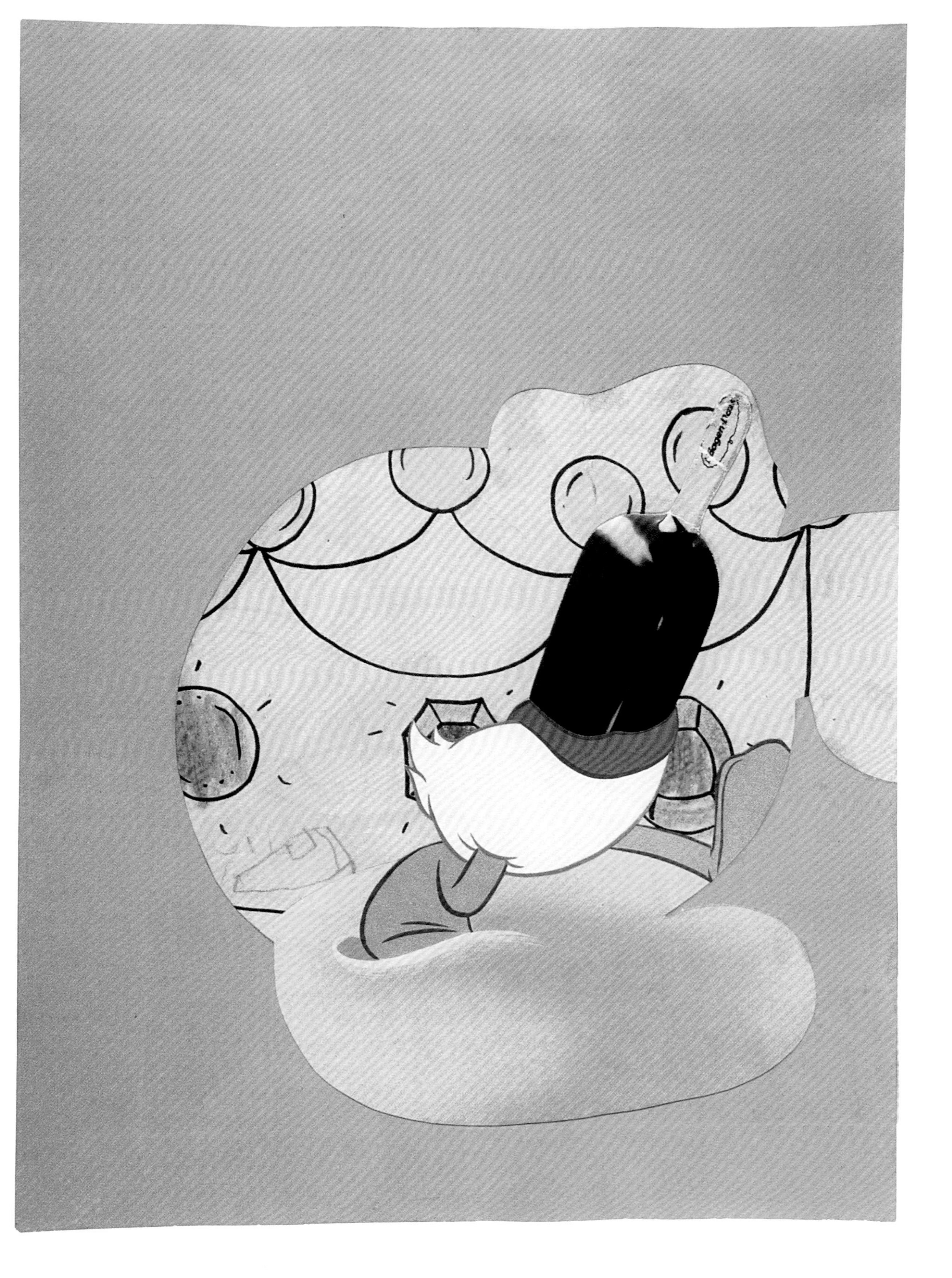

asked
"Sleepy,"
very
urry and get dressed,"
"I'm going
ke French toast."
Goody," said Sharon and starte
out of bed.
eaping, she was very surp
find herself
queen, slowly and rega
Her body felt
very hea
but smooth and sort
floaty. It w
pleasant.
ron's usual
stom in the morning was to jerk
o hard, they almost always ca
all
mped everything on the floor
er to her bureau to get so
d for
drawer handles and was sur
refully her fingers grasped
em.
wers out but her arms mov
back
pulled out gently and
far
to reach her socks wi
out any
ished she tried to give
drawer
ldn't come away.
shed the
on her
though
that
end.
73

Arturo Herrera

From the European cubists and surrealists of the early twentieth century, to the work of the British-based Independent Group in the 1950s, to American pop art in the seventies, artists have incorporated popular print material such as advertising imagery in collage to critique and celebrate the dominant culture. More recently, practitioners seem to have approached the potential of collage for dismembering and reassembling by way of an interest in the grotesque or carnival figure—one who, in Bakhtin's theory, has been turned "inside out" and displays its openings on the surface. This "body collage" has taken many forms, most famously, perhaps, in Cindy Sherman's photographs of pieced-together body parts, or in the sensationalist installations of Jake and Dinos Chapman, whose disfigured, child mannequins have been endowed with surplus or enlarged orifices. In such artworks—antiportraits—the boundary points of the body, normally guarded by taboo, become confused. The sense of an individual person or self evaporates.

Arturo Herrera's collages join these three elements of collage—the critical, the celebratory, and the grotesque—and add to this gene pool strains from the already bizarre world of fairy tales and folklore, where ideas of innocence and deviance are first introduced to the child's imagination.

Herrera's mix of cut, pasted and painted fairy-tale figures, coloring book images, advertisements, and abstract, painterly marks creates a region of *collision*, a liminal zone in a state of constant penetration and transformation. Here, no single image is allowed autonomy. Each element in a single work is occluded, violated, played with. In one example a shiny, chocolate-covered Häagen-Dazs ice cream bar from a magazine ad protrudes, not so innocently, from the striding legs and torso of Donald Duck. This duck-cum-ice-cream has been isolated in the rounded frame that typically comes at the end of a television cartoon—the type that gradually closes around the image, like an iris in a lens. In the mostly obscured background of this bubble, which is surrounded by an expanse of monotone beige, pictures from a coloring book have been partially filled in, or their boundaries exceeded, with an innocent sense of disregard for the prescribed dictum to stay within the lines. In another collage, Herrera has scribbled furiously in pink crayon over cartoon figures and furniture, causing Tweety Bird to dissolve into the support on which he stands. Tweety looks over—bewildered—at the scene beside him, in which a teddy bear has been flattened by the combined pressure of a Wonder bread wrapper and a phallus-shaped cutout. A brownish abstract wash seeps out from underneath the bear. Here and elsewhere, the complex layering precludes logical visual decoding—which scene came first, what figure went under where, and whether, in the end, abstraction or figuration wins out.

In his collages, Herrera creates a childlike site of "imagination" with a sophisticated sense of the interpretive implications—psychological and cultural—of his archives. The resulting images toy with our desire to recognize forms or characters in much the same way that we try to decipher the abstract and read meaning into gesture and color. Herrera's collages thwart our attempts to identify a cohesive tale, but in searching for a plot we become happily lost in leapfrogging, associative, and impulsive reading of his hybrid maps.

Jessica Morgan

JO ANN WASSERMAN

Portrait

In Kentucky there are pancakes for breakfast and coffee tasting of donations, precisely ironed, creamer, Chinese blue and white.

Black, what a lot of black. How do you cut that down to size? She was a famous widow. A small seat for a large widow. I could not eat straight all the way through. “If it could be a bit longer so as to extend above the piano,” they instructed. They used words like genius. “American genius.” They said, “Color is your strength.”

Two years of cold hands while I imagined Kentucky or Kansas or any place people eat from steamy bowls. Today there is a famous widow pressed dark iris in the pages of these thin walls. “It just doesn’t suit,” they concluded. Small and at the bottom remains a child’s prayer, “Gift of Madame . . .”

Miracle Cure

She chewed it into poultice, a flowering rose, shreds of newspaper. Face shiny as an island vacation. Unfortunately I could not say exactly where to and so she smiled frozen cocktail sunshine, the straw bag dangling from her wrist. This won't hurt a bit, she said, placing a spoonful of the rose poultice on my tongue. Purple fan skirts, the brushing suede of steps close to my right side. My peripheral vision is all shot to hell. It's no good. I can't tell you what she is up to now. I hear sounds of pigeon wings, twirling skirts and the first time I dove perfectly into green water. I was willing. Swallowed. I wanted it to work.

Commerce

Rust in the pipes, in the food,
In the air of the storeroom,
Virginia creeper covering the screens

Where the men peer, disease in the air,
Just what the ladies fear,
They can't win and they fucken know it,
Says Frank.
Or as they stand and smile for the TV woman
Next to the camera. All these years
And we're still heroes

* * *

The rest of life always less noisy.
Cleats
On concrete where the ballfield
Turns into factory property.
All of it, behind the heat,
Behind the sawdust of breath,
Behind the torpor

* * *

Stepping to the curb
From the bistro, youthful windows
Higher up where music pounds.
The ladies know all about it

Angry rain on a copper roof

Zigzag line in the tree trunk—

Near the fields
Where condos are rising,
Empty hayracks in moonlight

The ladies applaud,
But the men have grown agitated,
Fingering their car keys. Losing their gravity

  Slippery road of sweat,
Puzzling your way to forgetfulness . . .

* * *

Cul-de-sac of stiff air, country good-will—
with everything they thought they'd left
Dangling in an alley, colloquies of sunlight
On scarred block

Everything resolved.
Bricks set so carefully
Into moist ground . . .

* * *

A recurrence

A sort of ticker-tape,
Bid and asked
Popping like a stick down a picket fence

Getting Purchase On Ice

That was a terrible time
When I came home from Canada

Found you in bed with the landlord.
Ha, she breathes

Black hair with flashes of white
Expectations wound with a piety

Elizabeth says, I've simplified,
Made order for myself

It's amazing what's happened

I don't even think about it.
(lying, of course)

What about Iris?

She asks.

Past willows, swans in open water—

Elizabeth
Moving in and out of enemy territory
Like a courier

You weren't any better, she says.

With dark bark of winter trees,
Hanging pines—a swivet
Out of nothingness. Shadow—

25 years,
I'm still hitching my breath

We took a walk on the country road
From the lake to the violin maker's house
For schnapps.
Sun out again, quiet, gravel slightly frozen,
A lip of dry snow

CONTRIBUTORS

Aron Aji, born in Izmir, Turkey, is an associate professor of comparative literature at Butler University in Indianapolis. He is the editor of *Milan Kundera and the Art of Fiction* (Garland Press) and has published articles on Salman Rushdie, Milan Kundera, Chinua Achebe, and others.

Yehuda Amichai's book of poetry *Open Closed Open* will be published by Harcourt Brace in the fall of 2000.

Manuel Bauer was born in 1966 in Switzerland and studied photography at the Zurich School of Art and Design. He worked as a freelance photojournalist in England, Egypt, Norway, India, Sri Lanka, Sicily, Germany, the United States, Spain, and Croatia until 1990, when he co-founded the Lookat Agency in Zurich. His prints and photo essays have been published in Europe and the U.S., in such journals as *Du*, *Geo*, and *Time*.

Ingmar Bergman was born in Uppsala, Sweden, in 1918. His work in the theater, opera, film, and television spans some sixty years and includes almost fifty films and more than 120 stage productions. He received the Academy Award for *The Virgin Spring*, *Through a Glass Darkly*, and *Fanny and Alexander*. His most recent film, *Faithless*, was produced this year for Swedish television. The interview in this issue of *Grand Street* was filmed for broadcast in Sweden, France, and Germany, and was a coproduction of Top Story Films, Arte Broadcasting, and Swedish Television.

Chana Bloch is a poet and translator and the director of the creative writing program at Mills College in Oakland. Her new book of poems, *Mrs. Dumpty*, will be published in the fall of 1998.

Don Bogen is the author of two books of poetry, *The Known World* and *After the Splendid Display*, both from Wesleyan University Press. He teaches at the University of Cincinnati.

Christian Boltanski was born in Paris in 1944. Recent exhibitions of his work have been held at the Villa Medici, Rome, the Belvedere du Chateau, Prague, and the Malmö Konsthall, Malmö, Sweden. He lives and works in Paris. His work is represented in the United States by the Marian Goodman Gallery.

Susan Breall has been an assistant district attorney in San Francisco since 1984. She has been prosecuting felony domestic violence cases exclusively since 1990, and is the Chief of the Criminal Division of the San Francisco District Attorney's Office for all crimes of violence against women, children, the elderly, and intimate partners. She specializes in working with underserved populations, in particular undocumented immigrant women who have been victims of domestic violence.

Bertolt Brecht was born in Augsburg, Bavaria, in 1898. He started writing both plays and poetry during the First World War. His career in the left-wing avant-garde theater in Berlin was interrupted in 1933 when he went into exile, at first in Denmark and then, retreating from the advancing German army, in Sweden and Finland. The poem in this issue of *Grand Street* was written in Svendborg, Denmark, in 1938. After living in California from 1941 to 1947, Brecht returned to East Berlin in 1949 where he founded the Berliner Ensemble. Among his plays are *Mother Courage and Her Children*, *The Good Woman of Sezchuan*, and *The Caucasian Chalk Circle*. He died in 1956. "A Visit to the Banished Poets" will appear in a forthcoming new edition of his poetry, edited and translated by Tom Kuhn and Michael Morley, to be published by Methuen in Britain and Arcade in the United States.

Guy Brett is a writer living in London. He was art critic for *The Times* during the 1960s and has contributed many articles to the international art press. His books include *Kinetic Art* (1968), *Through Our Eyes: Popular Art and Modern History* (1986), *Transcontinental: Nine Latin American Artists* (1990), and a monograph on David Medalla, *Exploding Galaxies* (London: Kala Press, 1995). He is currently putting together a book and an exhibition of the work of Li Yuan-chia.

Andrew Bromfield was born in Hull, England, and graduated in Russian studies from the University of Sussex. His career has included teaching Russian for twelve years, as well as teaching English in Yerevan, Soviet Armenia. From 1988 to 1993, he lived and worked in Moscow, where he was involved in founding *Glas*, an English-language journal of contemporary Russian writing, which he coedited. His translation of Victor Pelevin's *The Life of Insects* (Farrar, Straus & Giroux, 1998) was recently shortlisted for the Weidenfeld Translation Prize in England.

Peter Brook was born in London. He received his M.A. from Oxford. He has directed over fifty productions since 1943, and has staged his work all over the world. In London, as the codirector of the Royal Shakepeare Company, his productions included *King Lear*, *Marat/Sade*, *A Midsummer Night's Dream*, and *Antony and Cleopatra*. In 1971, he founded the Centre International de Créations Théâtrales in Paris. His theater productions at Bouffes du Nord have included *Timon of Athens*, *Measure for Measure*, *Conference of the Birds*, *The Cherry Orchard*, *The Mahabharata*, *The Tempest*, *The Man Who*, *Oh les beaux jours*, and most recently *Je suis un phénomène*. His films include *Lord of the Flies*, *Marat/Sade*, *King Lear*, and *Meetings with Remarkable Men*. He is the author of several books including *The Empty Space*, *The Shifting Point*, and *Threads of Time: Recollections*, published in 1998 by Counterpoint.

Juan Cameron was born in Valparaíso, Chile, in 1947. He spent some years in Argentina in the early 1970s and ten years in exile in Sweden during the later years of the Pinochet dictatorship. With the return of the democratic government in Chile, he returned to the city of his birth. Under very difficult circumstances, first the dictatorship and then while in exile, he wrote and published ten volumes of poetry. He has won numerous literary prizes including the 1997 Premio Internacional de la Poesía "Encina de la Cañada."

Peter Constantine was born in London and grew up in Greece. He has written on the languages and cultures of the Far East and has had pieces published in *The New Yorker*, *Harper's Magazine*, *Fiction*, and *London Magazine*, among others. His most recent book of translations, *Six Early Stories* by Thomas Mann, published by Sun & Moon Press, was awarded the 1998 PEN/Book of the Month Club Translation Prize. He is the translator of *The Undiscovered Chekhov: 38 New Stories*, to be published by Seven Stories Press in the fall of 1998.

Joseph Cornell was born in 1903 and died in 1972. He lived and worked on Utopia Parkway in Queens, New York. A large selection of his work will be presented in the exhibition *Joseph Cornell/Marcel Duchamp: In Residence*, which will open in October 1998 at the Philadelphia Museum of Art and will travel to the Menil Collection in Houston, Texas.

C.A.A. Dellschau (1830–1923), inventor, scientist, and visionary, was born in Prussia, and immigrated to the United States in 1853. Dellschau lived in Texas and possibly California, serving in the Civil War with the Confederacy. After 1900, Dellschau lived in Houston and devoted himself to the making of his aeronautical notebooks until his death. These notebooks resurfaced in the 1960s, barely escaping destruction at the city dump. Examples of his work are currently at the Menil Collection, Houston, and the San Antonio Art Association Museum. Selections from Dellschau's oeuvre of five thousand notebook drawings were recently exhibited at Ricco/Maresca Gallery in New York, the first time they had been seen outside of Texas.

Diastème is the author of *Les papas et les mamans*, published in 1997 by Editions d'Olivier, from which "Like, My Father" is excerpted in this issue. He is a contributor to the magazines *Première* and *20 Ans* and lives in Paris.

Jörn Donner was born in 1933 in Helsinki. An author, film director, and producer, he wrote and directed two films on Ingmar Bergman, *The Bergman File* and *Three Scenes with Ingmar Bergman*, and was the producer of *Fanny and Alexander*. Donner has served as a member of parliament in Finland and was the Finnish cultural attaché in Los Angeles from 1995 to 1996. He lives in Stockholm.

Thomas Sayers Ellis's poetry has appeared in *The American Poetry Review*, *AGNI*, *Best American Poetry 1997*, *Boston Review*, *GrandStreet*, *The Kenyon Review*, *Ploughshares*, *The Southern Review*, and *The Garden Thrives: Twentieth-Century African-American Poetry*. He has received fellowships from The MacDowell Colony, The Fine Arts Work Center in Provincetown, and Yaddo. In 1993 he coedited *On the Verge: Emerging Poets and Artists* (Faber & Faber). His first collection, *The Good Junk*, was published in the Graywolf Annual *Take Three* in 1996. He is currently assistant professor of English and African-American literature at Case Western Reserve University.

Laurent Feneyrou has written widely on music in France and Italy, and has worked with the Festival d'Automne in Paris and the Festival International d'Art Lyrique at Aix-en-Provence. His collection of interviews with the composer Philippe Fénelon, *Arrière-Pensées* (Musica Falsa) was published this year to accompany a production of Fénelon's *Salammbô* at the Bastille Opera in Paris. He lives in Paris.

Cola Franzen is the translator of Juan Cameron, Alicia Borinsky, and Saúl Yurkievich. Her recent translations include Borinsky's *Dreams of the Abandoned Seducer* (University of Nebraska Press). Forthcoming work includes *Horses in the Air: Selected Poems* by Jorge Guillén (City Lights, fall 1998) and *Background Noise* by Saúl Yurkievich (Sun & Moon Press, summer 1998).

Arthur Goldhammer was recently awarded the French-American Foundation Translation Prize for his translation of *Realms of Memory*, edited by Pierre Nora and published by Columbia University Press.

Lynda Roscoe Hartigan is deputy chief curator of the National Museum of American Art at the Smithsonian Institution in Washington, D.C. Since 1978 she has been the curator of the museum's Joseph Cornell Study Center.

Robert Hass was Poet Laureate of the United States, 1995–97, and is a professor of Slavic languages and literature at the University of California at Berkeley.

Arturo Herrera was born in Venezuela in 1959. In 1992 he received his MFA from the University of Illinois at Chicago. Then in 1997 he took up residence in New York City, having received awards from the Louis Comfort Tiffany Foundation and the Marie Walsh Sharpe Art Foundation. In 1998 he had solo shows at the Worcester Art Museum in Massachusetts, the Renaissance Society of the University of Chicago, and Wooster Gardens. He will be a resident at ArtPace in San Antonio, Texas, in 1999. He is represented in New York by Wooster Gardens/Brent Sikkema.

Susan Hiller was born in Tallahassee, Florida, in 1945 and has lived in London since 1973. Hiller has been the subject of several one-person museum exhibitions, including a retrospective in 1986 at the ICA, London, and in 1996 at the Tate Gallery, London. Her work in media ranging from drawing to video, has been seen most recently in group exhibitions at the Louisiana Museum of Modern Art, Humleabaek, the Tate Gallery, London, and in the 1997 Sydney Biennial and the 1998 Adelaide Festival. Hiller's large-vitrine installation, *From the Freud Museum*, will be exhibited at the Museum of Modern Art, New York, in 1998. She will have solo exhibitions in the same year in Caracas, Oslo, London, and New York. She has recently been awarded a Guggenheim Fellowship.

Andrew Hurley's translation of the *Collected Fictions* of Jorge Luis Borges will be published by Viking in September 1998. He has translated widely in Latin American literature, including most recently, *The Color of Summer* by Reinaldo Arenas, which will be published by Viking in 1999.

Franck André Jamme lives and works in Paris and in Burgundy, France. Since 1981, he has published eight volumes of poetry and fragments, such as *Absence de résidence et pratique du songe*, *La Récitation de l'oubli*, *De la multiplication des brèches et des obstacles*, and *Pour les simples* as well as numerous limited editions illustrated by such artists as Zao Wou-Ki, Acharya Vyakul, Olivier Debré, James Brown, Marc Couturier, and Monique Frydman, among others. His poetry was included in the anthology *The New French Poetry* (Bloodaxe Books).

Chana Kronfeld is an associate professor of Hebrew and comparative literature at the University of California at Berkeley. She is the author of *On the Margins of Modernism*.

Tom Kuhn is a literary scholar and translator who teaches at St. Hugh's College in Oxford. He is a general editor of the Methuen English edition of the collected works of Brecht, in which his translation of the verse play *Round Heads and Pointed Heads* is forthcoming. A further volume of poems in translation is also in preparation.

António Lobo Antunes, born in Lisbon in 1942, is a psychiatrist by training and still practices his profession on a part-time basis. He has published twelve novels and has been translated into a dozen languages. *The Inquistor's Manual*, his penultimate novel and a best-seller in Germany, will be published in 2000 by Metropolitan Books. His other novels include *Explanation of the Birds*, *Fado Alexandrino*, and *Auto dos Danados*.

Bernadette Mayer is the author of three books, *Midwinter Day*, *The Bernadette Mayer Reader*, and *Mutual Aid*. Her most recent book, *Two Haloed Mourners*, will be published in 1998 by Grand Army Press.

Susan Meiselas is an award-winning documentary photographer best known for her work in Central America. In 1978 Meiselas received the Robert Capa Gold Medal for "outstanding courage and reporting" in recognition of her coverage of the Nicaraguan insurrection that same year. In 1992 she was named a MacArthur Fellow. Her photographs have been published worldwide in the pages of *Time*, *The New York Times*, *Paris Match*, and *Life*, among others. She is the editor of *Learn to See* (Polaroid Foundation, 1975), *El Salvador: Work of 30 Photographers* (Writers & Readers, 1983), and *Chile from Within* (W.W. Norton, 1990). Her most recent book, *Kurdistan: In the Shadow of History* (Random House, 1997), is a hundred-year pictorial history of the Kurdish people. The portfolio of work featured in this issue of *Grand Street* is part of her current work in progress, *Archives of Abuse*. Meiselas is a member of Magnum Photos and lives in New York City.

Charles Merewether is a collections curator and specialist in the area of Spanish- and Portuguese-language cultures at the Getty Research Institute, Los Angeles. He has taught at the Universidad Nacional de Bogotá, the University of Sydney, the Universidad Autonoma, Barcelona, and the Universidad Iberoamericana, Mexico City. He is the author of the forthcoming *What Remains: Ana Mendieta*, as well as *Art and Social Commitment: An End to the City of Dreams 1931–1948* (Art Gallery of New South Wales, 1984). He has written extensively on the reinvention of modernism in non-European cultures, especially in Latin America, and more recently, on cultural memory and monuments. He is currently writing a book on art and the archive.

Czeslaw Milosz received the 1978 Neustadt International Prize in Literature and the 1980 Nobel Prize in Literature. Since 1961 he has been a professor of Slavic languages and literature at the University of California at Berkeley. His new book, *Road-Side Dog*, translated by Czeslaw Milosz and Robert Hass, will be published in November 1998 by Farrar, Straus & Giroux.

Jessica Morgan is curator of contemporary art at the Worcester Art Museum in Worcester, Massachusetts. She is currently working on an exhibition of art, architecture, gender, and urban space featuring the work of Marjetica Potrc, Sophie Tottie, and Rita McBride. She lives in Cambridge, Massachusetts, and New York City.

Peter Nagy is an American artist who is based in New Delhi. The most recent exhibition of his works was held in June 1997 at the Nicole Klagsbrun Gallery in New York. From 1982 to 1988 he was the director of Gallery Nature Morte in New York's East Village. He has recently resurrected Nature Morte as a commercial curatorial project in New Delhi, combining Indian and international contemporary art.

Bruce Nauman was born in 1941 in Fort Wayne, Indiana. Initially a painter, Nauman had abandoned the medium by the mid-1960s for sculpture, performance art, and film. His first solo museum exhibition was co-organized by the Los Angeles County Museum of Art and the Whitney Museum of American Art, New York, in 1972. In 1994, a retrospective of his work was organized by the Walker Art Center, Minneapolis and traveled to the Hirshhorn Museum, Washington D.C., and the Museum of Modern Art, New York. Currently, an exhibition *Bruce Nauman: Image/Text, 1966–1996* is on view at the Hayward Gallery in London, and will travel to the Museum of Contemporary Art in Helsinki in October 1998. Nauman lives and works in Galisteo, New Mexico. His work is represented in New York by Sperone Westwater Gallery.

Michael O'Brien's *The Floor and the Breadth* was published by Cairn Editions in 1994. His seventh book of poems, *Sills*, is forthcoming from Zoland Books.

Alan Michael Parker's first collection of poems, *Days Like Prose*, was published by Alef Books in 1997; his second, *Poems About the Vandals*, will be published by BOA Editions in 1999. He teaches at Davidson College in North Carolina.

Victor Pelevin was born in Moscow in 1962. He has received degrees from the Moscow Institute of Power Engineering and from the Russian Institute of Literature. His work has been translated into French, German, Japanese, and English. His collection of short stories, *The Blue Lantern* (New Directions), won the 1993 Russian Booker short-story prize, and his novel *Omon Ra* (Farrar, Straus & Giroux) was among those nominated for the 1993 Russian Booker Prize. "Sleep" will be included in *A Werewolf Problem in Central Russian and Other Stories*, a collection forthcoming from New Directions in November 1998.

Edgardo Rodríguez Juliá was born in Río Piedras, Puerto Rico, in 1946. He is the author of eleven works of fiction and several collections of short stories and essays, and teaches Hispanic literature at the University of Puerto Rico. In 1982 he was a Guggenheim Fellow. His first novel, *La renuncia del héroe Baltasar*, was published in translation as *The Renunciation* by Four Walls Eight Windows Press in 1997. "Up on the Roof" is an excerpt from his 1988 book *Puertorriqueños: Album de la sagrada familia puertorriqueña a partir de 1898*, published by Editorial Plaza Mayor in Madrid.

Daniel Rothenberg teaches in the Law & Society Program at the University of California at Irvine. For two years he was an outreach worker and paralegal with a federally funded legal-services program for migrant workers in Florida. This article is based on excerpts from *With These Hands: The Hidden World of Migrant Farmworkers Today*, which is being published by Harcourt Brace in October 1998.

Rianna Scheepers was born in Vryheid, Natal, South Africa in 1957, and grew up on a farm in Zululand. A white Afrikaner, she has been deeply involved in Zulu culture and has taught at the University of Zululand. Since the easing of South African censorship in 1990, she has written one novel and five short-story collections. Scheepers has received the Eugene Marais Literary Prize awarded by the South African Academy of Arts and Sciences, The Afrikaans Language and Culture Association Prize, and The Association of Afrikaans Culture Prize. She is an editor at Tafelberg Publishers in Cape Town, and in 1997 brought out an anthology of South African women's writing in Afrikaans.

John Sidgwick is the program translator for the Festival international d'art lyrique at Aix-en-Provence.

Charles Simic is a poet, essayist, and a translator. His new collection of poems, due in spring 1998 from Harcourt Brace, is called *Jackstraws*. He won the Pulitzer Prize in 1990.

William Steen is an artist, collector, and connoisseur of self-taught art and Tibetan ritual art, a BACA horseshoe champion, and frame designer at the Menil Collection in Houston. Since 1985 Steen has studied, collected, and worked with Texas prison visionary artists, Frank Jones and Henry Ray Clark, a.k.a. The Magnificent Pretty Boy. Steen currently exhibits paintings and drawings at the Moody Gallery in Houston. During the last three years, Steen has traveled to India and Nepal to research and document the miniature ritual images of Tibetan Bon (the indigenous religion of Tibet predating Buddhism).

Terese Svoboda's most recent book of poetry is *Mere Mortals* (University of Georgia Press). Her second novel, *Ghost Test*, will be published by Counterpoint Press in the spring 1999.

Joan Tate translated Ingmar Bergman's latest television film, *Faithless*. She also translated his novels *Private Confessions* and *The Best Intentions*, both published by Arcade, as well as *The Magic Lantern: An Autobiography* (Viking, 1989). Her other translations include novels by Kerstin Ekman, and Marianne Fredriksson. She lives in Shrewsbury, England.

Latife Tekin was born in 1957 in the central Anatolian city of Kayseri. She and her family moved to Istanbul in 1966. Her first novel, *Dear Shameless Death*, was published in 1983, followed by *Berji Kristin, Tales from Garbage Hills* (1984), *Night Lessons* (1986), and *Swords of Ice* (1989). She has been translated into English, French, German, Dutch, Persian, and Spanish. In 1998 the French translation of *Dear Shameless Death* was named one of the year's ten most important European novels. The excerpt included in this issue of *Grand Street* is from her novel *Night Lessons*.

Robert VanderMolen lives and works as a house painter in Grand Rapids, Michigan, where he was born in 1947. His most recent collection of poetry, *Peaches*, appeared in 1998. Other works include *Of Pines*, *Night Weather*, *Circumstances*, and *Along the River*. He received an NEA Fellowship in 1995. In recent years his poems have appeared in *Grand Street*, *Sulfur*, *Epoch*, and *Parnassus*.

Alicia Vogl Sáenz lives in Los Angeles and is currently working on her manuscript *Hair Pieces*.

Acharya Vyakul was born in 1930. He began to paint in secret in the early 1950s, and did not show his work publicly for almost forty years. His work was first introduced in the exhibition *Magiciens de la Terre*, Centre Georges Pompidou in Paris which was curated by Jean-Hubert Martin. Since then, Vyakul has had exhibitions in a number of countries, including France, England, South Africa, Turkey, and the United States. He lives and works in Jaipur, India.

Jo Ann Wasserman is a poet currently living in San Francisco. Her work has previously appeared in *The World* and *The Poetry Project Newsletter*.

Bengt Wanselius is a theatrical photographer based in Stockholm. His photographs of Ingmar Bergman's production of *The Bacchae* appeared in *Grand Street* 42.

Christian Wiman's first book of poetry, *The Long Home*, won the Nicholas Roerich Prize and will be published in November 1998 by Story Line Press.

Richard Zenith, who was awarded a National Endowment for the Arts Fellowship to translate two novels by António Lobo Antunes (both published by Grove Press), is now translating Antunes's *The Natural Order of Things*, to be published by Henry Holt in 1999. Zenith also writes and translates poetry. His *Fernando Pessoa & Co.— Selected Poems* was published earlier in 1998 by Grove Press.

Grand Street would like to thank **Stéphane Lissner** and **Anita Le Van** of the Festival international d'art lyrique at Aix-en-Provence, and **Arthur Goldhammer**, for their help with the **Peter Brook** conversation, and **Natasha Parry Brook** for recommending the interview with **Ingmar Bergman**. *Grand Street* is also grateful to **Ann Temkin** and **Ben Anastas** for their assistance with this issue.

Grand Street would like to thank the following for their generous support:
Edward Lee Cave
Cathy and Stephen Graham
Dominic Man-Kit Lam
The New York State Council on the Arts
Betty and Stanley K. Sheinbaum

JACOB'S
RITZ
PHILEAS FOGG
Thankfully Cool
TORTILLA

ILLUSTRATIONS

Front Cover
Arturo Herrera, Untitled, 1997–98. Mixed-media collage on paper, 12 x 9 in. Courtesy of the artist and Wooster Gardens/Brent Sikkema, New York.

Back Cover
Bruce Nauman, video still from *Green Horses*, 1988. Two color video monitors, two videotape players, one video projector, two videotapes (color, sound), one chair. Dimensions variable. Collection of Mr. and Mrs. Szwajcer, Antwerp. Copyright © Bruce Nauman/Artists Rights Society (ARS), New York.

Title Page
Marcel Duchamp, *With Hidden Noise (Ball of Twine)*, 1916. Assisted Readymade: ball of twine between two brass plates, joined by four long screws, containing a small unknown object added by Walter Arensberg, 5 x 5 x 5 1/8 in. Collection of the Philadelphia Musuem of Art, The Louise and Walter Arensberg Collection. Photo courtesy of the Philadelphia Museum of Art.

Table of Contents
Packing lettuce near Bakersfield, California, 1996. Photograph by Daniel Rothenberg.

pp. 17, 22, and 26 All photographs courtesy of the Association pour le Festival international d'art lyrique et l'Académie europćene de musique d'Aix-en-Provence.

pp. 32–41 Joseph Cornell, *L'agriculture pratique*. Twelve pages from Untitled Book Object (*Journal d'agriculture pratique et Journal de l'agriculture*), c. 1933–mid-1940s. Volume twenty-two altered with collages, cutouts, and pen-and-ink designs; folder containing seventeen additional collages, 1 3/4 x 7 3/8 x 10 5/8 in. (closed). Copyright © the Joseph and Robert Cornell Memorial Foundation. Photos courtesy of the Joseph Cornell Study Center, National Museum of American Art, Smithsonian Institution, Washington D.C.

pp. 65–68 Susan Hiller, *The Secrets of Sunset Beach*. Four color photographs from *The Secrets of Sunset Beach*, 1987. Ten hand printed R-type photographs, each 22 1/4 x 18 5/16 in. Courtesy of the artist.

pp. 98 and 102 Photographs courtesy of Edgardo Rodríguez Juliá.

pp. 104–108 Five paintings by Acharya Vyakul. Titles and dates appear with images. **p. 104** 9 3/16 x 6 13/16 in. **p. 105** 10 7/16 x 7 13/16 in. **p. 106** 8 3/16 x 11 15/16 in. **p. 107** 5 3/4 x 5 11/16 in. **p. 108** 8 9/16 x 6 3/16 in. All natural pigment on paper. Courtesy of the artist and Galerie du Jour Agnès B., Paris.

pp. 112, 114, 116, and 120–121 All photographs by Daniel Rothenberg. **p. 112** Tomato picker, Mendota, California, 1996. **p. 114** Woman harvesting grapes near Delano, California, 1996. **p. 116** Harvesting celery near Salinas, California, 1996. **p. 120–121** Hand-harvesting lettuce, Huron, California, 1996.

pp. 137–140 Susan Meiselas, *Archives of Abuse*. Four collages from a work in progress, 1992/1998. Color photographs, xeroxed reports, felt-tip marker, and paper clips, all 11 x 8 1/2 in. Courtesy of the artist.

pp. 151, 152, 155, 156 and 158–159 Christian Boltanski, *Reserve Detective III*, 1987. Mixed-media installation. Wooden shelves with cardboard boxes, photographs, stories, and twelve black lamps. Courtesy of the artist and Marian Goodman Gallery, New York.

pp. 162–163, 164–165, 168, 169 and 170 Three works by Bruce Nauman. Titles and dates appear with images. **pp. 162–163** Photographs and tape, 20 x 30 1/4 in. **pp. 164–165** Two color video monitors, two videotape players, one video projector, two videotapes (color, sound), one chair. Dimensions variable. Collection of Mr. and Mrs. Szwajcer, Antwerp. **pp. 168, 169, and 170** Two color video monitors, two videodisc players, two videodiscs (color, sound). Dimensions variable. Marx Collection, Berlin. All images copyright © Bruce Nauman/Artists Rights Society (ARS), New York. Photographs courtesy of the artist.

pp. 173–176 C.A.A. Dellschau, *Sky Lubrication*. Titles and dates appear with images. All watercolor, pencil, and black ink on paper with newsprint. **p. 173** 18 x 16 1/2 in. **p. 174** 16 5/8 x 19 in. **p. 175** 14 x 18 1/2 in. **p. 176** 17 x 19 in. Courtesy of the Menil Collection, Houston.

pp. 180 and 188 Photographs copyright © Bengt Wanselius.

pp. 196–202 Manuel Bauer, *The Sinicization of Tibet*. Eight black-and-white photographs, all 1996. Captions appear with images. All images copyright © Manuel Bauer/Lookat Photos, Zurich.

pp. 225–228 Five collages by Arturo Herrera from a group of untitled collages, 1997–1998. All mixed-media collage on paper, 12 x 9 in. Courtesy of the artist and Wooster Gardens/Brent Sikkema, New York.

Treat yourself. Treat a friend.
NEW LETTERS
"One of the best literary journals in this country."
Charles Simic, Pulitzer Prize for Poetry
New Letters quarterly has, for more than 60 years, published fiction, art, poetry and essays by the world's finest new and established writers, including Pulitzer Prize winners, National Book Award winners and Nobel Laureates.
NEW LETTERS
LITERARY AWARD WINNERS
NEW LETTERS
NEW LETTERS
THE WRITER'S VOICE
"New Letters is one of the very few indispensable literary magazines."
— Susan Fromberg Schaeffer, novelist
Often selected for The Best American Poetry, The Best American Essays, Prize Stories: The O. Henry Awards, The Pushcart Prize Anthology and many other honors. Join our family of subscribers.
Magazine subscription rates
Individuals: $17 one year
$28 two years
$55 five years
Libraries: $20 one year
$34 two years
$65 five years
New Letters, University of Missouri-Kansas City, Kansas City, MO 64110

GRAND STREET
BACK ISSUES
GRAND STREET 59 TIME
Fetishes
GRAND STREET 53
Egos
GRAND STREET 55
Dreams
GRAND STREET 56
Edward Ruscha
Terry Southern
Dirt
GRAND STREET 57
GRAND STREET 58 DISGUISES
GRAND STREET 60 PARANOIA
GRAND STREET 61 ALL-AMERICAN
William T. Vollmann
Octavio Paz
Peter Sellars
Reinaldo Arenas
Mike Davis
Doris Salcedo

36
Edward W. Said on Jean Genet; Terry Southern & Dennis Hopper on Larry Flynt
STORIES: Elizabeth Bishop, William T. Vollmann; PORTFOLIOS: William Eggleston, Saul Steinberg; POEMS: John Ashbery, Bei Dao.

37
William S. Burroughs on guns; John Kenneth Galbraith on JFK's election
STORIES: Pierrette Fleutiaux, Eduardo Galeano; PORTFOLIOS: *Blackboard Equations*, John McIntosh; POEMS: Clark Coolidge, Suzanne Gardinier.

38
Kazuo Ishiguro & Kenzaburo Oe on Japanese literature; Julio Cortázar's HOPSCOTCH: A Lost Chapter
STORIES: Fernando Pessoa, Ben Sonnenberg; PORTFOLIOS: Linda Connor, Robert Rauschenberg; POEMS: Jimmy Santiago Baca, Charles Wright.

39
Nadine Gordimer: SAFE HOUSES; James Miller on Michel Foucault
STORIES: Hervé Guibert, Dubravka Ugrešić; PORTFOLIOS: *Homicide: Bugsy Siegel*, Mark di Suvero; POEMS: Amiri Baraka, Michael Palmer.

40
Gary Giddins on Dizzy Gillespie; Toni Morrison on race and literature
STORIES: Yehudit Katzir, Marcel Proust; PORTFOLIOS: Gretchen Bender, Brice Marden; POEMS: Arkadii Dragomoshchenko, Tom Paulin.

41
Nina Berberova on the Turgenev Library; Mary-Claire King on tracing "the disappeared"
STORIES: Ben Okri, Kurt Schwitters; PORTFOLIOS: Louise Bourgeois, Jean Tinguely; POEMS: Rae Armantrout, Eugenio Montale.

42
David Foster Wallace: THREE PROTRUSIONS; Henry Green: an unfinished novel
STORIES: Félix de Azúa, Eduardo Galeano; PORTFOLIOS: Sherrie Levine, Ariane Mnouchkine & Ingmar Bergman—two productions of Euripides; POEMS: Jorie Graham, Gary Snyder.

43
Jamaica Kincaid on the biography of a dress; Stephen Trombley on designing death machines
STORIES: Victor Erofeyev, Christa Wolf; PORTFOLIOS: Joseph Cornell, Sue Williams; POEMS: Robert Creeley, Kabir.

44
Martin Duberman on Stonewall; Andrew Kopkind: SLACKING TOWARD BETHLEHEM
STORIES: Georges Perec, Edmund White; PORTFOLIOS: Fred Wilson, William Christenberry, POEMS: Lyn Hejinian, Sharon Olds.

45
John Cage's correspondence; Roberto Lovato: DOWN AND OUT IN CENTRAL L.A.
STORIES: David Gates, Duong Thu Huong; PORTFOLIOS: Ecke Bonk, Gerhard Richter; POEMS: A. R. Ammons, C. H. Sisson.

46
William T. Vollmann on the Navajo-Hopi Land Dispute; Ice-T, Easy-E: L.A. rappers get open with Brian Cross
STORIES: David Foster Wallace, Italo Calvino; PORTFOLIOS: Nancy Rubins, Dennis Balk; POEMS: Michael Palmer, Martial.

ORDER
WHILE THEY LAST

47
Louis Althusser's ZONES OF DARKNESS; Edward W. Said on intellectual exile
STORIES: Jean Genet, Junichiro Tanizaki; PORTFOLIOS: Barbara Bloom, Julio Galán; POEMS: John Ashbery, Ovid.

48
OBLIVION
William T. Vollmann: UNDER THE GRASS; Kip S. Thorne on black holes
STORIES: Heinrich Böll, Charles Palliser; PORTFOLIOS: Saul Steinberg, Lawrence Weiner; POEMS: Mahmoud Darwish, Antonin Artaud.

49
HOLLYWOOD
Dennis Hopper interviews Quentin Tarantino; Terry Southern on the making of DR. STRANGELOVE
STORIES: Paul Auster, Peter Handke; PORTFOLIOS: Edward Ruscha, William Eggleston; POEMS: John Ashbery, James Laughlin.

50
MODELS
Alexander Cockburn & Noam Chomsky on models in nature; Graham Greene's dream diary
STORIES: Rosario Castellanos, Cees Nooteboom; PORTFOLIOS: Katharina Sieverding, Paul McCarthy; POEMS: Robert Kelly, Nicholas Christopher.

51
NEW YORK
Terry Williams on life in the tunnels under NYC; William S. Burroughs: MY EDUCATION
STORIES: William T. Vollmann, Orhan Pamuk; PORTFOLIOS: Richard Prince, David Hammons; POEMS: Hilda Morley, Charles Simic.

52

GAMES

David Mamet:* THE ROOM*; Paul Virilio on cybersex and virtual reality

STORIES: Brooks Hansen, Walter Benjamin;
PORTFOLIOS: Robert Williams, Chris Burden;
POEMS: Miroslav Holub, Fanny Howe.

53

FETISHES

***John Waters exposes his film fetishes; Samuel Beckett's* ELEUTHÉRIA**

STORIES: Georges Bataille, Colum McCann;
PORTFOLIOS: Helmut Newton, Yayoi Kusama;
POEMS: Taslima Nasrin, Simon Armitage.

54

SPACE

***BORN IN PRISON: an inmate survives the box; Jasper Johns's* GALAXY WORKS**

STORIES: Vladimir Nabokov, Irvine Welsh;
PORTFOLIOS: Vito Acconci, James Turrell;
POEMS: W. S. Merwin, John Ashbery.

55

EGOS

Julian Schnabel:* THE CONVERSION OF ST. PAOLO MALFI*; Suzan-Lori Parks on Josephine Baker

STORIES: Kenzaburo Oe, David Foster Wallace;
PORTFOLIOS: Dennis Hopper, Brigid Berlin's *Cock Book*;
POEMS: Amiri Baraka, Susie Mee.

56

DREAMS

Edward Ruscha:* HOLLYWOOD BOULEVARD*; TERRY SOUTHERN AND OTHER TASTES

STORIES: William T. Vollmann, Lydia Davis;
PORTFOLIOS: Jim Shaw, ADOBE LA;
POEMS: Bernadette Mayer, Saúl Yurkievich.

57

DIRT

John Waters & Mike Kelley:* THE DIRTY BOYS*; Rem Koolhaas on 42nd Street

STORIES: Mohammed Dib, Sandra Cisneros;
PORTFOLIOS: Langdon Clay, Alexis Rockman;
POEMS: Robert Creeley, Thomas Sayers Ellis.

58

DISGUISES

***Anjelica Huston on life behind the camera; D. Carleton Gajdusek:* THE NEW GUINEA FIELD JOURNALS**

STORIES: Victor Pelevin, Arno Schmidt;
PORTFOLIOS: Hannah Höch, Kara Walker;
POEMS: Vittorio Sereni, Marjorie Welish.

59

TIME

***Mike Davis on the destruction of L.A.; John Szarkowski:* LOOKING AT PICTURES**

STORIES: Naguib Mahfouz, Nina Berberova;
PORTFOLIOS: Spain, Charles Ray;
POEMS: James Tate, Adonis.

60

PARANOIA

Fiona Shaw on life in the theater; Salvador Dalí on the paranoid image

STORIES: David Foster Wallace, Nora Okja Keller;
PORTFOLIOS: Tom Sachs, David Cronenberg;
POEMS: Fanny Howe, Lawrence Ferlinghetti.

61

ALL-AMERICAN

***William T. Vollmann tracks the Queen of the Whores; Peter Sellars:* THE DIRECTOR'S PERSPECTIVE**

STORIES: Reinaldo Arenas, Guillermo Cabrera Infante;
PORTFOLIOS: Rubén Ortiz-Torres, Doris Salcedo;
POEMS: Octavio Paz, Aimé Césaire.

62

IDENTITY

Edward W. Said on Mozart's dark side; actor Marcello Mastroianni explores his past

STORIES: Can Xue, Marcel Beyer;
PORTFOLIOS: Mona Hatoum, Robert Rauschenberg;
POEMS: Christopher Middleton, Robin Robertson.

CALL
1-800-807-6548

Please send name, address, issue number(s), and quantity.

American Express, Mastercard, and Visa accepted; please send credit-card number and expiration date. Back issues are $15 each ($18 overseas and Canada), including postage and handling, payable in U.S. dollars. Address orders to GRAND STREET, *Back Issues, 131 Varick Street, Suite 906, New York, NY 10013.*

63

CROSSING THE LINE

John Waters interviews "drag king" Mo B. Dick; Elias Canetti's aphorisms and adages

STORIES: Franz Kafka, Patrick Chamoiseau;
PORTFOLIOS: Lygia Clark, Justen Ladda;
POEMS: Guillaume Apollinaire, Hilda Morley.

64

MEMORY

A "lost" play by Tennessee Williams:* NOT ABOUT NIGHTINGALES*; David Mamet recalls his* SALAD DAYS*;

STORIES: José Saramago, Murathan Mungan;
PORTFOLIOS: Tony Smith, Nancy Spero;
POEMS: John Ashbery, Pablo Neruda.

65

TROUBLE

William T. Vollmann's treatise on violence:* RISING UP AND RISING DOWN*; Fiction and reportage from Algeria;

STORIES: Christopher Fowler, Einar Már Gudmundsson;
PORTFOLIOS: Larry Burrows, Sam Taylor-Wood;
POEMS: Zbigniew Herbert, Gillian McCain.

Bookland of Brunswick, Brunswick, ME
University of Maine Bookstore, Orono, ME
Books Etc., Portland, ME
Raffles Cafe Bookstore, Portland, ME

Pages, Toronto, CANADA

Dartmouth Bookstore, Hanover, NH
Toadstool Bookshop, Peterborough, NH

Wootton's Books, Amherst, MA
Boston University Bookstore, Boston, MA
Harvard Book Store, Cambridge, MA
M.I.T. Press Bookstore, Cambridge, MA
Cisco Harland Books, Marlborough, MA
Broadside Bookshop, Northampton, MA
Provincetown Bookshop, Provincetown, MA
Water Street Books, Williamstown, MA

Northshire Books, Manchester, VT

Main Street News, Ann Arbor, MI
Shaman Drum Bookshop, Ann Arbor, MI
Cranbrook Art Museum Books, Bloomfield Hills, MI
Book Beat, Oak Park, MI

Afterwords, Milwaukee, WI

Accident or Design, Providence, RI
Brown University Bookstore, Providence, RI
College Hill Store, Providence, RI

Farley's Bookshop, New Hope, PA
Faber Books, Philadelphia, PA
Waterstone's Booksellers, Philadelphia, PA
Andy Warhol Museum, Pittsburgh, PA
Encore Books, Mechanicsburg, PA
Encore Books, State College, PA

Yale Cooperative, New Haven, CT
UConn Co-op, Storrs, CT

Rosetta News, Carbondale, IL
Pages for All Ages, Champaign, IL
Mayuba Bookstore, Chicago, IL
Museum of Contemporary Art, Chicago, IL
Seminary Co-op Bookstore, Chicago, IL

Encore Books, Princeton, NJ
Micawber Books, Princeton, NJ

Community Bookstore, Brooklyn, NY
Talking Leaves, Buffalo, NY
Colgate University Bookstore, Hamilton, NY
Book Revue, Huntington, NY
The Bookery, Ithaca, NY
A Different Light, New York, NY
Art Market, New York, NY
B. Dalton, New York, NY
Coliseum Books, New York, NY
Collegiate Booksellers, New York, NY
Doubleday Bookshops, New York, NY
Exit Art/First World Store, New York, NY
Gold Kiosk, New York, NY
Gotham Book Mart, New York, NY
Museum of Modern Art Bookstore, New York, NY
New York University Book Center, New York, NY
Posman Books, New York, NY
Rizzoli Bookstores, New York, NY
St. Mark's Bookshop, New York, NY
Shakespeare & Co., New York, NY
Spring Street Books, New York, NY
Wendell's Books, New York, NY
Whitney Museum of Modern Art, New York, NY
Syracuse University Bookstore, Syracuse, NY

UC Bookstore, Cincinnati, OH
Bank News, Cleveland, OH
Ohio State University Bookstore, Columbus, OH
Student Book Exchange, Columbus, OH
Books & Co., Dayton, OH
Kenyon College Bookstore, Gambier, OH
Oberlin Consumers Cooperative, Oberlin, OH

Indiana University Bookstore, Bloomington, IN

Iowa Book & Supply, Iowa City, IA
Prairie Lights, Iowa City, IA
University Bookstore, Iowa City, IA

Louie's Bookstore Cafe, Baltimore, MD

Box of Rocks, Bowling Green, KY
Carmichael's, Louisville, KY

Xanadu Bookstore, Memphis, TN

Bridge Street Books, Washington, DC
Chapters, Washington, DC
Franz Bader Bookstore, Washington, DC
Olsson's, Washington, DC
Politics & Prose, Washington, DC

Daedalus Used Bookshop, Charlottesville, VA
Studio Art Shop, Charlottesville, VA
Williams Corner, Charlottesville, VA

Library Ltd., Clayton, MO
Whistler's Books, Kansas City, MO
Left Bank Books, St. Louis, MO

Paper Skyscraper, Charlotte, NC
Regulator Bookshop, Durham, NC

Chapter Two Bookstore, Charleston, SC
Intermezzo, Columbia, SC
Open Book, Greenville, SC

Square Books, Oxford, MS

Books & Books, Coral Gables, FL
Goerings Book Center, Gainesville, FL
Bookstop, Miami, FL
Rex Art, Miami, FL
Inkwood Books, Tampa, FL

Lenny's News, New Orleans, LA

And at selected Barnes & Noble and Bookstar bookstores nationwide.

GRAND STREET

NEXT ISSUE:

FIRE